HANG TIME

HANG TIME

ZEV CHAFETS

WARNER BOOKS

A Time Warner Company

The events and characters in this book are fictitious. Certain real locations and public figures are mentioned, but all other characters and the events described are totally imaginary.

Warner Books, Inc., 1271 Avenue of the Americas, New York, NY 10020

 A Time Warner Company

First Warner Books printing: April 1996
10   9   8   7   6   5   4   3   2   1

Library of Congress Cataloging-in-Publication Data

Chafets, Ze'ev.
    Hang time / Zev Chafets.
        p.   cm.
    ISBN 0–446–52047–0 (hardcover)
    1. Basketball players—United States—Fiction.   2. Americans—Travel—Israel—Fiction.   3. Terrorism—Israel—Fiction.
I. Title.
PS3553.H225H3   1996
813'.54—dc20   95-41981
                                                                            CIP

Book design by H. Roberts

For Mookush, Shmuelik and Coby,
with all my love

HANG TIME

CHAPTER ONE

THEY CAME STRUTTING THROUGH THE LOBBY OF THE TEL AVIV Hilton like an honor guard, the stubby, gray-haired American in the black suit flanked by two towering young men, one black and one white. The black man moved languidly, his eyes turned inward, listening to Ice-T through a small headset clamped over his gleaming, shaved skull. The white man, pug-nosed and crew-cut, with angry acne scars on his face, kept his gaze fixed straight ahead. Only the short, gray-haired man acknowledged the stir in the lobby, nodding smartly to the surprised tourists and gawking Israelis they passed on the way from the elevator. Although he was by far the least physically impressive of the three, he carried himself with the regal self-assurance of a man used to hearing the word "legendary" precede his name.

Just outside the hotel, the tall white man, whose name was Greg Bannion, scanned the waiting cars and taxis. He saw a skinny, kinky-haired driver with a knit beanie on his head emerge from a black Mercedes limousine, smile broadly and wave. "That must be the limo," he said. "Christ, I hope there's enough legroom. How long a drive is it to Jerusalem?"

"One hour," said the gray man in the authoritative tone of someone accustomed to things running precisely on his schedule.

Bannion looked at his watch, recently set on Tel Aviv time, and scowled. "It'll be fucking midnight before we get back," he said. "I don't see why they had to schedule this fucking dinner on our first night."

"The foreign minister's leaving for Japan day after tomorrow. This was the only time he could see us," said the gray man, moving toward the limo.

"Foreign minister my ass," said Bannion. "How many people live here anyway?"

"Five point three million," said the gray man. "Eighty percent Jews, twenty percent Arabs. Not counting the West Bank and Gaza. It's in the information packet you got in New York."

"There's more people than that in L.A.," said Bannion. "Shit, there's probably that many in metro Detroit. Tyrone, how many people in Detroit?"

The black man turned his head slightly and shrugged. Bannion and the old man had been at each other ever since last night at Kennedy. He didn't like the idea of spending three weeks with either one of them, and he sure as hell had no intention of taking sides.

"You don't know how many people in your own hometown?" Bannion demanded.

"Census bureau," said Tyrone Holliman. That was the way he talked to white people, in broken phrases and sentence fragments. It made them shake their heads and think he was stupid, because they didn't know how to translate. In Tyrone-talk, what he had just said was, "I ain't the census bureau, you big, ugly, bristly-haired, spot-faced motherfucker."

"Don't worry about it," said the gray man. "For fifty thousand bucks you can stay up all night to talk to the goddamned mayor of Peoria."

The little driver was out of the car now, next to the open back door, ushering them in with a shy smile and a grand, sweeping gesture. The gray man inspected his body at a glance, an instinct from his recruiting days. Good set of shoulders for such a skinny guy, but pipestem legs and no butt. He'd be willing to bet the kid couldn't jump a foot straight up.

The driver noticed the gray man's inspection and his smile widened. "Welcome," he said. "Please."

"*Please* and *welcome* in the same fucking sentence," said Bannion. "You're a polite little guy, aren't you?"

The driver looked at him puzzled, turned down the smile a notch and closed the door after them. Then he climbed behind the wheel and fired up the engine.

"You know where we're going, Jocko?" barked the gray man. The driver nodded emphatically as he eased the Mercedes into the crowded evening traffic on Hay-arkon Street.

"Speak any English, my brother?" asked Tyrone in his soft voice.

"Leetle," said the driver.

"They got some weird-looking Jews in this country," Bannion said. "This one's got hair like you, Tyrone, if you had any hair."

"He's probably a Yemenite," said the gray man. "Israel's got Jews from all over the world."

"Never seen a Jew behind the wheel of a limo before," said Bannion. "Usually they own the damn company." He grinned and raised his voice. "You own this limo, pal?"

"Please?" said the driver, making one right and then another, heading the car away from the Mediterranean.

"You're welcome," said Bannion. He winked at the others, but Tyrone pretended not to see and the gray man merely shook his head.

They were on a dark street, still in Tel Aviv, when the driver hit the brake. "My cousin," he said, pulling over to the curb. A small man dressed in Israeli army fatigues, with an Uzi submachine gun slung over his shoulder, opened the front passenger door and slid in. "We give him ride to Jerusalem, okay?"

"Cousin my ass," snorted Bannion. "You're probably going to charge him for the ride."

"Please?" asked the driver.

"Yeah, no problem," said the gray man. "Just get us there on time."

The cousin turned, looked at the three Americans and smiled. Then he said something rapid-fire in a foreign language they didn't understand. What he said was: "They won't all fit into the trunk."

"What do we do?" asked the driver.

"Leave one," said the cousin. "In the grove near Ashkelon."

The Mercedes emerged from city traffic onto a modern six-lane freeway. The blue sign read: BE'ER SHEBA, ASHKELON. "Hey Jocko, we're going to Jerusalem," said the gray man.

"Shortcut," said the cousin. "Don't worry."

"Jew driver, naturally he's gonna be taking a shortcut," said Bannion. "Probably save a few pennies on the gas. Tyrone, you got a Jewish agent?"

"Business," said Tyrone, meaning: "I wouldn't tell you my business if you were the head of the motherfucking FBI."

They drove for a while longer and the gray man said, "This doesn't look right. I don't see any Jerusalem signs."

"My cousin is make wrong turning," said the soldier. "One minute." He said something to the driver, who sped off an exit ramp and down a dirt path.

The gray man consulted his watch. "Pull over at the first gas station," he commanded. He was annoyed but working to keep it under control. Before leaving the States his daughter Ellen had warned him to hold his temper. "Try not to run the whole country while you're over there, Dad," had been her exact words. He was trying, but now he was late, and he hated tardiness. "I want to call, tell them we're running behind schedule."

The driver ignored the request. After a minute or so the gray man tapped him hard on the shoulder. "I said to stop at the first gas station," he barked. "Get it?"

"We are here," said the soldier as the driver brought the car to a stop.

"Where?" asked the gray man, peering into the dense darkness. "I don't see any telephone."

"Get out," said the soldier, turning toward the back-seat and leveling his Uzi at the Americans.

"What the fuck—" exclaimed Bannion.

"Do you know who I am?" demanded the gray man.

"No problem, my brother," said Tyrone. He was the only one who had ever had an Uzi pointed at him before. Slowly he opened the door and climbed out, motioning for the others to follow. They stood in the sand, feeling a cool salt breeze, and waited, three Americans, two white and one black, two tall and one short, two young and one old.

"*Allah hu akbar,*" said the cousin with the Uzi.

"*Allah hu akbar,*" replied the driver, producing a six-inch butcher knife that flashed in the moonlight.

"*Salaam aleikum,*" said Tyrone, who had learned the Arabic words from his big brother Rasheed in Detroit.

"Fuck this shit," said Bannion, advancing on the two little men.

"*Allah hu akbar!*" screamed the driver as he drove his knife into Bannion's chest. The big, crew-cut American slumped and fell to the ground, groaning. The driver pounced on him, straddling his wide body, plunging the knife into him again and again until the cousin, who was pointing the Uzi at the other two Americans, said, *"Bas."* Enough.

"Jesus," said Tyrone. The gray man, for once, was speechless.

"Sit," commanded the cousin, who was no longer smiling. The driver produced a shovel from the trunk and began digging a hole.

"You're making a big mistake, Jocko," said the gray man, trying to recover his bluster. "You don't know who you're fucking with. We're official representatives of the U.S. government—"

"No mistake, Mr. Bronstein. You are a prisoner of war."

"My name's not Bronstein. I'm Digger Dawkins, you dumb-ass."

"No," said the little man, suddenly agitated. "No tricks." He walked over to the gray man, smashed him in the face with the wooden butt of the Uzi and watched as he crumpled in the sand. Then he pointed the gun at Tyrone again.

"I got a brother in Detroit named Rasheed," said Tyrone. "He's a Muslim, same as you."

"Lift," said the cousin, gesturing to the prone body.

"Reason I'm telling you that, I think you making a mistake. See, this guy ain't no Mr. Bronstein. He's Digger Dawkins, just like he said. Basketball coach. And I'm Tyrone Holliman. Detroit Pistons? Small forward? NBA?"

"Lift," repeated the cousin, waving the Uzi. Tyrone bent down, slung the gray man over his shoulder, and hoisted him gently into the spacious trunk.

"Now you, get down," said the cousin.

"You gonna shoot me or hit me?" asked Tyrone in an even tone, measuring the distance between himself and the gunman. Then he heard a noise behind him and felt the thud of a shovel on his bald skull.

"Help me," the cousin with the Uzi said to the driver, who dropped the shovel and grabbed Tyrone under his arms. Together they lifted him into the trunk. Then, with their feet, they pushed Bannion's body into the shallow hole and began covering it with sand.

CHAPTER TWO

ROSENTHAL LIT UP A KENT, WAITED FOR THE SNIFF OF DISAP-proval from Stacy, and then rapped lightly for order. It didn't take much of a rap; there were only four men gathered around the conference table in the small Tel Aviv office located near the Ministry of Defense.

On the Israeli side were Kedmi, chief of the national police, a large, powerfully built, phlegmatic man with a bald head and hair growing out of his ears, and Benny Rosenthal himself, the bland deputy head of the Shin Bet Internal Security Service. The Americans were Stacy, the CIA station chief, and Carl Berger, the president's special envoy, who had arrived in Israel that morning. Rosenthal was well acquainted with Stacy and, of course, Kedmi. Berger, a thin, hard-looking man with short brown hair and a strong jaw, he knew only by reputation.

"We'll start with an update," said Rosenthal. "Kedmi?"

"Nothing new," said the police chief. "Dawkins, Holliman and Bannion were last seen two nights ago, around nineteen hundred hours, getting into a black Mercedes limousine in front of the Hilton Hotel. The doorman says the driver was small and dark, wearing a knit yarmulke. We showed him pictures, but he can't identify him. Nobody noticed the license plate."

"Still no ransom note?" asked Stacy.

"If there was a ransom note I would have mentioned it," said Kedmi.

Berger absorbed the testy exchange in silence, content to leave the talking to others for the moment.

"If it was a criminal kidnapping there'd be a note by now," said Stacy.

"Probably," said Kedmi. "But they could be waiting, letting the suspense build. That happens sometimes."

"Who's 'they'?"

Kedmi shrugged. "The Russian mafia, maybe. Or some local freelancers."

"Or Americans," said Rosenthal. "Gamblers."

"Like in the movies," said Kedmi with a smile.

Stacy asked, "What about the terrorist angle?"

"Our informants in the West Bank haven't heard a thing, and Arafat's people in Gaza swear they don't know, either. They've just disappeared."

"Well," said Rosenthal to Berger, "that brings you up to date. Any questions?"

"I do have just one question," said Berger in a deferential, surprisingly high-pitched tone. "What will I tell the president?"

"That we're doing everything we can."

"No," said Berger, "I don't think I can tell him that. We're not talking about three backpackers here. These men are household names in America, sports heroes. And do you know what happens when three American heroes vanish? The media goes berserk. Larry King, Dan Rather, Tom Brokaw, Ted Koppel, Rush Limbaugh, *TIME*, *Newsweek*, the whole national press corps, everybody wants to know what's happened to them."

"We're aware of that," said Rosenthal, "we know they're important—"

"Not important," said Berger, cutting him off. "Much more than important. The president wants to go on TV and tell the American people that Israel, our friend and ally, is turning the country upside down looking for these men. But based on what I just heard, I don't think he can say that."

"We're doing our best—"

"No sir, you are not," said Berger curtly. "What you are doing is going through the motions, talking to the usual suspects, holding little meetings over coffee and cake and waiting for something to turn up. That's not what I call doing your best."

"What do you expect?"

"Call out the national guard—"

"They don't have a national guard here," Stacy said.

"It's an expression," said Berger impatiently. "Call out the army, declare a state of national emergency, let the kids out of school to hunt for them. You people are getting three billion dollars a year in aid, and the president wants a three-billion-dollar search. And he goddamn good and well wants it to look like one, too. Do you understand what I'm telling you?" He was glaring at the Israelis when the door opened and a middle-aged woman entered the room. She bent over Kedmi, whispered something in his ear; he rose and followed her out the door.

"It wasn't a rhetorical question," said Berger to Rosenthal. "I want an answer."

"I'll tell the prime minister you said so," said Rosenthal blandly.

"Fine, do that," said Berger. "Tell him we expect to get our money's worth on this one."

The door opened and Kedmi returned, a strange look on his face. "News," he said. "We know where they are."

"Where?"

"Reuters in Lebanon just reported receiving a phone call from Hizbollah. They're holding them captive in Beirut."

"Since when does Hizbollah kidnap people in Israel?" asked Berger.

"They don't," Rosenthal said. "They probably got cooperation from Islamic Jihad or one of the other local extremist groups. After all, Lebanon's an easier place to keep hostages than here."

"How the hell could they get them out of the country?" asked Stacy.

"By boat, probably," said Kedmi. "From Gaza. It's only a few hours."

"It doesn't matter how they got there," said Berger. "The question is, how do we get them back? What do they want?"

"The release of fifteen hundred terrorists," said Kedmi. "They're going to send us a list tomorrow. That's all they want from us."

"All," said Rosenthal. "Some all."

"The prestige of the United States is involved here. And American public opinion," said Berger sharply.

"So is Israeli national security," said Rosenthal.

"They have one other condition," said the big police chief in an expressionless voice. "They want a televised public apology on CNN, begging forgiveness from Allah for anti-Islamic policies."

"Well, if that's what it takes," said Berger.

"The prime minister will never agree to it," said Rosenthal.

"He won't have to," Kedmi said, looking directly at Berger. "They don't want an apology from him. They want it from the president of the United States."

CHAPTER THREE

TYRONE HOLLIMAN OPENED HIS EYES A CRACK AND, THROUGH the dim light, saw the little driver sitting across from him on a torn wicker chair. He had an AK-47 assault rifle across his legs and a mouthful of pita bread and hummus. Tyrone closed his eyes again to think. There was a terrible pounding in his skull and his mouth was dry. He was lying on some kind of straw mattress, covered with a rough, nasty-smelling blanket. The room was cold, and it reeked of bad odors—cheap disinfectant, onions, spent cordite and stale urine. He had no idea where he was, and no memory of getting here, but he knew he didn't have amnesia, because he had no trouble remembering the skinny little knife-murderer sitting ten feet away eating his lunch.

Tyrone lay still, controlling his breathing, trying to fight down the nausea and the throbbing. What did he know for sure? He had been kidnapped. The kidnappers were some bad motherfuckers, no doubt about that. What he needed to do was communicate with them, let them know that, whatever their ransom demands, the Pistons would pay. His brother Rasheed had taught him that when somebody's got hold of you, it's up to you to help him find a good reason for letting you loose.

Tyrone heard a groan; Dawkins was alive, too. Tyrone wasn't sure if that was good news or not. Dawkins didn't seem like the kind of white man who knew how to talk his way out of trouble. If he came on with that General Patton attitude of his, Tyrone knew that he could piss off a whole tribe of little kinky-ass, knife-stabbing brothers and get them both killed.

"Tyrone," Dawkins called, causing the guy with the AK-47 to stir. Through narrowed eyes Tyrone watched the guard walk to the far corner of the room, bend over the coach and say, "Please?"

Dawkins ignored him. "Tyrone, goddamnit, are you alive?" he demanded in a strong voice.

Tyrone licked his dry lips and cleared his throat. "Yeah, I'm alive."

"Thank God," said Dawkins. "Where the hell are we?"

Suddenly the guard banged a hammer against a water pipe, filling the room with an earsplitting clang.

"Stop making that damn racket, you little cocksucker," snapped Dawkins.

"Man, be cool," Tyrone said softly. "These cats got a short fuse."

"They're gonna have a short life by the time this is over," said Dawkins. "They don't know who the fuck they're dealing with."

A metal door opened above them and they heard heavy footsteps on concrete stairs. Dawkins and Tyrone, squinting into the dimness, saw a large man dressed in a long white robe and knitted white skullcap enter the room. He said some Arabic words to the guard, who nodded and scurried up the stairs.

"I am glad you are finally awake," said the Arab in fluent, American-inflected English. "You will have some tea and bread in a few moments. My name is Abu Walid."

"Do you know who I am?"

"You are Dawkins."

"I'm a personal friend of the president of the United States of America is who I am."

"Yes," said Abu Walid. "In the past two days I have learned that you are both very famous men."

"Two days?" said Dawkins. "We've been here that long?"

"You were given something to make you sleep," said Abu Walid. He walked over to Tyrone, knelt down and ran his fingers gently over his skull. "How is your wound?" he asked.

"Hurts."

"It will heal."

"What are you, a doctor?" said Dawkins, annoyed at the big man's casual dismissal of his presidential connections.

"Yes," said Abu Walid. "A doctor of surgery."

"A doctor. Jesus, thank God," said Dawkins. "Listen, Doc, these two assholes hijacked us by mistake—"

"Yes, it was a mistake," said Dr. Abu Walid. "Do not blaspheme."

"Get to a phone, call the American Embassy, tell them where we are—"

"Man's telling you he's one of them," said Tyrone.

"I am truly sorry," said the doctor. "But, under the circumstances, you will have to stay here."

"But you said yourself it was a mistake," Dawkins said. "The guy they were looking for, Berstein—"

"Bronstein," said Dr. Abu Walid. "Mr. Arthur Bronstein. He is the chairman of the International Zionist Congress."

"Well, I'm no Zionist," said Dawkins. "I'm a goddamned Methodist—"

Abu Walid reached out and slapped Dawkins hard across the face. "I said, do not blaspheme," he snapped. The coach, stunned, stared up at him. "Ahmed was expecting an old man with two bodyguards. He mistook you"—he gestured with his head to the silent Dawkins—"for Bronstein."

"Should have asked first," said Tyrone.

"He forgot the words in English."

"Damn," said Tyrone softly. "Whole country full of Jews and he picks us."

"At first I was upset," said Abu Walid. "But Allah is great. When I learned your identity from the radio, I knew that He had given us two famous Americans instead of one famous Zionist."

"Correction," said Tyrone. "Coach Dawkins is an American; I'm an African-American. Kareem Abdul-Jabbar? Muhammad Ali? Elijah Muhammad? You know who I'm talking about?"

"But you are on an official American State Department tour," said Abu Walid. "Is that not so?"

"Wasn't my idea," said Tyrone. "See, I owed the league a considerable sum of money for a disciplinary situation. Bannion did, too." He paused for a moment, remembering the bloody corpse in the sand, and shuddered slightly. "Only reason we came, the commissioner said he would cancel the fines if we did."

"This disciplinary situation, what was it?"

Tyrone licked his lips, giving himself a chance to be creative. He didn't think this guy would be sympathetic to a drug abuse problem. "Ah, I got into a fight," he said. "This player on another team was disrespecting Allah and I punched him out, broke his nose. Commissioner's a Jew, so naturally he took the other cat's side, fined me fifty thousand dollars."

"You are a Muslim?" asked Abu Walid, sounding genuinely surprised.

"Ah, not officially, not yet, but I've been considering it," said Tyrone, seeing a chance. "My brother Rasheed in Detroit, he's a Muslim. We're real close."

"I lived in Dearborn for eleven years," said Dr. Abu Walid. "I studied at Wayne State and interned at Ford Hospital."

"For real?" exclaimed Tyrone, flashing his warmest smile. "Man, we homeboys. Dearborn, huh? Michigan Avenue, all right! Ford Motor Company. You a big guy; you play any ball while you was at Wayne?"

Dawkins lay on his mattress listening to Tyrone and the Arab chat with a feeling of frustrated injury. Tyrone Holliman was nothing but a street punk with a jump shot and a quick first step. He was Digger Dawkins, coach of four NCAA champs. His picture had been on the cover of *TIME*. He was friends with Jay Leno and Lee Iacocca. He played golf with the goddamned vice president of the United States at Burning Tree. And this raghead doctor had slapped him for cursing, like a schoolboy. Yet here he was, talking amiably with Tyrone Holliman. With dismay, Dawkins remembered that during the embassy takeover in Iran, Khomeini had freed the black hostages and kept the whites.

"I am not interested in games," Abu Walid told Tyrone. "My son is a sportsman. He would like to meet you."

"That wasn't him guarding us down here?"

Abu Walid made a face as if he were smelling the basement for the first time. "Ahmed? No, of course he is not my son. My son is not a driver or a guard."

"What's his name?" asked Tyrone quickly; you could never tell what might insult these people, set them off.

"Walid," said the doctor. "That is why I am called Abu Walid. It means 'father of Walid.' "

"Right," said Tyrone. "You mind if I ask you a question? You been in touch with the Pistons already?"

"No," said Abu Walid. "Why should I be in touch with a basketball team?"

"Well, you're gonna have to talk to them to get your money," said Tyrone easily. "How much you asking for?"

"Only criminals kidnap for money," said Dr. Abu Walid. "I am not interested in money."

"Yeah, course, not for you personally, I know that," said Tyrone. "But for the cause—"

"I have already informed the world what my conditions are," Abu Walid said. He turned to Dawkins and stared at him a moment. "You say that the president of the United States is your friend. He will now have a chance to prove it."

The metal door at the top of the stairs opened, and Ahmed the driver came down with his AK-47 strapped over his back and a brass platter of tea and bread in his hands. He set the tray between Dawkins and Tyrone and silently resumed his seat in the torn wicker chair.

"I must leave you now," said Abu Walid. "When there is news, I will let you know. In the meantime, do not make difficulty and you will not be harmed."

"Can I have my Walkman and my tapes back?" said Tyrone. "I'm stuck down here, I want to hear some tunes."

"I will see to it," said Abu Walid.

"And an English copy of the Koran."

"Yes, with pleasure." He turned to the coach. "Would you like one, too?"

"Hell, no," snapped Dawkins, preparing himself for another slap.

"As you wish," said Abu Walid mildly. "It is a matter of your choice. You may read and you may listen to songs. Do not try to escape; there is no way to leave here. If you do, and you are lucky, Ahmed or one of the other guards will shoot you."

"That's lucky?" said Tyrone with what he hoped was a disarming smile.

"Compared to the alternative," Abu Walid said.

"What's the alternative?"

"Punishment," said Dr. Abu Walid with a bleak smile. "If you do not cooperate, I will hurt you in ways you cannot even imagine."

CHAPTER FOUR

SECRETARY OF STATE LUCIEN DRAPER WAITED UNTIL THE TWO women were arranged comfortably beside him before smiling a signal for the press conference to begin. It was a smile of calibrated discretion, telegenic without seeming lighthearted. The occasion, after all, was a solemn one.

"Good morning, ladies and gentlemen," he said in his finely modulated Yankee drawl. "Before taking your questions, I'd like to introduce the two women with me on the dais, Professor Ellen Dawkins, daughter of Digger Dawkins, and Ms. Dre Holliman, mother of Tyrone Holliman. Ms. Nancy Bannion, the wife of Greg Bannion, was unable to be here today because of an illness in the family. This morning has been the first opportunity we've had to meet in Washington and fully discuss the present situation. Now, if there are any questions?"

"Mr. Secretary, can you tell us if there's any new information on the hostages?"

"I'm afraid not," said Draper. "As far as we know they are being held somewhere in Lebanon, apparently by a faction of Hizbollah."

"Are you in communication with the kidnappers?" asked a woman in a bright red suit.

"Not directly, no."

There was an eager rustling among the reporters. "Does that mean you have an indirect channel?" one called.

"I wouldn't care to comment any further," said the secretary.

"Professor Dawkins, are you satisfied that the government is doing everything possible to bring about your father's release?" asked a man from UPI.

Ellen Dawkins, professor of sociology at the University of California, Berkeley, stepped forward and squared her already erect posture. She was a small woman in her late thirties with gelled, fashionably short black hair, a prominent nose, a strong chin and narrow, darting brown eyes. In the past three days she had been on television often, her appearances characterized by a thinly controlled, articulate indignation. "I sincerely hope not," she said. "I mean, whatever the government's done until now, my father's still a captive, so obviously I hope that more can be done." She looked up at Secretary Draper, whose expression was warily composed, and added, "And will be done."

"Does that mean you think the State Department should pressure Israel to release the Islamic prisoners?"

"Absolutely," she said.

Draper stepped forward. "I want to make it clear that our policy is not to put pressure on any friendly government to make concessions to terrorists," he said.

"What about that, Professor Dawkins?" asked a young man. "The argument that giving in to the terrorists will only encourage future acts of kidnapping?"

"Let's use that one when it's your father who's being held captive," she snapped.

The secretary shifted his weight and tried to look statesmanlike. The press conference was becoming a fiasco. It had been the White House's idea, forced on a reluctant Lucien Draper, who believed with professional certainty that hostage families should be neither seen nor heard.

"What about you, Ms. Holliman?" a reporter asked. "What do you think the government should be doing?"

"I'm just a mother," said Dre Holliman in a quiet, rich contralto. Her dark, round face shone with the mournful humanity that had captivated America for the past few days. "I'm praying that the men who took Tyrone and the others will honor God by letting them go."

A murmur of sympathetic admiration swept through the room and Secretary Draper patted Mrs. Holliman's plump arm. Eight hundred miles away, in Detroit, Rasheed Holliman watched his mother on television with a wry smile. When the State Department people had informed her of the kidnapping, her first words had been: "I hope they catch those A-rab fuckers and cut their damn heads off with a sword." It wasn't until she had seen

Dawkins's daughter Ellen on TV, acting all arrogant and pissy, that she had decided that what this story needed was a sweet, maternal heroine. In her long life Dre Holliman had been a dancer at the Flame Show Bar, a police dispatcher, the wife of one of Detroit's leading numbers operators and, for the past decade, a precinct captain in the mayor's machine. The one thing she had never been before was a humble, God-fearing black church lady.

Not that she wasn't genuinely concerned about Tyrone; Rasheed knew she was. But she was convinced that he would be all right. "If it was him alone, I'd be scared," she confided. "But long as he stays with that old white man, they'll get 'em all out."

Rasheed wasn't so sure. Two years of infantry duty in Vietnam and twenty in the Detroit Police Department, the last eight as captain, had given him a poor opinion of the government's operational prowess. Not only that, his dealings with Detroit's Lebanese underworld had taught him a healthy respect for Arab cunning and determination. Rasheed had no doubt that his baby brother was in serious trouble.

"Do you think the president of the United States should publicly apologize for American crimes against Islam?" Rasheed heard a reporter ask.

"Absolutely," said Ellen Dawkins.

"But don't you think that sends a very bad message—"

"I think it's the simple truth," said Professor Dawkins. "The West has behaved disgracefully toward the Muslim world for centuries. An apology is long overdue."

The Secretary of State's long, patrician face reddened, but he said nothing. The president would be furious, but he could hardly get into a televised pissing match with the distraught daughter of a political prisoner.

"Ms. Holliman, do you share Professor Dawkins's view?" asked a blond woman from CNN.

"I support the president," she said—which was technically true, since she was a Democrat—"and I have faith that he'll do what's right"—which was totally false. Dre Holliman had never trusted a white man in her life.

"And on that note—" said the Secretary of State, eager to end his ordeal. Rasheed hit the remote control and the television fell silent. Then he picked up the telephone and dialed. After the third ring he heard a heavily accented voice say, "Hallo."

"Hey, Marwan," he said. "How you doin'?"

"*El hamdelilah,* one hundred percent," Marwan said. "All praise to Allah."

"That's cool," said Rasheed. "You ready for a round of golf?"

"You have a job for me?"

"Naw," said Rasheed. "All I want is fresh air and some sportsmanlike competition."

"We will be playing for money?"

"I believe so," said Rasheed. "Yeah."

"Excellent," Marwan said. "In that case, I will meet you in one hour."

CHAPTER FIVE

ON THEIR FOURTH DAY IN CAPTIVITY, DIGGER DAWKINS AND Tyrone Holliman had a visitor. They didn't know what time he arrived because their watches had been taken away and because the weak light in the hazy, windowless cellar never brightened or dimmed. They didn't even know exactly how many days they had been held, although Dawkins made a periodic estimate, which he scratched on the stone floor with a small pebble.

There were always two armed guards in the room. They spoke to each other in Arabic and occasionally issued a command or answered a question in broken English, but they were totally unresponsive to efforts at establishing any kind of rapport. Every few hours one bent down on a rug to pray while the other remained seated, with an AK-47 on his knees. When the first one was finished, they traded places.

The prayers were one constant in the cellar's routine. Meals were the other. They were always the same—tin plates of hummus and pita bread, onions and olives and, to drink, strong mint tea. The food, like the droning prayers, the guards' blank indifference, the constant damp chill and the unvarying pale light dulled Dawkins. Despite his best efforts to stay alert and angry, he found himself more and more often in a state of drowsy, timeless semiconsciousness.

Tyrone had more or less shut down, too. The first day, as they talked, Dawkins had naturally taken command, proposing various whispered escape schemes, sharing his experiences under stress in the Korean War and trying to buoy up Tyrone's confidence by assuring him that Dawkins's influential friends would protect them from any real harm. He also tried to pass the time by resorting to the one topic they had in common—basketball.

"You young kids, the salaries you get nowadays, you're too busy making gym shoe commercials to really learn the game, study it the way we did," he explained.

"Any five guys from my neighborhood could beat the old-timers' all-star team," Tyrone replied, putting on his earphones and lying back on the filthy mattress, moving to the music like he was at the beach instead of a goddamn Arab dungeon in the middle of nowhere.

Dawkins hoped Tyrone's unfriendly mood would pass, but it didn't. He spent his time listening to his Walkman, reading from the Koran and dozing off for long stretches. Sometimes he did sit-ups and push-ups and ran in place, all under the watchful eyes of the guards.

Dawkins had tried to give him some exercise tips, but Tyrone ignored him. Eventually Dawkins realized that there was nothing for him to do but wait, alone, for liberation.

A loud noise at the top of the stairs interrupted Dawkins's thoughts. He heard muffled words in Arabic and then the sound of heavy footsteps. Tyrone, plugged into Snoop Doggy Dogg, his eyes shut, didn't seem to notice. After a moment Dawkins, who had grown accustomed to the dim light, looked up and saw Dr. Abu Walid accompanied by an extremely tall young man in a long robe and large white skullcap. Automatically he took in the boy's wide shoulders, narrow hips and big feet; he put him at six-nine, six-ten maybe, around two hundred and thirty pounds.

Abu Walid hadn't been in the cellar since that first night. Dawkins, who hadn't been able to get the doctor's slap—or his threat—out of his mind, was surprised to see a mild, almost friendly expression on his darkly bearded face.

"Hello," said Abu Walid politely. "I hope you are being treated well."

"Are we getting out of here?" Dawkins asked, roused into a moment's wild optimism by the unexpected visit and the civil words.

"Soon, I hope," said Abu Walid. "It is no longer in my hands."

"Whose hands is it in?"

"It is a matter for the Americans and the Zionists," he said. "When we have a positive response, you will be free to leave."

"Shit," said Dawkins.

"Please," said Abu Walid in an almost diffident tone. "Do not curse in front of my son." He looked up at the tall boy, who smiled shyly, and rubbed his hand lovingly across his smooth cheek. There was an expression of unadulterated love on the doctor's face that Dawkins had seen only once before in his life: the night his team had won its first NCAA championship and the university president had come to the locker room to hug and kiss center Earl Ruffin for hitting the winning shot at the buzzer.

"You got a fine-looking boy," said Tyrone, joining the conversation in a slow, easy voice. "You Walid, right?"

"In America I'm called Wally," the boy said softly, looking down at the floor.

"Yeah, that's right, your daddy said you lived in Dearborn," said Tyrone. "You a Pistons fan?"

"Isaiah Thomas, Joe Dumars, Bill Laimbeer," said the boy. "Tyrone Holliman."

"Yeah!" said Tyrone, with a sharp laugh. The exclamation shocked Dawkins, who couldn't imagine such a joyful sound coming from the morose Tyrone. "You play any ball yourself, Wally? You a ballplayer?"

"I was in America," said the kid. "Here there's nobody to play with."

"That's a bitch, man," said Tyrone. "How come you don't play in the local league, big as you are?"

"First we must redeem our homeland from the enemies of Islam," said Abu Walid. "Then there will be time for leagues and games."

" 'Cept by then, Wally here might be too old to play," said Tyrone. "Besides, I know lots of Muslims play ball."

Walid turned to his father and began speaking in Arabic. The only words Tyrone understood were "Hakeem Olajuwon" and "Kareem Abdul-Jabbar." At first the doctor shook his head, but as the boy continued talking, the older man's eyes grew soft. Finally he smiled and put his hand on Walid's cheek.

"My son may spend some time with you, discussing basketball," he said.

"If you don't mind," said the boy.

"Naw, that's cool," said Tyrone. "It's cool with you, ain't it, Coach Dawkins?"

Dawkins tried to speak, but his throat was too tight. For a moment he considered expressing his feelings by spitting on the floor, but then he remembered Abu Walid's warning about noncooperation and nodded his head resentfully.

"All right," said Abu Walid. "These are the rules. You will not curse in front of my son or blaspheme in any way. And you will not discuss with him anything other than basketball. Is that clear?"

Dawkins nodded again and looked at the ground. Tyrone nodded, too, then smiled and said, "Motor City."

"Good," said Abu Walid. He didn't understand that in Tyrone's private language, he had just been told: "This gawky, basketball-talking kid of yours is gonna help me get my ass back to the Motor City."

There was no mention of Coach Digger Dawkins.

CHAPTER SIX

MARWAN EL KASSAM SMASHED HIS CLUB ON THE GROUND, missing Rasheed's feet by inches. "Damn," he shouted. "Damn you to hell for eternity." He was talking to his golf ball, which had sliced off into the trees.

"Easy, Marwan," Rasheed said, picking up the two-iron and handing it back to him. "I'll let you have a Mulligan. Go ahead."

"Thank you," said Marwan. He teed up a white Titleist in the middle of the fairway and hit it with a three-wood. The ball flew toward the distant green. Marwan smiled broadly.

"I only let you do that 'cause we playin' this hole for money," said Rasheed.

"How much?" asked Marwan. They were on the eighteenth fairway, and Marwan had been waiting patiently for Rasheed to come to the point.

"One thousand dollars," said Rasheed, climbing in the golf cart, letting Marwan drive. "You hear about Tyrone?"

"A terrible thing," said Marwan, sincerity shining from his dark, liquid brown eyes. "It is a great crime. It makes me ashamed to be an Arab, a Muslim. I curse the men who have done this to Tyrone. I curse on the graves of their forefathers—"

"You got any idea who they are?" asked Rasheed. He knew from experience that Marwan's tirade would last until it was stopped. When it came to denouncing injustice, Marwan could talk some eloquent shit.

"How could I know such a thing?"

"By asking around," said Rasheed. "Talk to your homeboys out in Dearborn, some of the brothers around the Big Sheikh. See can you find somebody to pull your coat about who's got Tyrone and where he's at."

"No one would tell me such a thing," said Marwan. "Even if someone knew."

"Someone knows," said Rasheed. "There isn't a thing comes down in the Middle East without the Sheikh knowing about it. The information's worth a lot of money."

"How much? Not that such a thing would be possible."

"Say, fifty thousand."

"That *is* a great deal of money," said Marwan thoughtfully. "But, of course, you *have* a great deal of money. And Tyrone is your brother, after all. It is no more than I would do for mine."

Rasheed had no idea if Marwan had a brother. He did know that he had once had a sister, but she was dead; Marwan had shot her after discovering that she was pregnant with the child of an Italian building contractor from Wyandotte. Rasheed also knew that Marwan had left Lebanon after being caught scamming his boss in a drug operation. The operation consisted of feeding plastic-wrapped bundles of opium to camels, riding them to Syrian ports and slitting open their bellies to extract the drugs. The boss Marwan had scammed was a Syrian general. That's how he had wound up in Michigan.

Rasheed had no problem with any of this. As far as killing his sister was concerned, Marwan had explained that it was the Arab way to preserve family honor. A life in the streets of Detroit had prepared Rasheed for this sort of reasoning; he had met plenty of guys who had shot or stabbed somebody for making a remark about their mother. It was stupid, but stupidity wasn't necessarily a bad thing, especially in people who thought they were smart.

The camel scam was cool, too. In fact, it had made Rasheed confident in his occasional dealings with Marwan. Any man greedy enough to stiff a Syrian general would be willing to do almost anything for money.

Rasheed Holliman, despite his name, was not a Muslim, but he knew plenty of Muslims—Syrians, Yemenites, Lebanese, Iraqis, Iranians, Palestinians. They controlled Detroit's retail grocery business and a lot of slum property in the city, as well as a good share of the illicit drug trade in the tri-county area. Lots of brothers considered them exploitative bloodsuckers, but Rasheed admired their entrepreneurial spirit, family loyalty and ruthlessness. Still, he was wary of them and he preferred to deal through middlemen like Marwan. Marwan knew the Arabs of Dearborn and their complex communities. He spoke their language. It was in that language that Rasheed was counting on him to ask around until he heard a whisper about his baby brother.

"It is conceivable that I might be able to find out where Tyrone is," said Marwan. He parked the golf cart near the eighteenth green and climbed out. "When would the money be payable?"

"Half up front," said Rasheed, who got out of the cart and followed Marwan to the green. "Half after."

"I see," said Marwan. He walked to his ball, took out a nine-iron and chipped the Titleist crisply to within a foot of the flag. "After what?"

Rasheed kicked Marwan's ball into the hole with his toe, took out his wallet, counted off ten hundred-dollar bills and handed them over. Then he climbed into the golf cart.

"After I bring him back," he said, and drove off in the direction of the clubhouse.

CHAPTER SEVEN

"DO YOU KNOW HAKEEM PERSONALLY?" WALID ASKED Tyrone. They were sitting across from one another on the floor of the cellar, their long outstretched legs taking up most of the room. Dawkins was curled on his mattress in the corner, trying to drown out the sound of the conversation by listening to the godawful sound of Queen Latifah on Tyrone's Walkman.

"Yeah, me and Hakeem are tight," said Tyrone. "I played against him in three all-star games. He's from Nigeria, but he's a real civilized cat."

"Is he a good Muslim?"

"Oh yeah, he's real deep into Islam," said Tyrone. "Prays five times a day, just like y'all. Goes to the mosque in Houston, goes on the road. I imagine when he's in Detroit he heads out to Dearborn."

"Sheikh Ibrahim is in Dearborn," said Walid. "He is my father's friend."

"He the deaf and blind one?" asked Tyrone.

"He is a very holy man," said Walid reverently. "My father says that Allah has closed his eyes and ears so that he may be reached only by pure thoughts."

"Must be nice, keep all the ugliness out," said Tyrone in a soft, seductive voice.

"Yes. Tell me, would you say Hakeem is the best center in the NBA?"

"Most definitely," said Tyrone. "But Shaquille is coming up."

"Shaquille is also a Muslim name," said Walid. "Did you know that?"

"Yeah?" said Tyrone.

"There are many other Muslims in the NBA, too," said Walid. "Abdul Rauf, for example, in Denver."

"Lot of Islamic brothers," Tyrone agreed.

"Nothing in the Koran prohibits playing basketball," Walid said in a slightly truculent tone.

"If it did, Hakeem wouldn't be playing," agreed Tyrone. "The man wouldn't disrespect his religion like that."

"That's what I think, too," said Walid. "Tell me, who is your all-star team?"

"All-time or playing now?"

"Now," said Walid.

"Well, you gotta start with Hakeem, like I said before. Power forward, I'd pick Shawn Kemp. Two guard, that's Michael. Point guard have to be Jason Kidd."

"You forgot the small forward," said Walid with a grin.

"I was just taking that one for granted," said Tyrone. "What's the deal, Big Wally, you got somebody else in mind for my slot?"

"Of course not," said the boy.

Tyrone laughed. "Maybe you figuring on taking over for me one of these days. That why your daddy hijacked me, give you a chance to break in with the Pistons?"

"I am very sorry about this," said Walid. "You must believe me. What my father is doing is necessary, but I wish it could be done without you."

"This ain't so bad," said Tyrone, gesturing around the room. "I been in worse places."

"In the black ghetto," said Walid. "Where you learned to play."

"Oh yeah," said Tyrone easily. "Way, way back in the ghetto, place we call Badass Street. Further you walk, badder it gets." He smiled at Walid, a smile of such charm and warmth that the boy blushed.

"Who is the toughest opponent for you to guard?" he asked.

"That's easy," said Tyrone. "Rasheed."

"Who does he play for?"

"Rasheed don't play, period," said Tyrone. "He's one serious motherfucker." He paused and looked at Walid. "Don't tell your father I was cursing, all right?"

"Shit," said Walid. "It is cool."

"My man," said Tyrone, reaching out and giving him five.

"Tell me about Rasheed. Who is he?"

"My big brother."

"You have a brother who is a Muslim?"

"Yeah, I told your daddy that first night," said Tyrone. "That's how come I know so much about it."

"But you yourself are Christian?"

Tyrone shrugged. "Way I see it, God loves everybody who serves Him."

"No," said Walid, his tone stiffening. "God loves only those who serve Him properly."

"Yeah, well, I'm no expert," said Tyrone quickly. "Except on basketball."

"Go back to Rasheed," said Walid. "Is he in the NBA?"

Tyrone shook his head. "Rasheed's nearly fifty," he said. "He could have played, but they sent him to Vietnam and when he got back he wasn't interested. The money in those days wasn't like it is now, and he figured he'd be better off staying in Detroit."

"What does he do?"

"Owns a big security company," said Tyrone. "Works mostly for GM. Before that he was a police captain. But when I was coming up, ten, twelve years ago? Rasheed would come by, pull off his uniform, take me out to the playground and plain kick my ass. He's the one who made a basketball player out of me."

"He was your coach," said Walid.

Tyrone gazed over at Dawkins, who had fallen asleep with the sound of Latifah blaring in his ears. "Coaches, man, that's X's and O's on a blackboard and bedtime curfews. The only way to get to be a ballplayer is competition. Get out there every day, go up against dudes better than you and let them school you. That's what Rasheed did for me. We'd go out, one on one, and have ourselves some wars."

Walid looked at Tyrone for a long moment. "Would you play with me?" he asked shyly. "One-on-one?"

"Man, how the hell we gonna play in a cellar?" asked Tyrone, feeling the excitement in his belly but fighting to keep his voice cool and uninterested.

"I know a court where we could go," said Walid. "It is outside, in a protected place. No one would see us."

"Forget it," said Tyrone. "Your daddy didn't even want you talking about basketball. I know damn well he ain't gonna let you and me shoot hoops outdoors somewhere."

"But if I can convince him?"

"I don't know," Tyrone said. "Your daddy think this is my idea, he's liable come down here and operate. Let's leave it alone, all right?"

"Please, let me talk to him," said Walid. "I promise he won't think it is your idea. He will not punish you for pleasing his son."

Tyrone took a deep breath. "I'd need some shoes, size fourteen. And warm-up clothes—these are too funky to play in."

"Then you agree?"

"Yeah, if it's all right with your daddy. Sure, why not?"

"You have made me very happy, Tyrone," said Walid in a boyish voice. "It is like a dream for me."

Tyrone looked at the kid's long, open face and smiled warmly. "Yeah," he said. "Tell you the truth, I'm kind of looking forward to it myself."

Chapter Eight

Carl Berger flew into Dulles, where he was met by his aide, Andy Stubbins. Like Berger, Stubbins was an army officer on loan to the National Security Council staff. Unlike Berger, he lacked a sense of civilian style—his blocky shoes, stiff bearing and overpressed blue suit made him seem like a soldier at a Halloween party. Berger, on the other hand, blended in, a skill he had cultivated since his cadet days at the Academy at the tail end of the Vietnam War.

"Good trip, sir?" asked Stubbins, taking Berger's flight bag but allowing him to carry his own leather briefcase.

"Carl," Berger corrected him. He regarded "sir" as an automatic term of military deference and therefore somehow worthless; it implied that, had their ranks been

reversed, it would be Berger calling Stubbins "sir."
"When does the president want to see me?"

"He's waiting for you now."

Berger climbed into the backseat of the limo,
snapped on the reading lamp and opened his briefcase.
"I'm going to go over my notes," he said. Stubbins, he
noticed, was suitably impressed; ten minutes off the
plane and the boss was already at work. The story would
circulate at the White House tomorrow, further buttress-
ing Berger's reputation for fanatical dedication.

Too young for Vietnam, Berger distinguished himself in Lebanon, Grenada and Panama. But it was at the
Pentagon, where he had served as a senior aide to the
chairman of the Joint Chiefs of Staff, that he had come
into his own. He was smarter than most of the career soldiers around him, including many of his superior officers, at home with the attitudes and manners of the
military bureaucrats, politically savvy and happy to serve
as a ramrod for the chief.

Carl Berger's success at the Pentagon, especially his
reputation for getting results, had attracted the attention
of President Edward Masterson. He brought Berger to the
White House, officially as deputy national security adviser, unofficially as the elegant young president's man
for special ops.

Berger was very good at running roughshod over
foreigners, like the Israelis, and sticking it to the soft
guys at State. But he felt out of his depth when it came to
dealing with the president himself. Teddy Masterson was
a subtle, witty, somewhat capricious man, the son of a

U.S. senator and a Rockefeller heiress, graduate of Princeton, the Sorbonne and Harvard Law. One term in the U.S. Senate had convinced 53 percent of the American electorate that, at forty-nine, he was ready to sit in the Oval Office. Now, three years later, his approval rating made him seem a likely candidate for reelection.

Berger found the president sprawled on the couch, one long leg dangling over the edge, gazing at a large television screen. "Larry King," the president said with easy derision. "He's got three former CIA heads kicking my ass over this kidnapping. How'd you like to be the head of the CIA, Carl? It would solve a problem."

"Sir?"

"All these ex-CIA guys are Republicans. If I replace McGinty with you, then he could go on some shows, give me a little Democratic balance."

Berger smiled, alerted by the president's tone that he was being ironic. Or sardonic, maybe—he could never remember the difference. He made a mental note to check the dictionary when he got back to his office.

"What'd you find out, Carl?" the president asked, keeping his eyes fixed on the screen. "What can you tell me that these Republican talk-show experts don't already know?"

"Not much, Mr. President," said Berger. In the past few days he had visited Tel Aviv, Beirut, Damascus, Cairo and, secretly, Tehran. "So far, I've come up empty."

"Empty, you say," exclaimed the president in a mock British accent. "I've had officers shot for less, Bosworth." It was another thing about Masterson that disconcerted

Berger, his weird sense of humor. What the hell was he supposed to reply? Something in a fake British accent? He didn't even know who Bosworth was.

"Take a seat, Carl," the president said, resuming his normal conversational tone. "What do the Israelis know?"

"Nothing," said Berger, relieved to be back on solid operational ground. "But they'll cooperate, you can be damn sure of that. I reminded them of their obligations to this country."

"Threatened to cut off their aid, did you?" said the president, amused. "How does it feel to make a three-billion-dollar threat?"

"I was acting on your instructions, sir."

"Damn straight," said Masterson. He rose, walked to his large oak desk and sat down in the leather swivel chair. "You know, in the old days, when something like this happened, we had excuses for doing nothing. The Russians, the Cold War, the balance of power, whatever. But nowadays we're the only superpower, which makes me the only super-president. If famous American citizens get abducted by a pack of bandit sheep-fuckers and I can't do a thing about it, it makes me look bad."

"Mr. President, I've got our people shaking every tree out there. It's only a matter of time before we find them."

Masterson thought about it for a moment and then rose. "Carl, I want you to come around here," he said, gesturing to his empty chair. "Take my place for a minute, see what it feels like. Go ahead."

Berger did as he was told, slipping into the president's chair and gingerly resting his forearms on the great oak desk. Masterson came around the other side and took Berger's seat.

"A lot of history has taken place where you're sitting," said Masterson. "This is where Truman stopped the buck. JFK sat here when he almost blew up the world to impress Marilyn Monroe. Ronald Reagan kept his jelly beans on this desk. It gives you perspective.

"Carl, I want you to imagine that you're me. If we find these hostages, then what? After Irangate I can't make a deal, it's political suicide. I can't hang around the Rose Garden wringing my hands—that's what got Carter defeated in 1980. I need action, no matter what."

"Sir, there are three American lives at stake here."

"Thanks for reminding me," said Masterson dryly. He gestured toward the window. "You know how many Americans die out there every day? Car wrecks, overdoses, drive-by shootings, just in Washington alone? You think these hostages' lives are special because they're rich and famous?"

"No sir."

"Goddamn right, no sir. They're special because they represent the prestige of the United States of America. My polls show that the American people are sick of getting kicked around by the Muslim extremists. Ergo, my dear Bosworth, the voters want some serious send-in-the-marines, John Wayne, one-American-can-lick-ten-foreigners shoot-'em-up action. And so do I."

Berger swallowed hard. "I'm a soldier, Mr. President, not a politician."

Masterson sighed. "You think I'm being cynical? Hell, Carl, you see the same intelligence reports I do. You know what these people are up to, right here in America."

Berger nodded. Recently there had been almost daily intelligence warnings about an Iranian-backed terrorist cell preparing to attack targets in New York, L.A., even Washington, D.C. The FBI hadn't been able to find the terrorists, but Berger had no doubt that they were out there.

"And another thing," said Masterson, pressing his case now, "you took this job in the first place because you believe in me, in my policies, and you want to help carry them out. Is that a fair statement?"

Berger nodded again. "It's fair," he said.

"But if I lose the election next year, you and I won't be able to carry out the policies we believe in," Masterson said. "And if this kidnapping drags on and on, that's just what will happen."

"What you're saying is the ends justify the means," Berger said.

"Obviously," said Masterson. "Especially in this office. If they didn't, Lincoln wouldn't have sacrificed hundreds of thousands of lives to preserve the union. FDR wouldn't have demanded total surrender. The whole reason for having means is to use them in the pursuit of your ends. And I assure you that I am not going to allow a pack of religious fanatics to decide who the next president of the United States will be."

Berger sat at the desk, tapping his fingers on its polished surface. For a brief moment he was tempted to tell Masterson to take his trick questions and patronizing manner and shove them up his ass. But twenty years of military discipline made that impossible. Besides, he was intrigued by the situation.

"Decisive action, Carl, that's what I want. Something that will stop this Muslim aggression in its tracks."

"And bring back Dawkins, Bannion and Holliman," added Berger.

The president looked at him blankly for a moment, then nodded. "That, too," he finally said. "Of course."

CHAPTER NINE

THERE WERE ELEVEN PATRONS IN THE SIDAH CAFE AND CAKE Shop at 9:00 A.M. All were men, all had dark mustaches and all were smoking harsh cigarettes and sipping potent Turkish coffee from tiny chipped cups. They sat at small tables in twos and threes, gossiping in the rich, sweet Arabic of southern Lebanon.

The Sidah Cafe and Cake Shop was decorated with large color posters of the Ayatollah Khomeini and other prominent Shi'ite clerics. Lebanese, Iranian and Islamic flags dangled limply on poles in the corners of the room. The far wall, painted greenish blue, was festooned with dozens of black-framed photographs of serious-looking young men. Over the photos was printed, in Arabic, the legend: "Our Holy Martyrs."

Marwan el Kassam sat at a table against the wall drinking coffee and smoking cigarettes with a droopy-eyed, gray-bearded man called Suliman the Nephew. In a different society such a nickname for a man in late middle-age might have seemed dismissive; but in this case it was an honorific title, public recognition that Suliman was the favorite son of the favorite brother of the childless Sheikh Ali Abdul Rachman, the Big Sheikh, spiritual leader of the Lebanese Shi'ites of Dearborn, Michigan, and much of the rest of America.

Sheikh Ali, as he was affectionately known to his thousands of followers, was a formidable old man with a long white beard and piercing gaze who had spent twenty years in America without bothering to learn a word of English. He wrote and preached in Arabic, vitriolic diatribes against the Great Satan, the Zionist Infidels and the abominations of Western immorality. The Sheikh had almost no contact with the America outside his simple, unadorned mosque. What intercourse there was took place through the agency of Suliman the Nephew.

This role, as the holy man's connection with the world, made Suliman a powerful and well-respected figure in the Shi'ite community of Dearborn. It was he who received and entertained visiting notables, managed the financial affairs of his uncle's mosque and dealt with the requests and problems of the congregation. It was he, too, who met with FBI agents, like the ones who had come earlier that morning to ask about the kidnapping of the three American basketball heroes in Lebanon.

"They were like all the others, two foolish, red-faced Americans," he told Marwan in a mocking tone. "They smelled of perfume, like women."

"Perhaps they were women," said Marwan. "In this country it is often impossible to tell the difference."

"The Americans have no women, only whores," said Suliman.

"That is true," said Marwan, bowing his head slightly. The remark was a tribute to the fact that he had killed his own dishonored sister in the proper way. "I hope these FBI women did not inconvenience the Sheikh."

"The Sheikh is well," said Suliman, noncommittally.

"Thank God," Marwan said. "I wonder what they thought he might know of such a matter."

"Marwan, do you know the parable about the man who travels the world around in order to sneak a look into his neighbor's back window?"

"No," said Marwan. "I am not well educated. Please, tell me this parable."

"There is no such parable," said Suliman the Nephew.

Marwan raised his eyebrows in puzzlement. "Oh?"

"Let's get to the point," said Suliman in Michigan-inflected English; he was unable to be curt in Arabic. "I don't intend to talk in circles like some Hollywood coffeehouse Arab."

Marwan smiled; he and Suliman the Nephew were old friends. "In that case, let's go for a walk," he suggested.

The two men strolled hand in hand, Lebanese fashion, down an American street lined with storefront mosques, baklava bakeries, shesh-besh parlors, "halal" butcher shops and walls marked with Arabic graffiti. "If they wanted to know about the basketball players," said Marwan, in English, "why did they come to you?"

Suliman the Nephew sighed. "Every time an American is abducted in Lebanon, the FBI agents come poking their noses up my asshole."

"Perhaps that is why they wear perfume," said Marwan in Arabic, and both men laughed. "What did you tell them?"

"Nothing. This kidnapping has nothing to do with us. It is not a Hizbollah operation."

"Naturally not," said Marwan. "I wonder who might be behind it."

"Ya, Marwan, why are you pumping me for information?" asked Suliman in English.

Once again Marwan smiled, but cautiously. He trusted Suliman's friendship, but he also feared it. Marwan knew very well what the penalty would be for treachery. Far better, he knew, to be candid. At least up to a point.

"I was approached by the brother of one of the hostages," he said in Arabic. "His name is Rasheed Holliman. He was a police captain in Detroit. You may know him."

"I did not realize that the basketball player was Rasheed Holliman's brother," said Suliman. "He is a very dangerous man."

"And very rich. He is prepared to pay a fortune for the return of his brother."

"To whom will he pay this fortune?"

"To the one who can provide information on the brother's whereabouts in Lebanon."

"The basketball players are not in Lebanon."

"But the message was received by Reuters in Beirut."

"My uncle made inquiries," said Suliman in Arabic. "He likes to be kept abreast of events at home. The hostages are not in Lebanon. Of this I am certain."

"You know where they are?"

"Not precisely."

"Even imprecise information would be very valuable."

"How valuable?"

"Ten thousand dollars," said Marwan. "And another ten after the brother is rescued."

"Ten thousand dollars isn't much," said Suliman, switching back to English. "You can't even buy a Chevrolet for ten thousand dollars. A man's brother should be worth more than a Chevrolet."

"Fifteen thousand, and the other five thousand comes from my share," said Marwan. He said this in Arabic, because blatant falsehoods came easier to him in his mother tongue.

Suliman tugged Marwan's hand, indicating for him to stop. They stood facing one another as the traffic on Michigan Avenue passed them by, oblivious to the transaction taking place. "Twenty," Suliman said softly. "For the name and the place."

Marwan hesitated and then nodded. "Twenty."

"The name means nothing to you," said Suliman. "It is a man called Abu Walid. He is a Palestinian physician."

"Hamas?"

"No. He is a disciple of the Deaf and Blind Sheikh, but he himself belongs to no group. I believe that he is trying to establish his own movement." Marwan nodded; the Deaf and Blind Sheikh, a Sunni, was a rival of Suliman's uncle. That fact made him trust the information he was getting.

"And the place?"

Suliman leaned forward and pressed his stubbly cheek to Marwan's right ear. "Al-Quds," he whispered thickly. "Jerusalem. That is where the basketball players are being kept."

CHAPTER TEN

TYRONE WAS HELPED OUT OF THE TRUNK BY THE ARMED guards. At their command he stood, hands at his sides, while one of them pulled the oily-smelling black cloth bag off his head. He blinked a few times and saw Walid looking at him, with a combination of embarrassment and boyish excitement.

"Are you all right?" he asked. "The road was bumpy."

" 'Specially all curled up," said Tyrone. The black Mercedes had been replaced on this trip by an elderly Peugeot, and Tyrone's brief trunk ride had left his stomach queasy and his long legs cramped. He had been in the cellar for almost a week, and the cool, sunlit breeze made his eyes water and his forehead hurt. He took a deep breath of clean air and coughed. "Lungs jacked out of shape," he muttered.

"I hope this will be all right," said Walid shyly. "It is not regulation court . . ." He let the words trail away as he followed Tyrone's gaze around the dusty cement-paved courtyard which was surrounded on all sides by a dilapidated two-story structure painted a faded tan. On the far end of the courtyard was a wooden backboard with a hoop and a torn net.

"It'll do," said Tyrone. "Let's stretch." He began a series of leg-flexing exercises and Walid did the same, imitating his movements. The two guards sat near the Peugeot at the entrance to the courtyard, holding AK-47s on their knees and chatting in Arabic.

After five minutes or so, Tyrone stopped. He was sweating lightly, a sign he was out of shape. "You bring a ball?" he asked.

Walid nodded and called to the guards. Tyrone noticed that with them, his manner was neither boyish nor shy; he spoke imperiously, in a tone reminiscent of his father's. One of the guards fetched a basketball from the Peugeot and kicked it, soccer style, toward them. Walid extended a large foot and let the ball roll up his leg into his hands. "It's a Spaulding," he said.

"All right," said Tyrone. "Let's take a few shots, warm up a little."

Walid dribbled toward the center of the courtyard, eighteen feet from the basket, jumped into the air and fired the ball. It missed not only the rim but the entire backboard, bounced off the wall and rolled back toward them. "Airball," he said in an abashed tone. "I am very nervous."

"No big thing," said Tyrone. "Try again."

This time Walid dribbled to his right, giving the ball a nice easy bounce. He jumped again, and the shot caromed off the rim.

"Getting closer," said Tyrone. One thing he didn't want to do was discourage the kid.

Walid scooped up the ball, drove toward the basket and leaped into the air. His arm soared over the rim, practically to the top of the backboard, and he hung there for a long moment before smashing a power dunk through the torn net.

"Man, you can jump," said Tyrone, genuinely impressed. "Sky like a brother."

"Thank you," said Walid. He picked up the ball and passed it to Tyrone. The American dribbled once or twice, the ball feeling both familiar and strange in his hands, and then launched a twenty-footer that sailed through the hoop.

"Beautiful shot," called Walid.

"Come on out here an' guard me," said Tyrone, retrieving the ball. Walid faced him and assumed a defensive stance, one hand extended at his hip, the other raised over his shoulder. Tyrone cradled the ball, took an explosive first step toward the basket and launched himself for a power dunk of his own. Suddenly he saw Walid's huge hand slap the ball harmlessly against the backboard. Tyrone came down, spun around and looked hard at the tall boy.

"I fouled you," said Walid, sounding apologetic.

"Clean block," Tyrone said. "Let's see you do it

again." He dribbled the ball out to twenty feet and faced the boy again. This time he threw him a head fake, watched him stumble over his huge feet and blew past him toward the basket. As Tyrone jumped for the rim he heard a loud Arabic exclamation and felt a hand on his arm.

"That time you fouled," said Tyrone. "But you got some reflexes, baby, getting back on me like that."

"I could never stop you."

"Not right this minute," agreed Tyrone. "But you a ballplayer, man. Get some competition, you gonna be bad. How old you say you are?"

"Seventeen. And a half."

"Get your ass in a college program, play with the brothers, you could be an NBA prospect in a couple years," said Tyrone. He was exaggerating, but not by much; the kid was an athlete, no question about that.

Walid smiled sadly. "My father would never permit me to attend an American college."

"You ask him?"

"I don't need to ask him. He considers basketball a waste of time. It was very difficult to get his permission to practice with you."

"He want you to be a doctor?" asked Tyrone.

"I don't know what he wants," said Walid, sounding like a young boy. "He won't allow me to participate in the *jihad* against the Zionists—"

"What's a *jihad*?"

"Holy war," said Walid. "That is the reason you and Coach Dawkins were taken prisoner."

"Man, do I look like a Zionist to you?"

Walid shrugged his bony shoulders. "That's my father's affair," he said. "I may not discuss politics with you."

"That's cool," said Tyrone. He heard the regret in Walid's voice, and for now that was enough; there would be other days, other chances. "How come your daddy won't let you be in this holy war of his?"

"I am too tall," said Walid, blushing slightly.

"Too tall?"

"Among the Palestinians I stand out," he said. "I am too easily identified."

"That what you are, a Palestinian?"

"Of course," said Walid. "What did you think?"

"Didn't know," said Tyrone. "Your daddy's been talking about Muslims, but he didn't mention Palestinians."

"Let's play some more," said Walid uneasily, glancing at the guards.

Tyrone looked around the deserted compound and beyond, to the bleak brown hills in the distance. The sky was the purest blue he had ever seen and the air was crisp and clear. He wondered what was beyond the walls. He wondered where Rasheed was right now. "Okay," he said. He threw an arm over Walid's shoulder and walked him to the far end of the courtyard. "When I slap the ball, head for the basket—full speed—and I'll hit you with a pass."

"Fast break," said Walid.

"That's right," said Tyrone. "Fast break. Most effective play there is for getting out of a trap."

CHAPTER ELEVEN

RASHEED HOLLIMAN CLIMBED DOWN THE METAL STAIRS OF THE El Al 747, followed by two security guards. They were the same two who had been tailing him from Kennedy, sitting nearby in the passenger lounge and directly behind him on the plane, in business class. He wasn't supposed to know that they were security guards, but he had made them at a glance, two rawboned guys with scalp-scraping haircuts, wearing oversized blue blazers, unfashionably wide neckties and thick-soled brown shoes.

Rasheed didn't mind being followed, any more than he resented the two-hour security grilling he had received at the airport in New York. He respected the Israelis for their thoroughness, and he was well aware that he fit their terrorist profile: a powerfully built, six-foot-five-inch black man with a shaved skull, a diamond stud in his earlobe and an Arabic name, traveling alone, for no discernible purpose, to Israel. He could have shortened the inquisition and dispensed with the security guards by mentioning the name of the man who was meeting him in Tel Aviv, but he didn't feel like doing that. He preferred to good-naturedly endure the probing personal questions of the pretty young airline security woman, the worried glances of his fellow passengers and the silent presence of the two Israeli boys in the misshapen sports-coats.

Rasheed slipped on his prescription sunglasses to soften the sharp Mediterranean glare and saw Kedmi standing on the tarmac, waving. He was in uniform, his large belly filling his blue tunic, a broad smile on his face. When Rasheed hit the ground, Kedmi embraced him in a warm hug. "My car is waiting," he said. "I'll get you through passport control in a minute and then we can go home. Ruthie's been cooking all day."

Rasheed looked over at the security boys, raised his sunglasses and smiled. As he climbed into the Volvo 740 parked near the plane, they were still staring. The car belonged to Yoav Kedmi, Israel's national police chief.

"Been a long time," said Rasheed, settling in next to Kedmi in the backseat. A thin-faced police driver was closed off from them by a glass partition.

"Too long," said Kedmi. "I'm sorry you have come under these conditions, though. I wish your first visit to Israel could be a holiday."

"Like your first trip to Detroit, you mean?"

Kedmi grunted. Eleven years earlier he had been

sent to Detroit to investigate an Israeli gang suspected of smuggling drugs and weapons across the river into Canada. On his second day in town, at a stoplight on Woodward Avenue, he had been forced out of his rented Chrysler LeBaron at gunpoint, smashed over the head and robbed. When he arrived, several hours later, at police headquarters on Beaubien Street, the story had already spread through the massive fortresslike building. Cops smirked at him as he walked through the hall to the small room he had been assigned. He had been at his desk only a few minutes when the door opened and a giant black man entered. "Heard you got an ass-whuppin' out on Woodward today," he said without preliminaries. "My name's Rasheed Holliman. Captain, second precinct."

"I don't wish to file a complaint," said Kedmi, feeling sheepish and annoyed.

"I don't wish to take one," said Rasheed. "Chief asked me to keep my eye on you while you're here. Make sure the citizens of our fair city don't stage a repeat performance."

"Please tell your chief I do not need a babysitter," said Kedmi. His English was slow but almost perfect, with only a mild foreign accent. "I have been in tough places before."

Rasheed gazed at Kedmi and felt instinctively that the big, slow-talking Israeli was telling the truth; he seemed like a man who could handle himself. Rasheed thought about how embarrassed he would be to get a public beating in a foreign city. "Look, man," he said, plopping down on the corner of Kedmi's desk, "you know how in all those police movies there's always two officers, one white and one black, who don't get along at first but then they become buddies? Well, let's just skip that first shit and go get us some lunch."

Kedmi smiled for the first time, a wide, gap-toothed grin. "Why not?" he said. Since arriving in America, Rasheed Holliman was the first man who had talked to him directly, Israeli-style, without phony politeness.

"Something special you want to eat?"

"I'll leave it to you," said Kedmi. "You look like a man who appreciates a good meal."

At Vanelli's, an Italian restaurant with murals on the walls and fresh flowers on the tables, they ordered ravioli and steaks and a bottle of Merlot. Kedmi lifted his glass and said, "*L'chaim*. To life."

"To life," said Rasheed, sipping the wine.

"I am surprised you drink," said Kedmi.

"You mean while I'm on duty? That's more movie bullshit."

"Your religion," said Kedmi. "Muslims aren't allowed to drink alcohol."

"Yeah, only I'm not a Muslim."

"But your name—"

"My real name's Ralph," said Holliman with a smile. "You ever see *The Honeymooners*?"

Kedmi shook his head.

"TV show when I was a kid. The main character was this fat white bus driver called Ralph. So I took Rasheed. Back to Africa, roots, you know?"

"Yes," said Kedmi. "When I came to Palestine from Poland I was nine years old and my name was Kasenovski. I changed it to Kedmi, in Hebrew."

"Well now," said Rasheed, "we got something in common. Both going under an alias."

"If I had had a gun today, they wouldn't have beaten me and taken my car," said Kedmi suddenly, a grim expression on his broad face.

"How come you weren't carrying one?"

"It is not allowed," said Kedmi. "In the United States a visiting policeman is not permitted to carry a gun."

"Maybe not in the United States, but this is Detroit," said Holliman. "Here, everybody packs. Hell, even my mother carries a .22 in her purse. What kind of weapon you use at home?"

"Smith and Wesson revolver," said Kedmi.

Holliman reached behind him and produced a snub-nosed revolver from a holster in the small of his back. "Take this for now," he said, handing it to Kedmi. "Go ahead, take it. It's not registered, nobody'll know where it's from. Besides, I got another one on me. Tomorrow I'll get you a Smith and Wesson."

"You carry two guns?"

"Always," said Rasheed.

"Thank you," said Kedmi, gazing evenly into Holliman's eyes as he slipped the pistol into his jacket pocket.

"Forget it," said Holliman, taking another sip of wine. "You'd do the same for me."

*　　*　　*

Yoav Kedmi spent four months in Detroit, much of it with Rasheed Holliman and his family. Rasheed was divorced and his ex-wife and three children had moved to Seattle. He lived at home with his mother and younger brother, Tyrone, in a huge brick house with a sculpted lawn and a swimming pool in the back, in the northwest corner of the city. The first time Kedmi saw it, he was shocked. "In Israel, not even millionaries have such homes," he said.

"Poor folks don't live in 'em here, either," said Rasheed. "My daddy bought this place, couple years before he died."

"What did he do?"

"For a living? Numbers. Gambling."

"That is legal here?"

"Highly illegal," said Rasheed with a smile. "Especially when you're as big as my daddy was."

"It wasn't a problem for you? Being a police officer, I mean."

"Naw, man. When I first started on the force the city was still white, and they didn't give a damn about black folks playing the numbers, long as they did it in their own neighborhoods. Then, after the riots, when the city turned black, well, the new administration was understanding. See, in the old days the only way for a black man to make any real money was undertaking, preaching, pimping or policy. The mayor needed friends with real money, especially since all the rich white men moved out the city. Matter of fact, this house used to belong to a doctor named Blumberg. One of your boys."

"My third cousin," said Kedmi, with a smile. "You grew up in this house?"

"Naw, I came up on the east side, off Gratiot. My brother Tyrone did, though. He's twenty-two years younger than me."

"He's lucky," said Kedmi, remembering the asbestos shack outside Jerusalem he had lived in as a boy.

"That's not what he thinks," said Rasheed. "Tyrone doesn't like being a rich kid. He's bright, makes all A's without trying, but all he wants to do is hang around the projects playing ball and acting slick. Thinks it makes him authentic."

"You're worried about him," said Kedmi. In Israel it was common for police officers and criminals to come from the same neighborhoods, even the same families. He had heard these kinds of stories before.

"I would be, 'cept for two things," said Rasheed. "The kid's a stone basketball player. Next year he's going to Michigan, and after that he'll play pro ball, no question about it."

"What's the other thing?"

"Me," said Rasheed. "There's some crazy mother-fuckers in this city, but none of them is crazy enough to fuck with my baby brother. He can't even buy weed on the street without me hearing about it. I got the whole damn city on his case."

Kedmi never cracked the Israeli smuggling ring in Detroit, but during his time there he became a member of the Holliman household. Rasheed's mother, Dre, reminded him of his Tante Fanya; like her, she was a self-centered, sharp-tongued, openhearted widow with an interest in money, politics and men, and a fierce resentment of aging.

Tyrone was unfailingly polite to his mother; Rasheed he idolized and resented. Rasheed was what Tyrone, at seventeen, longed to be—a legendary badass on the streets of Detroit. Rasheed seldom talked about his exploits, but Tyrone often recounted stories about his big brother's career. Kedmi had considered these tales a form of worshipful exaggeration. Until the night at the Brewster Projects.

Kedmi and Rasheed were in the Athens Cafe having an after-work beer when Rasheed was called to the phone. He listened impassively, took out a pad, wrote down an address and then hung up without saying goodbye. "I've got to go," he told Kedmi. "Finish your beer and I'll see you tomorrow."

"What's the matter?"

"Tyrone," said Rasheed. "He's down at a crack house in the projects."

"Is he selling or buying?"

"He'd never use that shit, he cares too much about his body," said Rasheed. "Boy's trying to be some kind of gangster. I'm gonna go fetch his ass out of there."

"I'll come, too," said Kedmi. "I've never seen a crack house."

"Yeah, okay," said Rasheed. "But this is an unofficial call. Tyrone's six months away from college, and whatever comes down, I don't want his name on any police reports."

Ten minutes later they pulled up in Rasheed's unmarked Ford in front of a dilapidated apartment building in a neighborhood full of boarded-up homes and abandoned stores. It was a warm spring evening and hundreds of people milled about on the street, visiting with one another, laughing and sipping from bottles wrapped in brown paper bags. A murmur went up when Rasheed arrived, and they cleared a path to the front door of the apartment building.

"You better stay in the car," Rasheed said.

"No way, baby," said Kedmi, who was proud of his newly acquired street English. "I'm the backup."

"Well, all right, but remember, whatever goes down, you didn't see it," said Rasheed. He climbed out of the car, took a heavy metal pipe from the trunk and went bounding up the stairs of the building. Kedmi followed, puffing by the time they reached the second floor. Without pausing, Rasheed smashed the metal pipe into the door, bursting the lock, and jumped into the room. Three young black men looked up with shocked expressions. They were seated at a card table, several thousand dollars worth of cash in front of them. One of them was Tyrone Holliman.

" 'Rone, get your ass downstairs to the car," Rasheed commanded in a harsh voice. "You other Negroes, put your hands over your heads."

"Come on, Rasheed, these are my friends," said Tyrone. "We just sitting here, man, ain't nobody doin' noth-ing—"

Tyrone Holliman was six-foot-seven, with an ath-lete's reflexes, but Rasheed knocked him off his seat onto the filthy linoleum floor with a massive forearm sweep before he could even raise an arm. With his other hand Rasheed dropped the metal bar and produced a .357 Magnum.

Tyrone climbed to his feet and stood glaring at his brother. He started to say something, but Rasheed pushed him toward the door, and after a moment's hesi-tation he walked through it and down the stairs. Rasheed stood facing the two young men, who had their hands over their heads.

"You know who you're fucking with?" one of them said.

"Who am I fucking with?"

"Man, we the Rivers," said the young man.

"The Rivers?" said Rasheed, sounding impressed. "Kedmi, we got us two members of the Dee-troit aristoc-racy here. You ever hear about the world-famous Rivers Brothers over in Israel?"

"Only the Kennedy Brothers," said Kedmi.

"Kennedy Brothers ain't shit compared to the Rivers Brothers," said Rasheed in an easy, conversational voice. "They some bad, drug-dealing Negroes."

"When my brother hear about this, he gonna fuck you up, cop or no cop," said one of the young men.

"Okay," said Rasheed. "You get on the phone, call your brother on his beeper and tell 'im to get his ass

down here right now. We gonna have a family conference."

Within an hour, Earl Rivers arrived, an older, thick-
bodied, scowling version of his brothers. Rasheed greeted
him amiably.

"Fred say on the phone you fucking with him and
Donald," said Earl. "I ain't got time to play with you,
man. What you want?"

"I want you to respect my family, Earl," said
Rasheed. "Tyrone's my baby brother. He's got a chance at
pro ball. You get him all confused in this drug shit, he
gonna wind up on the Jackson Prison Globetrotters."

"Man, your brother ain't my business," said Earl
Rivers. "You got problems at home, settle 'em at home."

"I want you to promise me you gonna leave Tyrone
alone," said Rasheed. "You and your brothers. Will you
do that for me?"

"And what you gonna do for me in return?"

"Let you live," said Rasheed.

Rivers laughed. "Shit, man, there's three of us and
just one of you, plus your white punk here."

"He's not in it," said Rasheed. "This is between us. It
doesn't have to get violent. All I want is your cooperation."

"Fuck that shit," said Earl, his eyes fixed on Holliman. "I don't cooperate with po-lice, they cooperate with
me." Kedmi decided that if there was shooting, he'd aim
for the two younger brothers at the card table. *You've sur-
vived five wars,* he thought to himself, *and now you're
going to die in a crack house in Detroit, Michigan.* He was

still thinking about that when Rasheed Holliman opened fire. The room exploded into noise, bodies crashing everywhere, blood and pieces of bone spurting against the walls. Within seconds, all three Rivers brothers were dead.

Kedmi looked at Rasheed, who was already bending over Earl Rivers's body. "I have never seen such a thing," Kedmi said. "You killed them all."

"Three sorry, drug-selling motherfuckers," said Rasheed. He put on a glove, fished an automatic pistol out of Earl's jacket, and placed it in his hand. As Kedmi watched, he did the same with the other two.

"None of the guns have been fired," Kedmi pointed out. "Won't that look strange? For the investigation?"

"Three armed Rivers brothers, dead in a crack house full of drugs and money? I'll get a departmental citation. Deserve it, too, taking this trash off the streets."

"That's not why you did it, though," said Kedmi.

Rasheed looked at Kedmi and nodded slowly. "Tyrone's special," he said. "He needs taking care of." There was an intense look of love on Rasheed's face; a look that Yoav Kedmi had instantly recalled when he had learned that Tyrone Holliman was one of the American basketball players kidnapped by Hizbollah. It had come as no surprise to him when Rasheed had called from Detroit to say he was coming to Israel.

Now they drove past the Tel Aviv bus station and Rasheed turned to Kedmi. "Who's all these hard-looking dudes with machine guns?" he asked.

"Off-duty soldiers," said Kedmi. "Or maybe some

settlers from the West Bank. They carry weapons wherever they go."

Rasheed peered at them. "They don't look like any Jews I've ever seen."

"One of the early Zionist pioneers said that Israel would be a real country when the first Jewish policeman caught the first Jewish criminal," said Kedmi.

"And you a real country now, huh?"

"A superpower," said Kedmi with a slow smile. "Maybe not like Detroit, but . . ." He reached under the front seat, took out a cloth tote bag and handed it to Rasheed, who looked inside and smiled; it contained a .357 Magnum and half a dozen clips of ammunition.

"My brand and everything," he said. "Thanks."

"You said I would someday do the same for you. There is one difference, however. This weapon is registered. When you go to Lebanon, you can take it with you."

"I'm going to tell you a secret," said Rasheed. "I'm not going to Lebanon. Tyrone's here."

"Here? Where?"

"In this country," he said. "I don't know where exactly. Thought you might be able to help me out on that."

"How do you know such a thing?"

"Information," said Rasheed. "Got the word from some Dearborn A-rabs from Lebanon who don't like the idea of this getting pinned on their kinfolk."

Kedmi looked at the driver, making certain that he was not eavesdropping. "Who else knows about this?" he asked.

"Just me and you."

"You didn't inform the American government?"

"Shit, no," said Rasheed. "And I don't want the Israeli government involved in this, either; they'd just tell the Americans. Is that a problem?"

"Rasheed, I am the chief of police."

"In that case, I'd appreciate it if you'd drop me off at the Hilton."

"I could have you followed," said Kedmi.

"Why bother? Look, Yoav, help me find Tyrone and you get credit for the bust of the damn century. What's the matter with that?"

Kedmi scratched his double chin. He had a high opinion of Rasheed Holliman's sources; if Rasheed thought Tyrone and the others were being held in Israel, they very possibly were. If so, he knew something that Shin Bet didn't. Finding the Americans before the security hotshots did would be a hell of a coup for the police, and for him personally. "I'm not taking you to the Hilton," he said. "I want you to stay with Ruthie and me. That way I can keep an eye on you."

"Is that a yes?" asked Rasheed. "You gonna help?"

"A temporary yes. Until we see where this leads."

Chapter Twelve

DIGGER DAWKINS SAT IN A BIG EASY CHAIR IN ABU WALID'S living room and sniffed the scent of roasted chicken wafting out of the kitchen. After a week in the cellar, the high-ceilinged salon, with its well-worn Oriental rugs, fake crystal chandelier and square-backed, mother-of-pearl inlaid chairs arranged around the walls seemed to him almost dizzyingly colorful and luxurious.

It was good, too, to be dressed in his suit again, instead of the stinking robe he had been wearing. The suit was freshly pressed, and although it smelled faintly of kerosene, it made Dawkins feel more like himself than he had at any time since the kidnapping.

Abu Walid was dressed in a long white *jalabiyya* and his thick black hair was covered, as usual, by a large white knitted skullcap. His demeanor was friendly, even respectful—a sure sign to Dawkins that the big Arab had finally figured out who he was dealing with.

Dawkins was especially gratified that Tyrone had been left downstairs. The fact that Tyrone had been allowed to leave the cellar each day to practice basketball with Walid had been a source of rage and humiliation. Here he was, the greatest basketball coach in the world, passed over in favor of a street punk. Not that Dawkins particularly wanted to teach the tall Arab boy to play, but his cavalier dismissal had been, in a way, the most threatening thing that had happened since his abduction. It was as if the terrorists had taken away his identity—an identity now being restored by the gracious hospitality of Dr. Abu Walid.

Walid appeared from the kitchen with a large platter of rice and meat, and placed it on a table near his father. The boy had been doing the serving all evening, first the fresh mango juice, then little fried football-looking hors d'oeuvres stuffed with chopped beef and pine nuts, and now the main course. Dawkins took a bite, smiled and said, "Delicious."

He hated the big Arab doctor, his giant son and the ferret-faced stooges who guarded him day and night, but this was no time for indulging his emotions. Early in his coaching career, Dawkins had often found himself in the living rooms of obnoxious but talented prospects and their even more obnoxious parents. He had mastered the art of insincerity, although he always made a point of paying back the kids when they arrived, on scholarship, at the university. There was no chance he could make

Abu Walid and his band of cockroaches do extra laps around the top of the fieldhouse or play with cracked ribs, but after his release, he would look for a way to get revenge. Maybe his friends in Washington would have some ideas. But for the moment, politeness was the ticket—especially since it was pretty clear from the warm food and the clean clothes and Abu Walid's deferential manner that he was finally on his way home.

The chicken was followed by little cakes drenched in honey and nuts, and potent black coffee. As he drained his cup, Dawkins wondered if he should belch to show his appreciation. He remembered seeing such a custom on a TV documentary, but he wasn't positive if it had been about Arabs or Eskimos, so he settled for a long, demonstrative sigh. "Great meal," he said. "My compliments to your wife."

A brief scowl passed over Abu Walid's face. Then he said, "I have something I would like to show you. Something you will find interesting, I am sure." He went to the VCR, which was resting on top of a bulky, old-fashioned German television, pressed a button and President Edward Masterson appeared on the screen. He was seated at his desk in the Oval Office, an American flag in the background and a stern look on his normally open, boyish face.

". . . Bannion and Tyrone Holliman are not only great athletes, they are innocent Americans," he was saying, "abducted while representing their country on an official tour. And Coach Digger Dawkins, as many of you may know, is not just a legendary figure in the world of collegiate sports, but a close personal friend—"

"I told you that you picked the wrong guy to Shanghai," said Dawkins, unable to restrain his delight. Abu Walid gave him a flat look and returned his attention to the screen.

". . . can say with confidence that these men would categorically support my decision not to bow to the terrorists and their outrageous demands. The United States of America does not negotiate with kidnappers. It does not reward lawlessness." The president paused, frowned and pointed his index finger decisively at the camera. "I warn the kidnappers: I will not, under any circumstances, agree to anything less than the immediate, unconditional release of our citizens."

Abu Walid gestured with his head to one of the guards, who flicked off the VCR. "It appears that your friend, the president of the United States, is a stubborn man," he said.

"I could have told you that," said Dawkins. "Hell, Teddy's famous for it." He kept his voice steady, although he felt so good that he wanted to shout; the president of the United States had put his power and prestige on the line for him, Digger Dawkins.

"Yes," said Abu Walid. "Well, since he has sent me a message, the only courteous thing is to reply." He said something in Arabic to the guard, who opened a nearby cupboard and produced a video camera. Suddenly Dawkins felt an electrical cord being wrapped around his body by another guard. "What the fuck—" he exclaimed as the guard took his right hand and tied it tightly to the wide pearl-inlaid arm of the easy chair.

"Do not curse," said Dr. Abu Walid. He wrapped a black and white *kaffiyeh* around his face, until nothing was visible except his brown eyes. Then he nodded to the guard with the camera and began to speak in Arabic. Dawkins sat, struggling, unable to understand a single word but aware that something very bad was taking place.

"In the name of Allah the All Merciful, all praise be unto Him," declaimed Abu Walid. "We, sons of the martyrs, enemies of the Great Satan and the Jewish dogs and monkeys who do its bidding, have heard the despicable insults of the Satanic American dictator. He has dared to point an insolent, threatening finger against the Avengers of God. To him, and to all nonbelievers, here is our answer."

Dawkins's eyes, which had been fixed on Abu Walid, widened in terror as he saw a gleaming stainless steel scalpel flash under the light of the fake chandelier. With slow deliberation the surgeon bent over Dawkins's right hand and, in plain view of the camera, calmly cut off the index and middle fingers. Dawkins watched in horrified shock as Abu Walid raised his bloody digits and said: "This is our answer to the threatening finger of the American president. If he dares to lift his voice against God, I will amputate the blasphemous tongue of his friend or one of the others. Respect the will of God, comply with our demands and these men will go free. Otherwise, they will be dismembered, as the West has dismembered the House of Islam. You have been warned. May the Almighty bless His faithful. Good night."

The camera stopped filming and Digger Dawkins passed out in his chair. Dr. Abu Walid unwound the *kaffiyeh* and, with deft movements, cauterized and bandaged Dawkins's amputated stubs. He dipped the severed fingers in a preservative solution, wrapped them in gauze and placed them in a plastic zip bag. "Deliver these, along with the videotape, to our friend," he said to Ahmed. Then he turned to Walid, who had gone pale during the procedure. "Have him returned to the cellar," he said, gesturing to Dawkins.

"Please, let me take him someplace else," said Walid. "I do not want to upset Tyrone."

"Very well," said Abu Walid. "Lock him in the safe room. But put a towel in his mouth; I don't want to hear his blasphemy when he awakes."

"Thank you, Father," said Walid.

"You are welcome, my son," said Abu Walid. Silently he thanked Allah for having given him such a fine, obedient boy. Although he considered basketball a waste of time, it pleased him that Walid was so happy playing each day with Tyrone. The guards reported that the black man had a respectful demeanor—so different from the blustering Dawkins—read daily from the Koran and behaved toward Walid in a warm, encouraging manner. When the time came to begin on him, Abu Walid would use an anesthetic; such a kindness would, he was certain, please his son greatly.

CHAPTER THIRTEEN

AHMED THE DRIVER SLIPPED INTO HIS ISRAELI CLOTHES—TENnis shoes, faded jeans, and a T-shirt that said HARD ROCK CAFE, TEL AVIV in Hebrew; hung a gold chain with a small Star of David around his neck and attached his knit yarmulke to his thick, kinky hair with a bobby pin. He put the videocassette and the severed fingers in a canvas gym bag and tossed it into the trunk of his Subaru 1600. The car, which was kept hidden in the compound, bore the yellow Israeli license plates he had bought from a Jewish drug addict who had stolen them from a parked car in Holon. On the seat next to him lay an M-16 semiautomatic, the same rifle carried by Israeli settlers in the West Bank. He ran his hand over the weapon, smiled and said, *"Ha'kol b'seder"*—a Hebrew phrase meaning "Everything's okay."

Ahmed, who was twenty-four years old, had been

speaking Hebrew almost as long as he had been using Arabic. As a small boy in Gaza he had sold pita and fruit to Israeli soldiers and visitors. In 1987, when the Intifada rebellion began and the tourists stopped coming, he improved his Hebrew by hurling jeers and curses as well as rocks at the occupation troops. But his real Hebrew education had come in Gaza Prison, where he spent six years. It was there he learned to read and write the language as well as speak it properly. His teachers were the prison guards. He studied their phrasing and pronunciation until he could amuse them by speaking fluent, grammatical Hebrew in a variety of ethnic Israeli accents—Yemenite, Iraqi, even the native Sabra dialect. It was a way to pass the time, although it embarrassed him when the guards singled him out and started calling him Avi, a Hebrew name.

It was Ahmed's flair for Hebrew that brought him to the attention of Dr. Abu Walid. The doctor was an aristocrat, a distant, deeply pious man from a well-known family. Prisoners from every Palestinian faction treated him with honor, and even the Israeli guards afforded him a grudging respect. Unlike Ahmed, who had been imprisoned for smashing an Israeli soldier over the head with a brick, Abu Walid was a political prisoner, a man of ideology and learning. It came as a great surprise to Ahmed when he approached him during an exercise period in the prison courtyard.

"You are the one they call Avi," he said.

"It is a stupid Israeli joke," said Ahmed. "Because I can mimic the way they speak." His voice shook as he explained; suspected collaborators were punished by death.

"It is a gift," said Abu Walid, "if it is used wisely."

"I am not wise," said Ahmed.

"You are young," said Abu Walid. "But you come from a good family. And you committed a brave act." He saw the surprise on Ahmed's face. "I have made inquiries about you."

"I am honored," Ahmed said, his voice once again betraying his nervousness. "My act was no more than the act of any good Palestinian. As for my family—"

"Do not be afraid," said Abu Walid gently. "You have a good father. Now you have two. You will be my son. Take my hand and walk with me."

And so Ahmed became a disciple of Abu Walid. They prayed together, five times a day in prescribed Islamic fashion, and took their meals together. In time, Ahmed was transferred from his large, crowded cell to Abu Walid's more spacious one. He did not know how this was accomplished, and it was not his place to ask. Dr. Abu Walid was his patron; expressing surprise at his powers would be a form of disrespect.

They spent less than six months together. Abu Walid was released, thanks to pressure from Amnesty International. On his last day in prison he took Ahmed aside. "I am not returning to Gaza," he said. "When you are set free, go home. Stay out of trouble, join no groups. Someone will contact you, and you will come to me."

"As you say," Ahmed murmured. He was young, with no wife, no money and no education to speak of.

But he felt lucky, because he had a future; he would follow Dr. Abu Walid.

Ahmed popped a cassette into the Subaru's tape deck—Danny Sanderson's greatest hits. Sanderson was an Israeli singer who wrote funny songs in Hebrew; Ahmed's favorite was one about boys and girls surfing in the Mediterranean. He had never surfed in his life; in fact he barely knew how to swim. He had never spent an afternoon in the sunshine with a pretty girl, either. His only encounters with the opposite sex had been with Jewish whores in the cheap hotels off HaYarkon Street in Tel Aviv. Dr. Abu Walid did not know of these occasional forays. He preached chastity until marriage, but Ahmed lacked the price of a decent bride. He knew that Dr. Abu Walid would eventually give him sufficient money, but in the meantime, whores were what he could afford.

Ahmed genuinely liked the Sanderson cassette, and it served as camouflage as well; he turned it up and sang along whenever he came to one of the military checkpoints that dotted the roads of the West Bank. It was for that reason, too, that he drove a Subaru; soldiers believed that Arabs drove European cars. Usually the Subaru with its yellow Israeli plates, the Sanderson songs, the yarmulke and Ahmed's breezy Hebrew were enough to get him through any roadblock. Just in case, though, he carried a forged driver's license and Israeli identity card issued in the name of Avi Halevi, which listed him as a resident of Ariel, an Israeli town in the northern part of the West Bank.

It was a three-hour drive to the Lebanese border,

two and a half if he really stepped on it, but Ahmed wasn't in a hurry. He knew this because Abu Walid hadn't told him to rush. One of the best parts of his life was that he didn't have to think for himself. The doctor was the most brilliant man he had ever met, perhaps the most brilliant man in the world, and following his orders gave Ahmed a sense of confidence he could never have achieved on his own. And if the doctor was sometimes cold, even harsh, Ahmed accepted it as the sternness of a father toward a son.

Not that he ever considered himself a true son to the doctor; that would have been presumptuous. Young Walid, whom he and the others called Walid-and-a-Half because of his amazing size, was his father's sole heir and greatest pride. Even in a society in which male children were loved extravagantly, Walid was especially cherished. Nothing else could explain the doctor's decision, so completely uncharacteristic, to allow the boy to play his basketball games each day with the black American.

Ahmed admired Abu Walid's fatherly indulgence as he admired everything about him. It was this admiration that kept him with Abu Walid and his small band of followers, praying, fasting and listening to long, cryptic sermons about the glorious future of Islam while other Palestinian men his age fought the Israelis in the street. "Do not be impatient," Abu Walid often said. "The time will come when we will do a great deed."

Ahmed understood that the time was now. As usual he was unable to fully comprehend the subtlety of the doctor's plans—why, for example, he had chosen to credit the kidnapping of the Americans to the despised Lebanese Shi'ites of Hizbollah, whom he, a Sunni holy man, always called "Evil Misleaders." But it was not his role to understand, merely to obey. Transporting the videocassette and the severed fingers to the north, like slaughtering the tall, ugly American on the beach near Ashkelon or standing guard over the hostages, was his small part in the doctor's unfathomable scheme.

In the distance, Ahmed saw the lights of Kiriat Sh'mona, the last Israeli city before the Lebanese border. He had booked a room at a small hotel in the center of town under his Israeli name. It was an inexpensive place, its lobby furnished with dusty chairs and plastic tables, its rooms barely large enough for a lumpy bed and a closet. He had stayed there before, posing as a salesman from Tel Aviv.

As he checked in, Ahmed joked casually with the night clerk, a Romanian immigrant named Marco. Then he carried his own bag up to his second-floor room, lay on the bed and thought about paradise. According to Abu Walid, paradise was a place where holy martyrs were rewarded with seventy-two lovely virgins and a permanent erection.

Ahmed felt himself getting excited. Tomorrow morning he would meet Maryuma, but she was no virgin and far from lovely. In her mid-thirties, she had pock-marked skin, oily black hair and wisps of hair on her fat chin and upper lip. But it was not her appearance that mattered, it was her address. Maryuma was a Lebanese Christian who lived in the town of Marjayoun, on the other side of the border. Each day she crossed into Israel to report for her job as a cleaning woman at the hotel. She had been working there for ten years and was subject to only the most perfunctory security check by the bored young women soldiers at the crossing point. There was virtually no chance that she would be searched tomorrow evening when she returned home, carrying her plastic bags of personal objects, which this time would include the cassette and Digger Dawkins's fingers.

Maryuma would take the bag to her father's home in Marjayoun and give it to her younger brother. He, in turn, would drive up to Beirut, where he would deliver it to a man who worked as a fixer for the international news agencies. Within hours, the entire world would see the mutilation of the American coach and listen to the fierce message of Dr. Abu Walid. Ahmed had no idea what would happen then, but he was certain it would be something of great importance. He stroked his erect penis and smiled; paradise, he knew, was just a matter of time.

CHAPTER FOURTEEN

WHEN WALID CAME DOWN TO THE CELLAR, THE FIRST THING Tyrone said was, "Where's Dawkins?" Since the night before, when the coach had been outfitted with clean clothes and taken upstairs, Tyrone had been afraid that Dawkins's presidential contacts had finally come through, leaving Tyrone as the only hostage. With Dawkins in captivity, the whole U.S. government would be involved; without him, there would just be the Pistons management and Jesse Jackson, hollering on television. And Rasheed, of course, but Tyrone couldn't imagine how even Rasheed could get him out of the cellar.

Walid blinked at the question and frowned. "He has been taken to a different place," he said.

"Your daddy's still got him?"

"Oh yes," said Walid. "I thought you would be pleased to be on your own. I know you do not like him."

"He all right?"

"Yes," said Walid. "Tell me, who is the most difficult opponent for you to guard? Man to man?"

"It's all man to man in the pros," said Tyrone. "Zone's illegal. Damn, Wally, you asking me questions like some reporter from *Sports Illustrated*. Cut that shit out."

Walid looked at the two guards seated against the peeling wall. Then he stepped forward and slapped Tyrone across the face hard enough to draw blood from his nose. The guards immediately raised their AK-47s, but Walid stopped them with a word and stalked out of the room.

When Walid was gone, one guard held his weapon on Tyrone while the other slipped the greasy black mask over his head and bound his hands with cord. Then they marched him up the stairs, out of the house and stuffed him into the back of the Peugeot. Ten minutes later, when the car came to the end of its bumpy journey, they released him, pulling the mask from his face, and he found himself in the concrete-paved courtyard. A serious-looking Walid stood staring at him, a basketball in his huge right palm. He signaled with his head and the guards untied Tyrone's hands.

"We will play H-O-R-S-E," he said. He dribbled to the center of the court, twelve feet or so from the basket, and launched a hook shot that rolled around the rim and fell through. He retrieved the ball and tossed it to Tyrone.

Tyrone bounced the ball easily on the cracked pavement, looking at Walid through narrowed eyes. Then he gracefully moved forward and threw up a hook that sailed cleanly through the hoop.

"Nice shot," said Walid. He scooped up the ball and, in a low voice, said, "I am very sorry about the slap. It was necessary."

"Why?"

"Last night my father cut off Coach Dawkins's fingers," Walid whispered. "You will not see him again." He dribbled to the foul line, a faded green line on the concrete, and shot a turnaround jumper that missed the rim and thudded off the wooden backboard into Tyrone's hands.

For a wild moment Tyrone was tempted to throw the ball at the guards, race for the Peugeot, grab a weapon and try to escape. But he knew that the little Arabs with their hot brown eyes and automatic rifles would cut him down before he got halfway there. And even if he did make it to the car, he had no idea where he was. He spun the ball in his hands, broke for the basket, leaped into the air, sank a reverse layup and then fell to the ground, holding his ankle and groaning. Walid raced over to him, bent down and inspected the injury. "Are you all right?" he asked with real concern.

"Your daddy gonna kill Dawkins?" Tyrone whispered.

Walid paused for a moment and said quietly, "Yes. If the infidels do not do as he says, he will kill him."

"And then he's gonna kill me."

"He would not do that," said Walid. "You are my friend. He would not harm my friend. Besides, the Americans and the Jews will do as he says after they see the film."

"What film?"

"They made a video film last night," said Walid. "My father warned that he will continue to cut Coach Dawkins apart until his conditions are met. Until there is justice."

"And you think that's right, cutting people up like a chicken?" asked Tyrone, staring hard into Walid's eyes.

The boy tried to hold the gaze, then looked away. "My father is a great man," he said. "I could never oppose him. It would be the same as opposing God."

Tyrone looked over at the watching guards, rubbed his ankle and stood gingerly. "Yeah, I understand that," he said, reaching out and ruffling Walid's hair.

"You are not angry with me?"

"Naw, man, I know this ain't about you," said Tyrone. "Go on over there and when I slap the ball, run full-speed for the basket. I'm gonna teach you how to do a Dee-troit, ally-oop dunk."

Walid walked to the spot that Tyrone had pointed to, waited for the slap and raced for the basket. Ten feet away he looked up and saw the ball, floating softly toward the hoop, framed against the pure blue sky. He left his feet, caught the ball in his right hand and, in one fluid motion, stuffed it through the hoop. Then he let out a wild whoop of pleasure that sent the two guards reaching for their AK-47s. "That was the greatest thing I've ever felt," he yelled.

"Guess you ain't tried sex yet," said Tyrone, smiling.

Walid blushed a deep red and giggled; in his world

the very mention of women was strictly taboo. He was seventeen and a half years old. His friend and hero Tyrone Holliman was not angry with him. He had just flown through the air like a mighty bird and made his first Dee-troit ally-oop dunk. And he had heard the word *sex* spoken out loud, conjuring mental pictures he could barely allow himself to glimpse. It was the most thrilling moment of his life, and his face beamed with excitement and happiness.

Tyrone smiled, too. He smiled because he'd put that look on Walid's face. It was a kind of power, the only kind available to him. Now all he had to do was find a way to use it, and to hang in there until he could. His Wally project was coming along, and his brother Rasheed was out there someplace, too. Sooner or later, something would happen. Until then, what he needed most was time. Hang time.

CHAPTER FIFTEEN

ROSENTHAL SAW THE VIDEO CLIP OF DIGGER DAWKINS'S
amputation on CNN. Journalists were always writing
about the incredible resources of the Israeli intelligence,
but Rosenthal knew that an increasing amount of information about the region was now being obtained cour-
tesy of CNN and the other satellite news networks. And
so he saw and heard what millions of other viewers witnessed—the terrified look on Digger Dawkins's face, the
sure, powerful strokes of the gleaming knife, the blood
spurting from the American's hand, his screams of pain,
the icy-cold brown eyes of the amputator whose face was
hidden in a white *kaffiyeh*, and the Arabic blessings and
threats and demands.

In the next twenty-four hours, as the clip was
played again and again over the world's airwaves, media
commentators agreed that it was one of the most grizzly,

and effective, pieces of terrorist theater ever shown. But the analysts of the Shin Bet weren't looking for drama. They went over the clip frame by frame. When they were finished, they brought their conclusions to Rosenthal, who took them to the prime minister.

Rosenthal knew Prime Minister Natan Peled well. Although they were almost a generation apart, they were both originally Galilee farm boys and, like many of the pioneer descendants, distantly related. They shared the rural Israeli traits of laconic understatement and personal simplicity. These traits misled many into imagining Peled to be a straightforward, unimaginative man. The press often described him as an improbably naive politician, but Rosenthal knew better. He had worked with a number of prime ministers over the years, most of whom prided themselves on their cleverness, but Peled had a farmer's cunning deviousness that the Shin Bet man viewed with admiration and wariness.

"What do you know and how do you know it?" asked the prime minister. He did not have the habit of saying hello to his visitors, or good-bye. Like many of the sons of the socialist pioneers, Peled regarded courtesies, even the most perfunctory, as effete.

"The kidnappers are Palestinians, not Lebanese," said Rosenthal. "Linguistic analysis is positive that the man on the tape is from the West Bank or Gaza. Well educated, from his accent and syntax. And most probably a physician."

"Why?"

"The professional way he severed the fingers," said

Rosenthal. "Another thing—he wants it to look like a Hizbollah operation."

"Terrorists take credit for their operations," said the prime minister. "If this is someone else, why would he give the credit to Hizbollah? Especially on such a successful kidnapping?"

"I don't know. But the accent is a dead giveaway."

"Lebanon's full of Palestinians," said Peled.

"There's another thing," said Rosenthal. "The chair Dawkins was sitting in was made in Bethlehem. We could tell from the inlaid mother-of-pearl. It's a style they don't use in Lebanon."

Peled tapped his fingers on his desk. "This was made in Denmark," he said, "but we're not in Copenhagen."

"Third, there are the shoes," Rosenthal continued. "The terrorist was dressed all in white, white *jalabiyya*, white trousers under the robe and white canvas shoes. The shoes were made by Gali. Israeli shoes."

"Gali exports all over the world."

"Not to Lebanon."

"You can buy anything in Lebanon, you know that. The whole country's one big black market."

"Prime Minister, my job is to give you our best evaulation. We think the hostages are being held in the territories. Probably the West Bank. We think the abductors are local Palestinians, Islamic fanatics, and their leader, or spokesman, is a physician."

"I see," said Peled. "How long will it take to run down the possibilities?"

"On an urgent basis? A few days at the most."

"All right, search," said the prime minister. "But this is extremely sensitive. No one else is to know about this. Not the police, not military intelligence, no one out of the agency. Anything you learn, anything you even suspect, you report to me immediately. Do you understand?"

"Yes, Prime Minister," said Rosenthal, although he didn't. He had no idea why Peled wanted the terrorists to be Lebanese. But Rosenthal had a maxim: Sometimes ignorance, not knowledge, was power—or at least survival and promotion. He wanted to find the hostages, but he had every intention of becoming the next chief of the Shin Bet. It wouldn't help to ask too many questions. And yet, as he walked down the corridor that led to the parking lot, he couldn't help wondering what the hell was really going on.

CHAPTER SIXTEEN

AT EXACTLY 8:00 P.M. EASTERN STANDARD TIME, PRESIDENT
Edward Masterson appeared simultaneously on all the
major networks. Initially they had been reluctant to pre-
empt their prime-time programs—especially ABC, which
had the Yankees-Indians game—but White House com-
munications director George Lione had convinced them
that what the president had to tell—and show—the nation would be more interesting than any sitcom or baseball game.

Masterson spoke from behind his oak desk in the
Oval Office, with nothing but the American flag in the
background. He was wearing a black suit, a somber tie
and, as the camera lights flicked on, his most presidential
expression.

"My fellow Americans," he began. "By now, you
have seen the footage of the mutilation of Digger

Dawkins, one of the three Americans kidnapped by criminal fanatics in Israel and transported to Lebanon. Like you, I am sickened and infuriated by this act of brutal lawlessness. As your president, it is my duty to act.

"As you know, the kidnappers have made two demands: that hundreds of their fellow terrorists be set free by our allies, the Israelis; and that I, as president, publicly beg forgiveness for so-called American crimes.

"Before I continue, let me say that these terrorists do not represent Islam, one of the world's great religions. They pervert their faith, cynically using it to pursue their sick hatred of civilization. And yet, it would be untrue to say that they are simply criminals. They are armed, trained and protected by terrorist states in the Middle East, first and foremost Iran. These states have hijacked a great religion and turned it into a movement to destroy democracy and decency.

"My fellow Americans, all of you remember the seizing of American diplomats in Tehran, the murder of U.S. marines by Iranian-backed fundamentalists in Beirut, the detonation of American civilian aircraft and skyscrapers. These outrages must stop. Tonight I am telling the terrorists in the clearest possible language: We will never apologize to barbaric murderers, and we will never submit to blackmail.

"In recent hours I have been in touch with the Israeli government. Prime Minister Peled has assured me that he will not give in to the extortive demands of the kidnappers. Israel and the United States have stood together many times in the past, and we stand together now, in the face of this most recent outrage.

"My fellow Americans. Too often we have allowed ourselves to be passive victims of the extremists' aggression. But the United States of America is not a nation without resources, and I shall use those resources to wage war against our enemies. Tonight, as I speak to you, American fighter planes are returning to their bases after having launched surgical strikes against Hizbollah bases in Lebanon's Bekaa Valley. We have already received, via satellite, the first footage of these missions, which I will show to you now."

Masterson's stern visage was replaced by grainy but distinct footage of targets caught in the sites of American fighter planes, the flight of missiles, smoke and fire rising from devastated buildings. The pictures ran silently, unaccompanied by narration, while tens of millions sat transfixed, watching U.S. planes pound targets six thousand miles away.

Masterson's face reappeared. "My fellow Americans," he said, "what you have witnessed is more than a display of prowess by the greatest military force the world has ever known. It is also an answer, clear and unmistakable, to the thugs who have seized our hostages and the outlaw government in Tehran that supports them. Today's mission was aimed at terrorist bases. But it was only the beginning. To the terrorists, I issue this warning: Release Dawkins, Holliman and Bannion now, immediately, and the use of American military power will cease. If you do not, you will bear responsibility for the consequences.

"My fellow Americans, these are strong words, and they may lead to even stronger action. But my predecessors in this office, great men like Lincoln, Roosevelt and Truman, did not shrink from the cost of using American power in defense of our national interests. Nor, my fellow citizens, will I. Good night and God bless America."

Teddy Masterson watched his image fade from the monitor, and heard the sound of applause. Lione and the other members of his staff were clapping and, astonishingly, so were the network cameramen and technicians.

"You were brilliant, sir," said Lione.

"You don't say?" said Masterson, his usual irony replacing the solemn television tone.

"I mean it," said Lione. "Just great."

"I second that, sir," said a balding cameraman. "I covered the Gulf War. We should have finished those guys off then."

"Yeah. And turned Iran into a parking lot after the hostages got out," said the TelePrompTer technician. "If you don't mind my saying so, Mr. President."

"I never mind hearing vox populi," said Masterson dryly. "Especially when it agrees with me. Thank you, ladies and gentlemen, for your support and your assistance." He rose and gestured to Carl Berger, who had watched the speech from a far corner of the office, to follow him into the small anteroom next door.

"Well, Carl, I didn't hear your voice in the chorus of praise," he said.

"No sir," said Berger.

"As a military man, I thought you'd be delighted by

today's response. Where's your fighting spirit, man? Whatever happened to damn the torpedoes, full speed ahead? Millions for defense but not a penny for tribute? Don't tread on me?"

Berger blinked; the commander-in-chief of the United States had all but declared war on Islamic radicalism, probably getting three Americans killed in the bargain, and here he was, lighthearted as a midshipman.

"Sir, we still aren't certain where these hostages are, or even who's holding them," he said.

"Well, we know goddamn good and well it's not the Daughters of the American Revolution, don't we, Carl? They're in Lebanon, in the hands of Muslim terrorists, and personally I don't see the difference which particular ones. Hizbollah, Islamic Jihad, Hamas or whatever."

"A few more days and we could have pinpointed them," said Berger. "You said you wanted an operation. I could have mounted one."

"That was before the goddamn videotape," said Masterson. "Our polls show eighty-two percent of the public wants immediate action and by God, they're going to get it." When Berger remained silent, the president scowled. "Goddamnit, Carl, I owe my first allegiance to the American people. They want retaliation, not to mention their money's worth from the defense budget. Right now there are two hundred million citizens across this great land who feel a whole lot better because they have a president who knows how to take care of business."

"The terrorists will probably kill the hostages now," said Berger.

"What if they do? We're in an undeclared war. Soon to be declared, if I have my way. And in wars, there are casualties."

"Wars have a way of escalating."

"No, really?" said Masterson.

Berger moved toward the door. "I will not be patronized, Mr. President," he said.

Suddenly, unexpectedly, Masterson laughed, a loud, genuine bark. "You crack me up," he said. "You're a colonel and I'm the president of the United States, and you don't want me to patronize you? That's what I *am*, your patron. Your boss. Not just in the chain of command, in real life. You think when I was a junior senator, the majority leader didn't patronize me? He fucking *humiliated* me, but so what? I had goals, I had a career, and so I kept a straight face and told myself that the guy was a schmuck. I'm not asking you not to resent me; I'm just telling you to keep it to yourself. Can you do that?"

"Sir, you asked me for my opinion—"

"No, Carl, I never did. You're not my adviser. I've got Draper and all the so-called experts at State for that, not to mention Thomas L. Friedman, Rush Limbaugh and the *Washington Post*. I don't need advice from you, Carl, I need loyalty. Competence. Assistance. Can I count on you? I mean, all the way?"

"Yes sir," said Berger. "It just—"

"You think what I'm doing is callous. But you can't be sentimental in this job. I admire Digger Dawkins even though I happen to know that he's a Republican. I like Bannion—hell, a white guy who can actually jump, he's practically a national asset. And Tyrone Holliman—not only am I a Pistons fan, but his mother is a big figure in Detroit politics. Did you know that?"

"No sir," said Berger.

"What I'm saying is, I'm sensitive to the situation. Message: I care. Remember George Bush? Jesus, what a stiff. One of the things that makes this job doable is realizing that not every one of your predecessors was Thomas Jefferson. But that's not my point—my point is, I want those guys saved every bit as much as you do. But there's a bigger picture. We've got to deal with the Iranians. This is a war. Not a declared one, not quite yet, but a war. Are you going to stay at your post?"

"Yes sir," said Berger.

"Carl," said Masterson, flashing a warm smile, "as of now, you're a brigadier general. I can do that."

Berger stared at Masterson for a long moment and then saluted. "Thank you, sir," he said.

"You're very welcome, General Berger. Now get out of here, go call your wife with the news."

"Yes sir," said Berger.

"And Carl? Be in bright and early. We've got a war to get rolling."

CHAPTER SEVENTEEN

THE NEWS OF THE BOMBINGS IN THE BEKAA VALLEY REACHED Dr. Abu Walid at 6:00 A.M. Jerusalem time. The doctor was an early riser, and he and Walid had already said their morning prayers when the speech was rebroadcast on CNN. It was a rarity, Abu Walid had observed, when prayers were answered immediately; which is why today, as the eastern sun lit the stones of Jerusalem pink and orange, he felt a special elation.

"Listen to him, Walid," he said, nodding toward the television. "The most powerful man on the planet and we have him jumping on a string like a foolish puppet, all praise to Allah."

"All praise to Him," echoed Walid. It was a great thing his father was doing, a holy thing, and yet it was difficult for Walid to see the agony on Digger Dawkins's face or to listen to his screams. He had no doubt that what was happening had to happen, but he regretted that it required the suffering of such a great coach of basketball.

Abu Walid consulted his watch. "He will know what we have done," he said. His son didn't have to ask who "he" was; the doctor was referring to the Deaf and Blind Sheikh in America.

Walid had heard the story of the Deaf and Blind Sheikh many times. It was a piece of family lore, at once a cautionary tale and a religious parable. How the young Abu Walid, scion of one of Gaza's oldest and wealthiest families, had come to Detroit's Wayne State University to study medicine. How he had lost his faith and his religion, eating unclean foods and polluting his body with alcohol. How he had stopped praying, failing even to fast during the holy month of Ramadan. How he had gone with women, American girls of low virtue who had soiled his spirit with their lewd behavior. How he had befriended infidels among his fellow students, even Jews, attending their parties, drinking forbidden beverages and taking part in profane conversations. And how, ultimately, he had renounced Allah for the gods of modernity and science. "I wanted to be a Western man," he often told his son, infusing the term with bitter mockery. "A man of science, a specialist."

As a young boy, Walid had listened to his father's stories of debauchery with dread, imagining him teetering on a pit of damnation, one foot over the side. Lately, though, they were having a different effect on him. He still condemned the wretched impiety of his father's youth, but somehow he couldn't stop himself from visualizing the wanton American girls, imagining the taste of illicit alcohol, wondering about the freedom of a day without prayer. He tried to banish these impure thoughts with redoubled religious devotion, but he could never quite keep them from returning, especially in his dreams.

Abu Walid was a stern father, but a loving and, in many ways, sensitive one. He saw in Walid the signs of his own youthful rebelliousness, and realized that the boy needed outlets for his energy and imagination. It was for this reason he allowed him to play basketball. It was for this reason that he made him, despite his young age, a confidant and partner in his Great Plan. And it was for this reason that he told him, again and again, tales of the Deaf and Blind Sheikh, the holiest man on the face of the earth.

He had first met the sheikh at the initiative of Abdullah Hassan, a fellow resident at the Henry Ford Hospital. He, too, was a Palestinian, from the West Bank town of Jenin. One day he sat down next to Abu Walid in the hospital cafeteria and said, in Arabic, "There is a man who cannot see who wishes to see you; a man who cannot hear who wishes to speak with you."

"There is a man who speaks drivel who wishes to spoil my lunch," said Abu Walid. He knew Abdullah to be an earnest, overzealous Muslim, constantly active in some cause or another. They were the only two Palestinian residents at the hospital, but they were separated by Abu Walid's superior social status—Abdullah was the son of refugees—and by Abdullah's censorious religiosity.

"Your lunch," he said, staring at Abu Walid's bacon sandwich.

"Protein," said Abu Walid with a smile.

"Cholesterol," said Abdullah. "And impurity. Infidel's meat. This man has something to say to you. Come with me to the mosque in Dearborn tonight."

"I've got rounds," said Abu Walid.

"I'll take your rounds," said Abdullah. "Go alone. It is important."

Abu Walid rubbed his eyes. He was permanently exhausted. A night off would be a wonderful gift. "Half an hour," he said. "I'll go for half an hour."

"Here is the address," said Abdullah, handing him a piece of paper. "He will be expecting you at seven o'clock."

Abu Walid took the paper. "Tell me something," he said. "Why is this sheikh so anxious to see me?"

"I do not know," said Abdullah, which was untrue; the meeting was part of a plot initiated by Abu Walid's wife, Fatima. She was a young, conventionally devout woman from a substantial Gazan family, and she was horrified by her husband's secular transformation in America. As a good Muslim wife she did not dare confront him. And so she had gone behind his back, to Abdullah, and begged him to do something that might return her husband to sanity.

Abdullah knew of many sheikhs in Detroit—there were almost three hundred thousand Muslims in the city—but he also knew that Abu Walid would be impervious to their sermonizing. He would need something dramatic, powerful, an argument that did not challenge, but transcended his newly acquired Western rationalism.

At precisely seven, Abu Walid arrived at the mosque in Dearborn. It was like dozens of others, small and dingy on the outside, brightly lit within. Abu Walid was a nonbeliever, but he had been raised properly; at the entrance he removed his shoes and socks, washed his feet in a nearby basin and entered the carpeted main room. A small boy, no older than seven or eight, barefoot and wearing a striped *jalabiyya*, looked up at him and smiled shyly. "Please, sir, follow me," he piped.

Abu Walid was led into an inner room furnished with large chairs placed around three walls, forming a U. In the center sat an old man of indeterminate age, with a long white beard, a powerfully hooked nose and sunglasses that shielded dead eyes. His head was covered in the traditional wrap of the Sunni sheikh, his thick body draped in a gray *jalabiyya*. He banged his hand on the seat next to him. The boy led Abu Walid to the chair, smiled again shyly, and then climbed up on the sheikh's ample lap.

"In the name of Allah the all-merciful I welcome you," said the boy in a bold voice shockingly different from his childish soprano. Abu Walid suspected a ventriloquist's trick, but the boy had clearly spoken from his own mouth.

"I am grateful for the invitation," said Abu Walid. "Grateful and puzzled."

"I will clarify everything," said the boy. Abu Walid looked from him to the old man, a bemused expression on his face.

"I am blind and cannot speak," said the boy. "I see through the boy's eyes and speak through his mouth."

"That is medically impossible."

"Yet it is so. It is a mystery."

"I am sorry, but I am a man of science," said Abu Walid. "I am trained not to believe things that cannot be explained."

"Move close to me," commanded the boy. The old man reached out his veiny hands and caressed the doctor's face. The touch was light yet firm, the touch of a sculptor lovingly working a piece of clay. Then he tightened his hands around Abu Walid's temples, squeezing them with sudden, surprising power.

"My thoughts have entered your mind," said the boy. "My spirit has mingled with your spirit."

Abu Walid felt nothing except an annoyance at the blind sheikh's foolishness; he assumed it was a prelude to asking for money. Anxious to go home to play with little Walid, he said to the boy: "Tell the sheikh that I appreciate his gesture and wish to reciprocate. I would like to donate fifty dollars to his charitable work." He reached for his wallet, but the old man extended a hand and stopped him.

"I do not want your money," said the boy.

"What do you want, then?"

"I want nothing but your belief. Soon you will begin having thoughts that are strange to you. You will feel an overwhelming love for Allah, and a desire to dedicate yourself to his service. You will struggle against these thoughts, but they will overcome you, and they will lead you to a path of repentance and purity. As I speak to you now through the boy's voice, so I will speak to you in the future through your own thoughts. I will instruct you. Listen to my voice, man of science, and obey, for it is the voice of your destiny."

Abu Walid sat speechless. He was a disbeliever, but he could not deny that the words, spoken from the boy's mouth by the ancient sheikh, thrilled as well as frightened him. He had questions, but before he could ask, the sheikh made a waving motion of his hand and the boy said, "Leave me now. Follow your heart. Listen to your thoughts. Allah is with you."

Abu Walid was led from the mosque by the boy. At the door he paused and said, "What will be my destiny?" The boy looked at him with large, black, uncomprehending eyes. "What is destiny?" he asked.

Abu Walid went home and resumed his routine. No revelations came to him in his dreams that night or in the nights that followed. No voices spoke to him. He worked at the hospital, played with his son, acted as a husband to his young wife. And yet, he found himself unable to forget the strange conversation with the Deaf and Blind Sheikh.

The changes came gradually. He lost his taste for pork and instructed his wife, much to her relief, that their meat should be purchased from a "halal" butcher. The smell of alcohol made him dizzy, and he poured his expensive bottles of French wines into the sink. And, without quite intending to, he gravitated to the sheikh's small mosque in Dearborn. The worshipers there were Sunni Muslims, Palestinians like himself, and they accepted his presence without comment or surprise.

On Fridays, the Muslim holy day, the Deaf and Blind Sheikh spoke through the small boy. His message was simple and direct: fidelity to God, brotherhood among true believers and *jihad*, holy war, against the enemies of Islam—Christian infidels, Satanic Jewish defilers and the false Muslims, followers of the Shi'a doctrine propagated by Iran. He taught that there was but one true path, Sunni, and that its goal must be to conquer and purify the world.

When Abu Walid began visiting the mosque, he expected the sheikh to reach out to him or at least acknowledge his presence. But neither the sheikh nor the boy seemed to notice him. Abu Walid could feel the power of Islam growing in his life, day by day, and yet he did not hear the inner voice of the sheikh, nor feel his spirit. He was caught, a man suspended between two worlds, not fully certain of the reality of either.

It was during the holy month of Ramadan that clarity finally came. Given the demands of his residency, the sunup-to-sundown fast was a genuine hardship. And yet he felt clean and strong—stronger than he had for many years. One morning he arose at four, made his ablutions and sat down to the predawn breakfast. Although he knew he needed to eat to maintain his strength, he was neither hungry nor thirsty. "I will go to the mosque," he told his wife.

Abu Walid climbed into his Oldsmobile Cutlass and took the familiar route down Telegraph Road from his home in Allen Park to Dearborn. Suddenly, a faint feeling came over him and he pulled the car into the parking lot of an all-night drugstore. Sitting behind the wheel, he heard what the sheikh had said he would hear, saw what the sheikh had promised he would see. The vision came in the form of a long mural, painted on a background of vivid blue, a tableau of pictures, each still and powerful in its detail. There was a depiction of Abu Walid leaving America for Gaza, a place of poverty and suffering he had abandoned forever; a picture of him dressed as a prisoner, in a Zionist jail; then, an image of himself and his son Walid, now grown tall and powerful, surrounded by a band of warriors. He saw these things clearly, and heard the sheikh's words spoken in the boy's voice: "Go home, ya Abu Walid, and lead the Avengers of God. That is your destiny."

And, as he had foreseen it that day, so had it occurred. As soon as his residency ended, he returned to Gaza with young Walid and his wife. There he set up a clinic, treating the ill, taking only the payment each could afford. He admonished his patients to believe in the Almighty and to fight the Israeli occupiers. It was this admonition, coupled with the fact that several kilos of TNT were found in his modest villa, that landed him in Gaza Prison.

The prison had been full of factions—Fatah, Communists, Hamas, Islamic Jihad—who vied to recruit the charismatic Doctor Abu Walid. He rejected them all. He was no one's follower, save Allah's and the Deaf and Blind Sheikh's. Prison was a place to gather disciples, not to become one.

The time he spent in the Gaza penitentiary was enough to recruit a band of loyal recruits. He chose them carefully—young, unmarried men of little education and modest family circumstances, without money or prospects, devout in their beliefs and defiant in their manner. Most of them had brothers or cousins who had been killed by the Israelis in the Intifada. When the time came, they would be the elite, the first shock troops of a mighty Sunni wave that would engulf not merely Palestine, or the Middle East, but the whole planet, turning the earth into the Dar al Islam, the House of Islam.

When Abu Walid left prison, he moved, with forged papers, to a small village just east of the walls of old Jerusalem. There he established his clinic and, in an abandoned school, his headquarters; gathered his followers as they left prison; and spun his plans. There had been moments, especially when he was in the midst of a surgical procedure or immersed in some medical text, when he doubted his own sanity. But the most rational proof, he told himself, was the objective one; and objectively, he now saw that his vision had succeeded beyond even his greatest expectations. Here he was now, locked in a struggle of wills with the president of the United States of America, as the entire world watched. It was not a struggle he intended to lose.

"Walid, tell Ahmed to bring me Dawkins," he commanded his son.

"Yes, Father," said the boy.

"And Walid? Make sure he brings the video camera."

CHAPTER EIGHTEEN

THE DAY AFTER MASTERSON'S SPEECH, AND ABU WALID'S RE-
sponse, Yoav Kedmi met Rosenthal at the Atara Cafe in
Jerusalem. Kedmi, large and bluff, dressed in the blue
uniform of the Israeli police, was a well-known figure,
and many of the cafe's patrons waved or smiled in his direction. After all, there was never anything to lose by
being on friendly terms with the nation's chief of police.

Rosenthal, on the other hand, attracted no attention. A stranger trying to guess which of Atara's customers was the deputy head of the Israeli secret service
would have picked out the elderly Polish waitress before
choosing him. He was round-faced, with long strands of
brown hair combed from the extreme right side of his
head in a futile effort to conceal his bald spot. He wore
thick glasses with old-fashioned black plastic frames. His

teeth were yellow and uneven, and there were spots of dried blood, shaving nicks, on his neck.

Rosenthal's demeanor was even less impressive than his appearance. He sat slumped in his seat, the posture of a defeated insurance salesman. From time to time he played distractedly with the little paper packets of sugar in the bowl, building small mounds that toppled over. When he drank, tea spilled from his glass and dribbled down his soiled white shirt.

People who didn't know Rosenthal well assumed that he cultivated his unkempt, unattractive appearance for professional reasons. But it wasn't true; Rosenthal hated his postal clerk's appearance. Years ago, when he had been a field agent, he had been a good-looking young fellow, a bit on the short side but thin and muscular with sparkling blue eyes and longish, curly hair. Not a movie star James Bond, by any means, but presentable enough to marry Lea Levi, a Shin Bet translator considered the sexiest woman in the entire agency.

But it had been a long time since he had done any real field work. He was an intelligence bureaucrat now, a powerful man who gave orders, attended meetings and travelled the world conferring with other powerful men. He had his suits tailor-made in London, but on his body they wrinkled as quickly as the cheapest off-the-rack schlock from Moe Ginsberg's. Monthly visits to the dentist failed to brighten his smile, various tonics did nothing to regrow his hair and, no matter how hard he tried, he couldn't get through a day without getting food stains on his shirt. Some men, he reflected, grew physically weak or intellectually vague with age; it was his fate to become messily unattractive.

Kedmi, he observed with envy, was just the opposite. Despite his large belly, he looked smart in his uniform. His skull seemed designed specifically for baldness, like Yul Brynner's or Kojak's. When he moved, his powerful muscles rippled gracefully. Kedmi's one great cosmetic flaw was the hair he allowed to grow from his ears. Rosenthal was often tempted to tell him to cut the damn things, or have them waxed off, but he never did. He figured that a guy as lucky as Kedmi could worry about his own ear hair. It was a petty form of jealousy and Rosenthal acknowledged it. He was a man who had built his entire career on one major attribute—the ability to be brutally honest with himself.

That honesty forced Rosenthal to concede that Yoav Kedmi was a good man. Competition between the police and the Shin Bet was a built-in feature of Israel's overlapping security system. They discreetly fought for turf, sometimes stole each other's successes, often blamed—anonymously, of course, and off the record—each other for security failures. They cooperated, too, but never without a cautious sense of imminent betrayal.

Kedmi and Rosenthal were about the same age, and they had known one another for many years. As they had risen in their respective organizations, they often found themselves working together on special task forces, serving on joint committees, sometimes even sharing cases. During all that time Rosenthal had kept a wary eye on the big police officer, searching behind his congenial front for signs of duplicity, bureaucratic backbiting or personal pettiness. He had found none. Rosenthal did not have a trusting nature, but after all these years, he trusted Yoav Kedmi as much as anyone he knew.

Kedmi had asked for today's meeting. Both of them had seen the horrifying video of the masked mutilator cutting off the right hand of an agonized Digger Dawkins, and heard him proclaim: "The president of the United States has unleashed the Satanic forces of his godless technology on the innocent people of God. He has warned us that his attack is only the beginning. This, too, is only the beginning. If he raises his hand against us again, we will amputate the remaining hand of this hostage and of the others. If he defames Allah with his tongue, we will cut out their tongues. We have no wish to hurt innocent Americans, but we can no longer allow our own innocent people to die at the hands of American bombs. It is written, an eye for an eye, a tooth for a tooth, a life for a life. Once again, President of America, I demand this: Release our warriors from your Israeli prisons. Confess your crimes against God. If you do, your hostages will rejoin their families. If you do not, the responsibility is upon your head. *Allah hu akbar, Allah hu akbar, Allah hu akbar.*"

"You remember when I was in Detroit, years ago on that Israeli drug smuggling thing?" asked Kedmi.

Rosenthal shook his head. "Don't think so," he said. There was no particular reason he should; criminal operations, at home or abroad, were the police's area.

"When I was there I became friendly with a Detroit

police captain," said Kedmi. "His name is Rasheed Holliman."

"Holliman? Any relation?"

"Tyrone's older brother. He's here now." Rosenthal sipped his tea, so interested he failed to notice the drops that fell on his white shirt, just below the second button. "He has information that someone is trying to make it look like a Hizbollah operation. He thinks the hostages are in the West Bank or east Jerusalem. His source on this is very close to the Big Sheikh."

Rosenthal nodded; he knew all about the Detroit-Lebanese connection, and the activities of Sheikh Ali, which had been the topic of more than one conversation with the FBI and Interpol. Sheikh Ali was one of the major Hizbollah fundraisers in America, as well as a powerful voice in its operational councils. "The prime minister says the hostages are in Lebanon," he said in a neutral tone.

"Does he?" said Kedmi. After all these years, he had perfect pitch for bureaucratic locution. Normally Rosenthal would have said, "We know the hostages are in Lebanon"; or "Our sources say they're not here"; or "Your friend's story is worth checking." By simply quoting the prime minister, he was telling Kedmi that he thought Rasheed Holliman might be right.

"Everybody makes mistakes occasionally," said Kedmi. "Even the prime minister." Rosenthal looked down at his tea and said nothing. "Look," Kedmi continued, "we can sit here and fence or we can come to the

point. You saw the same tape I did. The Palestinian accent, the furniture."

"The shoes," said Rosenthal.

"What?"

"The amputator or whatever you call him was wearing Gali shoes," Rosenthal said.

"Good catch," said Kedmi. "We missed that. Did
you tell the Old Man?"

Rosenthal nodded. "Which is when he informed me
that the hostages were in Lebanon."

"I see," said Kedmi. "Any idea why?"

"I could speculate," Rosenthal said. "So could you."

"What are you doing tomorrow night?"

Rosenthal shrugged. "Lea makes the Friday night
plans."

"Come to our place for dinner," said Kedmi. "Ruthie
will cook up something good. I want you to meet
Rasheed."

"Why?"

"Because I was once in a room with him and three
armed criminals who were trying to corrupt his brother.
Rasheed killed all three of them."

"At the same time? How?"

"Shot them in the head, one bullet per customer,"
said Kedmi.

"That's something," Rosenthal said. He had once
shot an Arab in the restroom of the Beersheba bus station. He had been standing at the urinal when the Arab
grabbed his briefcase and ran for the door. Rosenthal,
caught in the middle, hadn't had much choice—the

briefcase contained information about the reactor in Dimona—and so he had shot the Arab. Rosenthal remembered it as a very unsettling experience. "This Rasheed sounds like a serious man."

"Very serious," said Kedmi. Coming from the understated cop, it was a tribute. "Tomorrow night you'll see for yourself. By then maybe you'll have time to check around, see what the Mossad and military intelligence know. And why the prime minister doesn't want to find the hostages."

"I didn't say that," said Rosenthal. Then he paused and added in a low voice, "You could be getting us both in a lot of shit."

"There's all sorts of shit," said Kedmi. "Israeli shit you and I know how to handle. Arab shit, too. But when Rasheed Holliman finds his brother, there's going to be a new kind of shit around here."

"What type is that?" asked Rosenthal, slightly amused that his friend seemed so much in awe of the American cop.

"Detroit shit," said Kedmi. "It's the kind that doesn't come off in the wash."

CHAPTER NINETEEN

PRESIDENT EDWARD MASTERSON'S RESPONSE TO THE SECOND videotape was calm and measured. After ascertaining that it had come from Lebanon, he dispatched the USS *Eisenhower* to the coast of Beirut and ordered it to open fire on the Shi'ite suburbs. He sent the air force to attack Hizbollah targets near the Syrian border. He met with the head of the CIA and reviewed contingency plans for the overthrow or assassination of the rulers of Iran. And he ordered the secretary of Defense and the chairman of the Joint Chiefs to begin preparing Operation Lionheart.

All that was accomplished by lunchtime. He ordered a BLT and home fries from the White House mess and ate while consulting his pollster, Irv Waters. After lunch he contacted the Speaker of the House and the Senate majority leader and raised the possibility of a presidential address to Congress sometime in the next few days. Then he met briefly with his chief foreign policy speechwriter, Danny Fless.

All in all a busy day, he reflected; the best by far of his presidency. He had discovered that the job, like all jobs, was what you made of it. You could spend your time trying to micro-manage the economy or handling the routine business that flowed up through the paper chain or playing party politics or golfing every day—it was up to you. Many of his predecessors had chosen such mundane approaches. They were the obscure portraits on the White House walls, the Millard Fillmores, Rutherford Hayeses, William Tafts and Gerald Fords— undistinguished men, historical footnotes, forgotten even in their own lifetimes.

The presidential portraits that held his attention belonged to the gilded few: Washington, Lincoln, FDR. Different men from different centuries but with one thing in common: They had all led America to victory in great wars. Masterson's idol, John Kennedy, had understood that presidential immortality demanded such a victory— it was the reason for his bellicose inaugural address, the Cuban Missile Crisis, the involvement in Vietnam. JFK had been looking for his war, and if he had lived, he would have found it. His death was merely a matter of bad timing.

The first years of Masterson's administration had been frustrating. With the USSR in pieces, the big foreign policy issue was commerce; and improving the country's trade balance was hardly the stuff of Mount Rushmore.

Lyndon Johnson had shown the futility of domestic crusades with the War on Poverty. Nobody except the poor gave a damn about poverty, and the poor didn't write history.

No, like his predecessors he needed a Great Foe— British colonialism, Confederate slavery, Nazi aggression, Communist expansion—but all he had were minor scrapes in the Balkans, African tribal bloodbaths and some skirmishing in Central America. It was a bad hand to be dealt, and for a long time Masterson had feared that it would remain that way, causing him to go down in history as a competent nonentity.

Until the kidnapping.

Masterson had instantly recognized the potential, especially after the first mutilation tape had been shown. Global television was truly a wondrous thing. In ten seconds an Arab with a scalpel had achieved what it had taken the British years of raped-nuns-in-Belgium propaganda to accomplish—the complete demonization of an enemy. Besides, during World War I, nuns were still venerated and their torture considered a high crime. These days, with them marching around in miniskirts in front of abortion clinics, nuns weren't much of a rallying point. But three basketball heroes were a different story. Central casting couldn't have chosen them better: a black city kid, an Irish boy from California, and a venerated old man being hacked apart on television by a crazed, masked fanatic. This was a situation that contained the grain of presidential immortality.

That grain had to be tended and cultivated. Right

now what he had was a crisis, dramatic but localized. He
needed to expand it into a confrontation, and turn the
confrontation into a crusade, a fight for Western civilization against a fanatical Iranian foe bent on world domination. That was something worth fighting for, a victory
that would put a Masterson Memorial on the Mall.

To make matters even better, it was a just crusade.
The Iranians and their extremist allies *were* bent on world
domination. If Jimmy Carter hadn't been such a Sunday
School teacher he could have put himself in the national
pantheon by bombing Tehran during the hostage crisis.
Bush could have done the same in the Gulf War, taking
Baghdad and then moving across the border to seize
Iran. But they were weak, cautious men and, to be
fair, they still had the Russians to worry about.
Besides, they had been afraid of a confrontation with
worldwide Islam.

In the past, Masterson had been careful to draw a
distinction between the religion of Islam and the Islamic
Republic of Iran. But from now on, he would begin to
make the connection, tie them together in the public
mind. Islam was un-American. It preached holy war
against Jews, subjugation of women, world conquest and
a whole list of other outrages that his staff had compiled
for him. He would take that list before the country, along
with a history of recent attacks on American interests and
the fact that the Iranians and their fellow Shi'ite Muslims,
far from being the victims of fanatical dictators, enthusi-
astically supported them.

And the public would buy it. Every guy who ever

clenched his fists in anger watching bearded fanatics burn the American flag would understand, every feminist who learned that Iranian women were forced to wear the veil, every New Yorker who recalled the World Trade Center bombing. Every basketball fan—and, according to Irv Waters, there were sixty-one million of voting age—would understand, too, as they watched the masked embodiment of militant Islam dismember Coach Dawkins and the others.

There would be opposition: academics, many of them funded by oil money, arguing that fundamentalist Islam was simply a perversion of a great creed; soft-headed liberals, sons and daughters of those who had screamed for Roosevelt to bomb German cities, insisting it was wrong to demonize and punish a whole country for the crimes of its leaders; Texas oilmen and Wall Street bankers scared stiff of losing their investments. But they would be drowned out in a chorus of patriotic approval.

Masterson thought for a moment about the crises that would turn him into a great president. Three basketball heroes made an improbable catalyst but, on reflection, no more improbable than Archduke Ferdinand. The man in the mask, like Ferdinand's assassin, was a crazed figure about to set loose forces he could never dream of. Who was he? It didn't matter. The mask was unnecessary—if he removed it, no one would recognize him in any case—but theatrically it was perfect. Masterson could not have dreamed up such a telegenic personification of evil. But there he was, scalpel, wild brown eyes and all: Masterson's Monster. And if the monster had to be fed on basketball players and obnoxious, self-important sports legends for a little longer, well, it was a small enough price to pay for setting into motion the Great Crusade.

Chapter Twenty

Tyrone bounced the ball, slow and high, tantalizingly close to Walid's outstretched hand, daring him to make a move. "Come on, Two Potata," he called softly, "let's see you take it away."

Walid lunged; his long right arm swiping at the ball. Tyrone smoothly crossed the ball between his legs, letting the off-balance kid trip and stumble as he dribbled past him for an easy dunk.

"Let me try again," said Walid.

"Try a thousand times, you never gonna stop me way you move them big-ass feet of yours."

Walid looked down at his size-eighteen Converse basketball shoes, which his father had especially imported for him, and shook his head. "I can't make them any smaller," he said.

"Not smaller, quicker. Lot of big-footed guys can

move. Lots can't, too. They tend to be white boys. Like yourself."

"I can't change that, either."

"Not necessarily. See, white and black ain't colors, they're styles. There's some clumsy-ass brothers play white, humping around the court like soft-legged camels. Then you take a white guy like Majerle, he can really play. Or look at Jason Kidd, man. He's half white, lighter than you, but he's the baddest point guard out there. 'Cause it's not about skin tone, it's about rhythm, gracefulness. And attitude."

"Something is wrong with my attitude, motherfucker?" said Walid. He was smiling, the way he always did when he tried acting up. It was the smile Tyrone wanted to see, the kind he had once given Rasheed: a little brother's smile.

"Something wrong with your pro-nunciation," he said. "For one thing, it's not mother-fucker, like you saying teeter-totter. It's muhfucker."

"Muh-fucker," said Walid.

"Yeah, better. Now, repeat after me: Two potata muhfucker, two-tone bitch, soupy shuffle muhfucker, you ain't shit."

"What is that?"

"My mumble," said Tyrone. "You gotta have a mumble. You got a game coming up and you're thinking about your opponent, how you gonna stop him, dominate him, humiliate his ass, and while you thinkin', you mumblin'. Then, when you get on the court, you look him in the eye and start again, under your breath so he can hear,

'Two potata,' like that. It makes your adrenaline speed up, gets you in a game mood. Understand?"

Walid nodded.

"Okay, you try it."

"Two potato—"

"Potata."

"Two potata, muhfucker two-toned bitch, suffi shuffle muhfucker, you ain't shit," said Walid, looking to Tyrone for approval.

"Not bad," said Tyrone, laughing. " 'Cept it's not suffi shuffle, it's soupy shuffle—"

"What does it mean?"

Tyrone shrugged. "Rasheed taught it to me. But the main thing is, you gotta say it with the right expression. Tighten your jaw."

Walid clamped his teeth together.

"Good. Now, narrow up your eyes a little, look mean." Tyrone demonstrated and Walid aped him, narrowing his eyes and scowling.

"All right, now you getting a game face. Your opponent sees a face like that he's not gonna think you some goofy white boy from Yugoslavia or Utah. He's gonna think he's up against somebody from the schoolyard. Now, keep that look on your face and use the mumble."

"Two potata muhfucker two-tone bitch, soupy shuffle muhfucker, you ain't shit," Walid declaimed.

Tyrone laughed and slapped him on the back. "By George, I think you've got it," he said in a mock British accent. "Seriously, man, I could hear the playground in your voice. Okay, now you got you an NBA game face and a badass adrenaline-making mumble, we got to start working on your agility. What kind of dancing you like to do?"

Walid shrugged. "I cannot dance."

"I can see that," said Tyrone. "I mean, when you dance with a girl, what kind of dances do you *try* to do?"

"None," said Walid, blushing furiously. "It is forbidden."

"Lotta things forbidden, don't mean they don't happen."

"No, honestly, I have never danced."

Tyrone shook his head. "Well, what kinda music you like?"

"The music at weddings, festivals. Arabic songs."

"The wailing I hear in the mornings? No offense, man, but you can't learn to move to that. I'm talking about MTV-type music."

"I do not watch MTV. My father does not permit it."

"No MTV, no dancing, no girls—Walid, man, what the hell you wanna be a basketball star for? You ain't gonna get no fun out of it anyway." He ruffled the boy's hair and winked. "Okay, put these on," he said, handing him the Walkman earphones. "Go ahead, they're not gonna bite you. Put 'em on."

Tyrone saw Walid glance across the courtyard at the guards, who were smoking cigarettes and gossiping, their AK-47s slung over their shoulders. By now Tyrone had given them all nicknames. The ones on duty today were Moonpie, a round-faced young man with red, rubbery lips; and Spaceman, a bony little guy with thick glasses and pointy ears. The others were Spots, whose face was covered with pimples; Pat Riley, a guy with slicked-back black hair; a muscular young man he called Brown Paper Bag because his skin was that color; and GI Joe, the hitchhiking soldier who had been in the Mercedes that first night. The smiling driver, Ahmed, who had torn Bannion's body apart with his knife, Tyrone had no name for. He tried hard not to think of him at all.

"Man, don't worry about them," he said, nodding across the courtyard. "It's just music."

Walid hesitated, took the earphones and slipped them on gingerly. His face broke into a comically puzzled look; Tyrone had a 2Live Crew tape in there, Luther rapping about putting his dick in some sister. "Now, dance to the beat," Tyrone commanded, moving his own body to demonstrate what he wanted.

Walid looked at the guards and began woodenly moving from side to side. "Shake your shoulders," Tyrone hollered. "Shuffle them big feet, dance and show off. You moving like Frankenstein."

Moonpie and Spaceman were watching now, nudging one another merrily as Walid danced. "Y'all want to hear some sounds?" Tyrone called to them. They were the nicest set of guards, the least sullen. He was never sure how much English they actually spoke, but he saw they understood his invitation. They exchanged glances and began walking toward the court.

"Yo, Walid," called Tyrone. "Take off the phones, let the brothers hear some sounds."

Walid removed the headphones and glared at the

approaching guards in a way that made them retreat to the Peugeot. "Such music is not appropriate for them," he said, sounding like his father.

"Whatever you say," Tyrone said, raising his hand; he had learned not to argue with Walid when he got in His Holiness mode.

"I do not need these," Walid said, holding the head-phones out for Tyrone. "Basketball and music do not go together."

"That's where you're wrong," said Tyrone. "Basket-ball is just a dance, like ballet, except the music is in your head."

"We do not see ballet," said Walid.

"Yeah, it is forbidden, I know."

"I am not responsible for the rules," said Walid, a hint of apology in his voice.

"Didn't say you were. But you wanna play ball, you gotta move like a ballplayer. If that's against your religion, maybe you should just drop the whole thing."

"No," said Walid quickly. "I will practice to the music. But—"

"What's the matter?"

"The words of the song are dirty."

"Forget the words," said Tyrone, delighted that Walid had been able to make them out. Sex was some-thing he wanted on the boy's mind. Sex and fame and money and how basketball could be the key to getting them. "Cat's just singing about making love to a woman, that's all. The language is a little rough, but the pussy's still soft. I know you can relate to that."

Once again Walid blushed violently and took a step back. "Please, Tyrone, do not discuss these things with me," he said.

"Why not? You not a sissy, are you?"

"Sissy?"

"Into boys."

"Of course not," said Walid indignantly.

"Hey, it's no big thing," said Tyrone. "I just wondered. Every time I mention girls you start acting all strange."

"Please, sex is not something I think about."

Tyrone raised his eyebrows. "When I was your age, that's all I thought about. It's nothing to be ashamed of."

"It is different for me," said Walid. "When the time comes, I will have a wife. Until then—"

"You saying you never got any? You a virgin? For real? Man, you don't know what you're missing."

"If my father knew we were talking about this, he would not let me practice with you."

"Well, I ain't gonna tell him if you don't," said Tyrone. "What you do is your business. But if you want to learn to play ball, you better keep on listening to the tapes, get yourself a sense of rhythm."

"Yes," said Walid. "I will do that."

"Good. Come by the cellar, I got some other tapes: James Brown, Prince, Queen Latifah—"

"Latifah is an Arabic name," said Walid. "Is she a Muslim?"

"Yeah, I believe so," said Tyrone. "Now, set those phones down and let's see you take the ball away from me. Remember what I told you, move with me, follow my rhythm." Tyrone dribbled up high, tempting Walid, whose eyes were narrowed and jaw clenched. Tyrone tossed him a simple head fake, bounced the ball through his legs as he broke around him, picked it up on the other side and stuffed it.

"Nice one," said Walid. "You are too quick for me."

"Give it some time," said Tyrone. "And remember, you gonna be a ballplayer, you can't ignore what's happening between your legs."

CHAPTER TWENTY-ONE

ON FRIDAY NIGHT, WHEN BENNY AND LEA ROSENTHAL ARrived for dinner, the Kedmis' modest stucco bungalow in the Tel Aviv suburb of Tzahala was filled with the aromas of Jewish Poland. Lea shook hands with Rasheed, introducing herself by mumbling her name in the Israeli way, and gave him an appraising look. Benny did the same.

"It smells wonderful in here," said Lea.

"Kreplach soup, pupiks, varniskes, potato kugel, all Rasheed's favorites," said Ruthie.

"Don't forget the tsimis," said Rasheed.

"You like Jewish food?"

"I was raised on it," he said. "We had a Jewish lady cooking for us when I was a kid." He watched her face for surprise, but she merely nodded, as if it were the most natural thing in the world.

"See, now, in America that would raise some eyebrows," Rasheed said. "Mostly over there it's the Jewish ladies got black women cooking for them. But there was this widow Jenya, came from Poland someplace, she lived nearby. When the neighborhood changed, she stayed put; guess she didn't have the money to move. So my mama hired her. She liked being the only black lady on the east side of Detroit with a Jewish maid. Know what she used to call her? The *schwartze*." Rasheed's booming laugh filled the small room and bounced off the walls.

"Well, it's time for the *schwartze* to get back to the kitchen," said Ruthie. She was a stout woman, around fifty, with laughing green eyes and an open, straight-talking manner. "Come on, Leahle, you can help me grate the horseradish."

When the women left, Kedmi turned to Rosenthal and said, "Like I told you, this is off the record. Rasheed's here because he thinks his brother is being held in the West Bank or Jerusalem."

"Once I met a journalist from Texas," said Rosenthal. "He told me that the West Bank is four times the size of the Dallas airport."

"Is that right?" asked Rasheed.

Rosenthal shrugged. "I never checked. The point is, it's a pretty small place. Usually when something happens out there, we hear about it. And so far we haven't heard a thing."

"You can talk to Rasheed," said Kedmi, and then, switching to Hebrew, he added: "*Hu mishelanu*"—one of us. It was a phrase to be taken seriously. If Kedmi had merely wanted to make an impression on Holliman, he would have said, in English, "Rasheed is like a brother to me," or some such stock insincerity. "*Hu mishelanu*" was different—it meant that the American had Kedmi's confidence, and that the police chief intended to help him. Rosenthal could do the same or not—Holliman was Kedmi's friend, after all, not his—but he couldn't simply dismiss him with vague phrases and sympathy.

"We're quite certain they're in Lebanon," Rosenthal said.

"But not positive," said Rasheed.

"I told him about the shoes and the furniture and the Palestinian accent," Kedmi said.

Rosenthal gave Kedmi a sharp look. He was sorry now he had agreed to come to dinner. He had misjudged Kedmi's commitment to the American. "Did you give him the secret plans to the reactor in Dimona, too?" he asked in Hebrew.

"Don't exaggerate," said Kedmi.

"Sorry, I don't speak Hebrew," said Rasheed easily. "Look, it wasn't Yoav told me Tyrone was here. I got that information on my own. You know something more, I'd like to hear it."

There was a stirring in the kitchen and Ruthie emerged, red-faced from the heat. "Dinner's ready," she announced loudly.

"Just a minute," Kedmi said. He turned back to Rosenthal and looked at him evenly. "*Nu?*"

The Shin Bet man blinked behind his thick glasses. "Let's eat," he said. "Then we can talk."

*   *   *

After dinner the men went out to the small patio, surrounded by lemon trees, while the women stayed in the living room.

"What do you figure's going to happen next?" Rasheed asked.

"I wouldn't be surprised if there's another video on the way," said Kedmi. Earlier that day President Masterson had announced the arrest of several hundred Hizbollah sympathizers in the United States and declared a freeze on the assets of a dozen Arab charitable foundations accused of fund-raising for the terrorists. "The amputator's bound to be angry."

"Tyrone could do something stupid any minute," said Rasheed.

"Tyrone's not stupid," said Kedmi.

"Naw, he's a smart kid," Rasheed agreed. "But he's got this street complex. He thinks because he didn't come up in the damn projects he's got something to prove. You remember him in that drug house, acting like Super Fly. That's how he got in trouble last season with drugs. Hell, he doesn't even use 'em, he just wants to be part of the scene. The way I figure it, wherever he is, he's plotting some slick move. And Tyrone ain't slick. That's why I've got to get to him soon."

"You're not worried about Dawkins or Bannion," said Rosenthal. There was no censure in the remark, just curiosity.

"Couldn't care less," said Rasheed. "I'm out of the

law enforcement business. All I'm worried about is getting Tyrone. Dawkins's brother can see about Dawkins."

Rosenthal nodded. It was a useful piece of knowledge. "Why do you think the amputator started with Dawkins?"

"You a basketball fan?"

Rosenthal shook his head. "Why?"

"If you were, you'd know that Tyrone and Bannion aren't worth as much," he explained. "Digger Dawkins is the Great White Father."

"Bannion's white."

"White Father's a little different than white. If it was Colin Powell in there with a couple ballplayers, they would have started with him."

"Powell is a national hero," said Kedmi.

"So's Digger Dawkins. Every middle-aged white man in America thinks he's a genius. He's like Vince Lombardi or Bobby Knight, coaches who can win with white players. The terrorists were smart to start with him. You think Masterson would be bombing Lebanon right now and calling up the reserves if it was just Tyrone and Bannion? But when you fuck with Digger Dawkins, you're fucking with American values."

"Why didn't you go to the Americans with this information about your brother?" asked Rosenthal abruptly.

"Because I don't trust them. Hate to say it about my own government, but there it is. I spent two years in 'Nam getting shot at over bullshit. Besides, over here I got Yoav."

Rosenthal glanced at Kedmi from the corner of his eye. The big policeman smiled but said nothing.

"What I don't understand is why Masterson is being so aggressive," said Rosenthal. "These kidnappers, wherever they are, they aren't bluffing. If Dawkins is as important as you say, why put him at even more risk?"

"Good question," said Rasheed. "Tell you the truth, quite a few times I find white people hard to understand."

Rosenthal frowned, and Kedmi laughed. "Don't worry, Benny, he doesn't mean us. Rasheed doesn't consider Jews white people." He glanced through the open patio doors and saw Ruthie and Lea deep in conversation.

"How old do you think he is?" Lea was asking.

"Yoav says they're the same age. Fifty."

"He looks about thirty," said Lea. "Thirty-five, maximum. His skin is so soft. There's no wrinkles on his forehead, even."

"I'll ask him what kind of cream he uses."

"Tell him I'd be happy to apply it, too." Lea laughed. "Probably need a lot. I wonder if it's true what they say about their size."

Ruthie shrugged her plump shoulders and giggled. "How would I know?"

"You've never been with a black man?"

"I've been with three men my whole life," said Ruthie. "One from Kibbutz Ein Hashofet, one an intelligence officer in the Golani brigade and Yoav."

"Who's the one from Ein Hashofet?"

"It was thirty years ago. More."

"*Nu?*"

"Nobody you'd know." Ruthie cut slices of home-made banana cake and handed Lea hers on a small plate. "How many have you been with?"

"Three," said Lea.

"Three! You're telling me you've only slept with three men in your life?"

"Three from Kibbutz Ein Hashofet," said Lea with a hoarse Chesterfield laugh.

"That's more like it," said Ruthie. They were old friends, members of the tiny fraternity of old-time Israel. Their parents had been Zionist pioneers from Poland and, although Ruthie was a kibbutz girl and Lea came from Haifa, they had grown up on the same songs and stories, experienced the same deprivations and hard-ships, developed the same soft stoicism and skeptical in-nocence typical of their generation of sabra women. They knew the same people, the same landscapes, the same ways of getting through life. They shared as much as most sisters, including decades-old images of each other. Lea still presented herself as an alluring, sexually avari-cious woman and Ruthie loyally paid obeisance to the pretense, despite the sagging skin around her friend's neck, the yellowing teeth framed by her too-red lipstick and the liver spots on her veiny hands. "I can't believe you've never been with a black man," said Ruthie.

Lea shook her head. "I'll tell you where I'd like to start, though," she said. "He's not married?"

"Divorced." She stared at Lea and said, "You're not serious?"

"Why not? You don't think he's attractive? Those long legs, those big powerful hands, that beautiful skin. And his voice is like music."

"Lea, stop," said Ruthie.

"When he laughs did you see that pink tongue of his?"

"I mean it," said Ruthie. "Leave him alone."

"What, you're becoming a puritan in your old age?"

"It has nothing to do with that," said Ruthie. Her generation of socialist girls had been reared to regard sexual promiscuity as an ideal, like physical labor or personal honesty. Now that she was a grandmother, her lack of experience no longer bothered her, but when she had been younger, it had made her feel inadequate.

"Don't tell me you're jealous," said Lea.

"I would be and it wouldn't be the first time," said Ruthie. She reached out and laid a fleshy hand on her friend's thin arm. "He's not over here on holiday, Leahle, he's looking for his brother."

"So I'll help him look. Under the bed."

"I'm not kidding. He needs Benny's help. I don't want you to upset him."

"Benny never finds out about my little stories. The master spy."

"He would this time," said Ruthie. "He'll be watching Rasheed." It was true, but it was also a kind thing to say. Ruthie was well aware from Yoav that Benny knew all about his wife's little stories, and had for years. The sad thing was, he couldn't have cared less.

After the Rosenthals left, Rasheed sat with Yoav and Ruthie in the kitchen sipping iced coffee with vanilla ice cream. "Lea found you very attractive," Ruthie said.

"Woman of taste," said Rasheed lightly.

"Be careful of her," Ruthie said, making Rasheed grunt with laughter.

"Nobody's said that to me since my mama told me be careful of girls," he said. "Course, she was absolutely right about that."

"Did you talk to your mother today?" Kedmi asked. He didn't like Ruthie talking this way about Lea; Rasheed was his friend, but so was Rosenthal. Besides, from what he had seen of Rasheed's social life in Detroit, Lea, with her vulgar bracelets and strawlike blond peroxide hair, wouldn't pose much of a temptation.

"This afternoon," said Rasheed. "She's starting to get worried. Said, 'When that old white man run out of thighs and breasts, they gonna start cuttin' up Tyrone.'"

"God forbid," said Ruthie.

"I told her to relax, but the way Masterson's playing this, she may be right." He turned to Kedmi. "What about Rosenthal?"

"What about him?"

"He gonna help?"

"He said he hasn't heard a thing from his sources in the West Bank," said Ruthie.

"That's what he said—wait a minute, you were in the kitchen when he said that," said Kedmi.

"I was setting the table, and I was eavesdropping. You'd have told me anyway." This was true. Kedmi, who lived in a world of secrets, had long ago decided that he wouldn't have any from his wife. Either he could trust her or he couldn't. He believed that he could, and in twenty-eight years of marriage she had never disappointed him.

Kedmi grunted his assent. "When Rosenthal says he hasn't heard a thing, that's probably true, but he hasn't exactly turned the territories upside down, either." He turned to Rasheed. "A while back some terrorists kidnapped one of our soldiers. They said he was being held in Gaza, but we had reason to believe he was someplace near Jerusalem. Benny found him, not more than five miles from the prime minister's office."

"How'd he do it?"

"He sent out every agent he had, arrested anyone even suspected of a connection with the Islamic fundamentalists and beat the crap out of them all until somebody finally talked."

"Good police work," said Rasheed. "What happened to the soldier?"

Kedmi looked down at his brown desert boots and then met Rasheed's eyes. "The terrorists murdered him during the rescue operation," he said.

"You think that's what he's afraid of? Failure?"

"No," said Kedmi. "Benny Rosenthal's only afraid of one thing, and that's making his boss angry."

"Who's his boss?"

Kedmi took a long slurp of iced coffee through his

straw and belched quietly. "Prime Minister Peled," he said.

They sat quietly for a while. Finally Ruthie yawned and said, "The *schwartze's* tired. I'm going to bed. Yoav?"

Kedmi looked at Rasheed, saw something in his eyes and said, "Go ahead, I'll be there in a minute."

When she was gone, Rasheed said, "You got yourself a good woman."

"Thanks," said Yoav. "What?"

"You," said Holliman. "When you picked me up, you said you were going to help me temporarily. Until you decided what to do."

"I remember," said Kedmi.

"Well?"

"I'm due to retire next year," said Kedmi. "You know what happens to retired police chiefs? They get made ambassadors to Argentina or Bolivia, someplace pleasant and out of the way. It's supposed to be a kind of bonus."

"Sounds nice," said Rasheed.

Kedmi snorted. "Can you imagine me as an ambassador? Drinking tea with diplomats and making speeches? Bullshit."

"What are you saying?"

"I'm saying that I'm with you," said Kedmi.

Rasheed nodded. "I appreciate it."

"Forget it," said Kedmi. "I want those terrorists. And besides," he said, rising, "if we screw up, at least I won't have to learn Spanish."

CHAPTER TWENTY-TWO

THE ROOM WAS DARK ALL THE TIME, BUT DIGGER DAWKINS was too sedated to mind. He didn't really mind anything—not the terrible stink from his unwashed clothing, not the itching of his beard, not the miserable food he choked down from time to time, not even the distant throbbing he felt through the filthy, bloodstained bandages on his hand. Dawkins realized that something truly horrible was happening to him, but in a weird way it felt magical as well. For the first time in his life, he had totally lost control. There were no orders to give, no scores to keep, only shadows and dreams.

The dreams brought back long-forgotten memories that ran together in odd, unintelligible sequences. He was crying because the kids laughed when he tried to hit a baseball and fell flat on his keister. His mother was the pitcher, and she was laughing at him, too, until he made her stop by bashing her over the head again and again with his Louisville Slugger. But she was made of rubber and kept bobbing up like a beach toy. Then he was on his Schwinn racer, in the sky over Waterloo, Iowa, his neighbors looking up and shouting to him although he couldn't make out a word. The bicycle landed in Korea, where he found himself in a foxhole surrounded by the players on his first NCAA championship team. They were waiting for him to give the order to go over the top, but when he opened his mouth only weird Arabic wailing came out. The players began to laugh and so did he, laughing and laughing until the man with the beard arrived to give him another shot.

Rough hands raised Dawkins from his cot and lifted him to a standing position. Odd words were spoken as he was moved from the dark room into a lit one. The bearded man was there and the tall boy. They were wearing dresses. Dawkins tried to smile, or maybe he just dreamed that he tried to smile. They didn't smile back, or maybe he just dreamed that they didn't.

"Your government is not cooperating," said the bearded man. "You understand?"

Dawkins nodded. He remembered his father saying, "Put your money in government bonds, the government never goes broke, they can print their own money." What had happened to Dawkins's father? "Put your money in government bonds," he mumbled. "Can't go wrong."

The bearded man said something in the strange language and they put Dawkins in the big chair with wooden armrests. Then a young man with a camera appeared. It must be his postgame wrap-up show, he thought. "We didn't lose, the time just ran out on us," he said. "No team of mine will ever run out of gas in the fourth quarter. Kids these days—"

"Your friend President Masterson is arresting our brothers in America and bombing innocent civilians," said the bearded man. "What do you have to say to that?"

"Put your money in government bonds, goddamnit," Dawkins said in a surprisingly clear voice.

"The president is turning a deaf ear to our demands."

"Keep up the pressure on the inside, double-team the center," Dawkins said. "The big guy will kill you from eight feet."

"I regret the necessity to do this," said the bearded man. "But I will reply to the American president, a deaf ear for a deaf ear." With that he lowered the gleaming steel scalpel across the side of Digger Dawkins's skull. Dawkins's left ear fell from his head onto the floor. The camera panned to it, and then back to the gaping, bloody hole where it had been. A large hand applied some white gauze to the wound, stanching the bleeding, and then the camera moved up, revealing that the hand belonged to the brown-eyed man whose face was hidden in a *kaffiyeh*.

"President Masterson, release our brothers," he said. "Stop the persecution of the believers in your country, and the bombing of mine. Do not utter a word against the people of God, or I will cut out the tongue of this man. *Allah hu akbar. Allah hu akbar. Allah hu akbar.*"

Dawkins fainted in the chair. Dr. Abu Walid gave him a shot of morphine and commanded Ahmed and two others to return him to his room. He sent Walid, who had gone pale and trembling, to his room to rest. Then he looked at the ear, which was still lying on the floor. Idly he wondered what secrets had been whispered into it over the years. It was the ear of an infidel, and it had no more importance to him than a piece of meat at the market. *We will see,* he thought to himself, *how much importance the ear of Digger Dawkins has to the Americans.*

CHAPTER TWENTY-THREE

CARL BERGER WAS UNCOMFORTABLE AROUND ANGRY WOMEN. His mother and sisters all had mild temperaments. His wife, Mandy, too, was easygoing, although she occasionally got snippish when he failed to get home within an hour or two of the appointed time. At the Pentagon he had a number of more or less permanently irritated female subordinates, but he had assumed, correctly, that their ire was directed more against institutional macho attitudes toward women than at him personally. Ellen Dawkins, sitting across from him in his office, glowering with fury, was a new experience.

"I just wondered how much more of my father they're going to hack apart before you put a stop to this," she snapped.

"Professor Dawkins, the president shares your concern—"

"Bullshit. He's hiding in his goddamned office, sending me to messenger boys like you. I can't believe I voted for that prick."

"It's a complex situation—"

"Save that crap for Our Lady of the Pancakes," she said. "I'm not some Aunt Jemima from Detroit. You could have him out of there in two seconds if you wanted to and we both know it."

"If we could, we would," said Berger, although he suspected she was right. Masterson was bringing this on himself.

"They cut off my dad's ear, for Christ's sake," said Dawkins, her voice rising but still under control. "What more do they have to do to show you they're not bluffing?"

"They have to understand that we're not bluffing, either."

"What does that mean?"

Berger looked at his watch. "I guess you may as well be the first to know. Our planes have just returned from Bushire."

"Where's that?"

"Iran," said Berger. "It's their main nuclear research center."

"Oh my God," said Ellen Dawkins. "They'll kill him now."

"I hope not," Berger said. "Maybe they'll finally get the message and release him and the others."

"What kind of name is Berger?" Dawkins asked suddenly.

"Huh?"

"It's a simple question. What kind of name is it?"

"German," said Berger. "Why?"

"German-Jewish," said Dawkins, her eyes narrowing. "That's what this is all about, isn't it, Mr. Berger? Fighting Israel's wars. And if a few Americans or Arabs or Iranians get killed along the way, well, it's a small price to pay."

"Sorry to disappoint you, but I'm just plain German, Professor Dawkins," said Berger coldly. "Fifth generation. I can show you my baptismal certificate if you want."

Dawkins took several deep breaths and worked a trembling smile onto her thin lips. "I'm sorry, that was a stupid, bigoted thing to say. It's just that I've been under so much stress. I don't know what to do or who to blame."

"How about the guys who kidnapped your father?"

"They have no other way to express their desperation," she said. "I'd like to tear them apart with my own hands, but facts are facts. In their position you'd be doing the same thing."

"Dismembering basketball coaches? I don't think so."

"How many innocent Iranian civilians were killed by American bombs today? How many Lebanese? What's the matter with you people, what are you—" Suddenly she stopped talking and swallowed hard. "Jesus, Ellen," she said to herself, "why do you always have to be so goddamned argumentative?"

Berger was moved by the despairing look on her

small, strong face. "Would you like a glass of water? Or a drink? I've got a bottle of whiskey in the drawer."

"A drink," she said. "Jesus, yes, a glass of whiskey."

Berger poured her one and one for himself. Normally he didn't indulge during working hours, but he didn't want her to drink alone. She gulped the Dewar's, shut her eyes while it burned down her throat and said, "I have contacts."

"What kinds of contacts?" asked Berger; he wondered if she was threatening to bring political pressure against the president.

"There's a man I know, a Palestinian from Beirut," she said. "I met him years ago in Berkeley. He was supposed to be a graduate student."

"Supposed to be?"

"He was connected to liberation movements in the Middle East," she said. "I don't know too many details, but he was definitely connected. Pretty high up, actually."

"You're sure? Sometimes people exaggerate."

"We lived together," said Ellen Dawkins. "For almost a year. Then he went back to Lebanon. I think maybe he'd be able to help."

Berger knew exactly what he should do at this point—shake Ellen Dawkins's hand, wish her good luck and usher her out of his office. He was the president's adviser, working under his direct command. He had no moral right, let alone legal authority, to discuss establishing a back channel with terrorists. It was the kind of thing that could end his career or worse. But it could also pacify Ellen Dawkins, keep her mouth shut. "What kind of help?"

"I don't know, exactly," said Dawkins. "Maybe convince them to lower their demands, even let my dad go for humanitarian reasons. I know he'd be willing to try."

"Then why haven't you asked him to?"

"I don't know where he is. Last I heard he was in Iran. You can't exactly get the Tehran phone book and look somebody up. Especially somebody with as many names as he has."

"Well, then." Berger shrugged.

"But let's say I could find him," Dawkins said, "trace him through friends, and get in touch with him. And let's say he'd be willing to talk to Hizbollah. He'd have to offer them something."

"That's impossible," said Berger. "The president will never deal with terrorists."

"It wouldn't have to be much," said Dawkins, pressing her advantage. "Not at first. A meeting with an American official, as a gesture of goodwill. It might set things in motion."

"If you're asking me to meet with these kidnappers, the answer is absolutely no."

"But would you be willing to meet Jamil? Would you at least talk to him?"

Berger hesitated. "Is he wanted for anything?"

"Not here," said Dawkins. "In Israel, but no place else. And under a different name."

Berger frowned, turning his half-full glass in his hands. "If you can find him, and he can get to America,

I'd be willing to talk to him privately," he said finally.
"But I want you to understand up front, I can't negotiate
through him or anyone else. I'd need the president's approval for that."

"Just talk to him," said Dawkins. "See where it
leads."

"On one condition," Berger said. "From now on,
you stay off television. And if you *are* interviewed, stop
bashing the president."

"Why should I?"

"Because it's my condition," said Berger. "Take it or
leave it."

As he watched her silently deliberate, Berger reflected on how much he had learned about politics in the
past few months, how cagey he had become. He would
go to Masterson and tell him that he had secured Ellen
Dawkins's promise to shut up. He knew how valuable
that would be to the president. He closed his eyes for a
moment and saw himself with a second star on his
shoulders.

"All right," she said. "If you talk to him, I'll keep
quiet, at least until after your meeting."

"Jamil what?" asked Berger.

"It was Imami when I knew him," she said. "I honestly don't know what it is now."

"Well, if you find him, let me know," said Berger. "In
the meantime, we'll do everything we can to get this over
with."

"Thanks," said Ellen Dawkins. Her eyes were clear
now, and her handshake firm. "I'll be in touch."

Berger waited two minutes and then buzzed for Andy. "She's gone?" he asked.

"Yep."

"Call the FBI, find out what they know about a Jamil Imami, graduate student at Berkeley a few years ago. Palestinian with a Lebanese passport."

"Yes sir," said Andy.

"Carl."

"Okay, Carl. Anything else?"

"Yes," said Berger, rubbing his eyes so that Andy couldn't read their expression. "Find out what they have on Ellen Dawkins."

CHAPTER TWENTY-FOUR

ROSENTHAL TOOK THE CROWDED ELEVATOR TO THE TOP OF the six-story office building and walked up a flight of stairs to a door leading to the roof. A young security guard wearing an earpiece, a tan safari suit and a Baretta nodded and opened the door.

Twenty yards away, near the edge of the building, the prime minister of Israel stood gazing eastward into the distance, humming a Russian folk tune, a loaf of stale bread in his right hand. He was dressed in a short-sleeved white shirt and a pair of rumpled khaki pants. Standing there among the bird droppings he looked like a broad-backed, red-necked, bow-legged farmer, which is what he had been before he went into politics.

Most mornings, Peled spent an hour or so on the roof, feeding the birds and looking silently at the land-scape. Effi Goren, his young press secretary, wanted to give the story to the press—he thought it made an endearing image, the elderly statesman-farmer communing with nature—but Rosenthal had scotched that. The last thing he wanted was some sniper in a helicopter taking potshots at the Old Man.

Predictably, Peled himself had shrugged off the debate between his subordinates. His line about the press—"Newspapers are like palms; I don't read either"—was an Israeli political classic. Rosenthal happened to know that Peled read the papers every day, and even an occasional book. But the public loved the image of Natan Peled, last of the rough-hewn Zionist pioneers. When it came to PR, thought Rosenthal, the Old Man knew more than a whole faculty of media experts.

The prime minister heard Rosenthal's footsteps, turned, nodded and shifted his gaze back to the landscape. That was his form of greeting. Now it was Rosenthal's turn.

"I met a man named Rasheed Holliman on Friday night," he said. "He's the brother of Tyrone Holliman, one of the hostages."

"Where did you meet him?"

"At Yoav Kedmi's. He was a police captain in America. Yoav knows him from there."

The prime minister extracted an unfiltered Camel from his shirt pocket and lit up. Cigarette smoking was another of his habits. The fact that he was well past seventy and still smoked three packs a day made him seem invulnerable to his countrymen.

"Holliman says he heard from Arab sources in Detroit that the hostages are in the West Bank or Jerusalem," said Rosenthal. "That jibes with what we surmised."

Peled lifted his gaze higher on the horizon. "You know what's going on out there?" he asked. Rosenthal, who made a habit of not answering rhetorical questions, didn't reply; in his experience, the response often wasn't nearly as obvious as it was supposed to be.

Peled threw more bread crumbs and hummed for a while as Rosenthal peered into the distance, waiting. Finally the prime minister said, "Mordechai laughed and Haman cried." It was from the Book of Esther, a reference to the victory of the Jews of Persia over a genocidal enemy more than two thousand years before. It told Rosenthal where Peled meant by "out there"—the Iranian nuclear facility that now lay in ruins under the pounding of American bombers.

"The work of the righteous is done by others," Rosenthal quoted; it was a well-known epigram by a rabbi of antiquity. Neither Peled nor Rosenthal was the least bit religious, but it was impossible to use the Hebrew language without tripping over Biblical or Talmudic pieties at the turn of nearly every phrase.

"This is just the start," said Peled. "I spoke with President Masterson last night. He's intent on stopping the spread of the cancer of Iranian radicalism. Unquote."

"And what does he want from us?"

"From us? Nothing."

"Since when do the Americans want nothing?"

Peled squinted into the sun and tossed crumbs. "Sometimes nothing is a great deal. Besides, this is his war. Finally we have an American president who's killing snakes."

"Killing snakes?"

The Old Man coughed and cleared his throat. "When a snake bites you, you don't go looking for the snake with the bloody mouth," Peled said. "You kill all the snakes in sight."

"Of course," said Rosenthal.

"You and I understand that because we live in the swamp. But it's not so clear to Americans. They want to find the guilty snake, read him his rights and put his trial on television. Right now, Masterson's killing snakes. I don't want that spoiled. This American police captain is looking for a particular snake with a bloody mouth. If he finds it, and that snake turned out to be, let's say, a Palestinian fanatic living in the West Bank instead of an Iranian-backed terrorist, it would make Masterson look foolish. It might even force him to stop killing snakes altogether."

"I don't see why," said Rosenthal. "Let's say the kidnappers are Hamas or Islamic Jihad; they're still Muslim extremists. A snake is a snake."

"I can't count on American public opinion being quite so discerning," said Peled. "I don't want anything or anybody to contradict Masterson. Is that understood?"

"No, Prime Minister," said Rosenthal. He had learned that "Is that understood?" was the most treacherous phrase in the language. It was what politicians said to civil servants when they wanted to protect themselves from accountability. As a young agent, eager to impress,

Rosenthal had once answered the question affirmatively, and it had almost cost him his career. He was prepared to do his duty—to follow Rasheed Holliman, arrest him, deport him, even have him eliminated for the sake of national security—but not without a direct, explicit order.

"You're getting slow, Benny," said Peled, dragging on his Camel. It was a bad sign; Rosenthal couldn't remember Peled ever calling him by his first name. "If you can't understand something this simple, maybe it's time for you to think about retiring."

"And do what? Sit on my porch and write my memoirs?"

"Memoirs," said Peled. "Are you threatening me?"

"No sir," said Rosenthal. "There are certain things I'd never mention."

Peled bent down slowly, picked up a pebble and threw it at a pigeon, which scurried out of the way. "What do you want?"

"To understand exactly what it is you want me to do," said Rosenthal. *And record it,* he added silently; he had a small machine in his jacket pocket.

Peled turned and looked at Rosenthal. He had known Rosenthal since he was a boy. He had served with Rosenthal's father in the Palmach, bought him sweets as a kid. And here they were, on the roof of the prime minister's office in Jerusalem, he and little Benny Rosenthal discussing matters that would change the course of world history. Natan Peled was old, but not too old to appreciate the improbability of the situation. "For the time being I don't want anyone to discover the identity or the whereabouts of the kidnappers or the hostages. If things change, say in a week, we can discuss it again. Is that clear enough?"

"Almost," said Rosenthal. "What are my limits?"

Peled turned and looked around. There was no one within earshot, no one at all except the young security man on the other side of the door. "Use the most gentle means possible. We don't want to hurt anyone. But if it requires force, then I authorize you to use force. Now, is *that* clear enough?"

"Yes, Prime Minister."

"Good," said Peled. He turned away and tossed more bread to the pigeons strutting boldly around the roof. Rosenthal had his tape now, and he would carry out orders. The Old Man knew that Rosenthal surreptitiously recorded their conversations, but he didn't give a damn. Especially now. Because he knew something that Rosenthal didn't—he was dying of lung cancer.

Peled wouldn't accept treatment—he was too old and too complete to wage agonizing chemical warfare against death. His doctor said he had three or four months left. With luck, it would be enough time to witness the dismantling of the Islamic threat to Israel. It was a legacy he intended to safeguard, even at the cost of a few innocent lives. History would judge him. That was all a dying old farmer could hope for.

CHAPTER TWENTY-FIVE

ON THE FIRST DAY AFTER THE AMERICAN BOMBING OF ITS NU-
clear center, there was a stunned silence from Iran. On
the second, the streets of Tehran filled with hundreds of
thousands of screaming protesters, and Dr. Abu Walid
flew to Detroit to confer with the Deaf and Blind Sheikh.
On the third day, the protests spread to other Muslim
countries. In Algeria, fundamentalists burned American
flags and stormed the U.S. Embassy. In Beirut, Damascus
and a dozen other Arab capitals, demonstrators hung
President Edward Masterson in effigy and called for
death to all infidels. An emergency session of the Islamic
Foreign Ministers Conference issued a stern warning to
the United States to stop its aggression. The Iranian ambassador to the UN called for holy war. And a Delta
jumbo jet en route from London to Atlanta blew up over
the Atlantic. All four hundred and eleven passengers and

crew were killed. Half a dozen Islamic organizations, including Hizbollah, claimed credit for what was called by the Iranian government "the just retaliation."

A few hours after the Delta bombing, Edward Masterson summoned the leaders of Congress to the situation room of the White House. There, against a dramatic background of modulated electronic beeping and scurrying general officers, he informed them that he intended to ask for a formal declaration of war. He outlined the case against the Islamic republic of Iran, briefly summarizing the speech he planned to deliver to a joint session on Capitol Hill. But when he asked the leaders, five Republicans and six Democrats, for bipartisan support, he was infuriated to find that they weren't enthusiastic.

"Mr. President, I think we need a little more time to see how this situation shapes up," said the majority leader.

"It'll shape the way we want to shape it," Masterson said.

"Well now, that might be true at the beginning, but wars have a way of getting out of hand," the leader drawled. "There's a billion of these Muslims and a lot of them got bad tempers."

"Come on, Frank, we licked the Germans, the Japs and the Russians. You saying we can't beat a pack of Muslims?" Masterson smiled, trying to hide his annoyance at the fact that the majority leader, who had graduated from a pissant cow college in Texas, was lecturing him in realpolitik like some prairie Pericles.

"Frank's right, Mr. President," said the minority

leader. "The Iranians aren't even claiming responsibility for the bombing. We should at least wait until we get all the facts."

"Jesus H. Christ on the Cross," Masterson said. "They spit in your face and you pretend it's rain. There are more than four hundred dead Americans floating in the Atlantic right now. According to the FBI, we've got an Iranian terror cell in the U.S. prowling around God knows where. We've had to evacuate our diplomats from most of the Middle East. You all saw what they did to Dawkins—"

"That was horrible," said the House whip. "An eye for an eye. Sickening."

"But still not enough to go to war over," insisted the majority leader.

"As the commander-in-chief, my judgment is that it's more than enough," said Masterson. "We've waited too long to fight back in this unholy war against America." He looked from one face to another for a reaction; the "unholy war against America" line was going to be the kicker in his speech.

"With all due respect, Mr. President, you've asked us for our counsel and—"

"It's a bunch of defeatist crap," Masterson finished the sentence. "Did it ever occur to you that in a state of national emergency I can go ahead with or without an official declaration?"

"Don't push your luck," said the majority leader, his Texas drawl becoming leathery. "You got away with the bombing and we let you because bombing Iranian nukes is popular. But it's unconstitutional to fight a war without congressional approval. Unconstitutional and impeachable."

"I'll go over your heads to the people, let them send you a message," Masterson snapped. "I'll get my votes."

"Maybe, but you don't have them now," said the Speaker of the House.

Masterson rested his head in his hands for a moment. "Jesus, you think FDR had to sit around pleading for support after Pearl Harbor?"

"Your problem isn't FDR, it's LBJ," said the Speaker in a kindly tone. "Half the damn Congress is made up of Vietnam draft dodgers. There's no way they're gonna vote for a shooting war, not at this point."

When the meeting broke up, the Speaker caught Masterson by the arm and took him aside. "You really want this war, don't you, Teddy?" he said.

"It's a crusade," said Masterson, "and you're goddamned right I want it." They were close friends whose alliance had been cemented on board a lobbyist's yacht in the Potomac years before. The lobbyist had provided them with three hookers and left, filming the ensuing fivesome with a hidden camera. Three days after sending copies to Masterson and the Speaker, he had fortuitously dropped dead on the eleventh fairway at Burning Tree. The knowledge that they had the capacity to destroy one another's careers had made them unshakable allies.

"Be patient and I'll get it for you," said the Speaker. "Let the mood ripen a little. Concentrate on Dawkins and the other hostages—"

"They're old news," said Masterson. "I've got four hundred caskets right now."

"But they're empty, Teddy; those passengers were blown to smithereens. Besides, nobody knew them. Keep Dawkins front and center, go on putting pressure on the Arabs and let the mood grow for a few more days."

"And then you'll get me the votes?"

"It'll cost you," said the Speaker. "Henry Morton on the Supreme Court. That nuclear-energy splitter thing for my district. And I don't want to see another health care bill before the coming of the Messiah."

"And that'll do it?"

"The Speaker nodded. "Course, I can't speak for the Senate."

"God knows what Frank'll want," said Masterson. "But whatever it is, it's worth it."

The Speaker extended his hand. "In that case, Mr. President, give me a few more days, another atrocity or two, and I'll get you your crusade."

Chapter Twenty-six

WHEN WALID SHOWED UP TO PLAY BALL, TYRONE WAS STILL asleep. Walid shook him by the shoulder and said, "Good morning. Let's go."

The light in the cellar was paler than usual. "Little early, isn't it?" said Tyrone. "Not that I got anything better to do, but ain't this your praying time?"

"I have already prayed," said Walid. He smiled briefly and added, "My father is away for a few days."

"Is that right?" said Tyrone, instantly alert. "Where'd he go?"

"I don't know," Walid lied. He was bouncing on his feet, full of nervous energy. "Come on, Tyrone, get on up, get on the scene. I feel like a sex machine."

"I see you been listening to my tapes."

"They allow these songs to be played on the radio in America? With dirty words?"

"Ain't nothing dirty about sex," Tyrone said. "Funky, yeah. Smelly when it's good and hot. But not dirty."

"Do you have a wife?" asked Walid. He seldom asked personal questions, and he had a bashful look on his face.

Tyrone shook his head. "What do I need with a wife?"

"For sex," said Walid, blushing.

"For sex? Man, you don't need a wife for sex. Cat your age, you don't know a damn thing, do you?"

"In Paradise, Allah gives each martyr seventy-two virgins," said Walid. "And a penis that is always hard."

"That a fact? Well, it's the same in the NBA, only you don't have to die to get the pussy. It waits for you in the hotel lobbies. Now, far as keeping your dick hard, that's up to you."

"Is there really so much sex in the NBA?"

"Is there snow in Alaska? Yeah, there's sex. We all grown men."

Walid stole a look at the guards. "What is it like?" he asked in a husky whisper.

A beatific smile came over Tyrone's face. "It's wonderful, man," he said. "I can tell you some stories make those martyrs of yours jealous. You ever hear of a chick can suck three dicks at the same time?"

Walid shook his head. "Is there truly such a chick?"

"Really and truly," said Tyrone.

"How does it feel?"

"You don't want me to tell you," said Tyrone. "Not

with Moonpie and Spaceman sitting here, watching *your* dick get all hard."

Walid looked down and saw Tyrone was right. "We can talk on the court," he said.

"Never mix business with pleasure," said Tyrone. "You wanna hear about sex, we need the right atmosphere."

"Like what?"

"Someplace don't smell like a sewer, for one thing," said Tyrone. "Place where we can kick back and talk with no guards standing around."

"We could go upstairs," said Walid tentatively. "There is no one there."

"Sounds good."

"But the guards will be outside," Walid added. "I am sorry for this, but it is my father's order."

They climbed the stairs to the first floor of the house, and Walid led Tyrone past a closed door to a large, square room filled with large, square furniture. "This your crib?" asked Tyrone. "Your house?"

"Yes," said Walid.

"Where's your mama? She go with your daddy?"

Walid waved his hand, dismissing the question. His mother was of no concern to Tyrone. He reminded himself that his friend was an American, unaware of Muslim customs and not intentionally insulting.

"Would you like something to eat or drink?" asked Walid. In the cellar, Tyrone was a prisoner; here, in his father's living room, he was a guest, and the amenities had to be observed.

"You got any fresh fruit? Oranges, bananas, peaches?"

"And dates," said Walid.

"I don't like dates, but I been dreaming about fresh fruit."

"I will bring it," Walid said. He went to the kitchen, leaving Tyrone alone for the first time since his capture.

Tyrone looked around wildly. His first impulse was to rush from the house, but he knew there were guards outside. The thing to do was peek around, find something that would help him escape later on. His eye fell on the closed door. When they had passed it before, it seemed to him that Walid had stiffened, like there was something important in there. With catlike steps he walked to the door, quietly turned its latched handle and swung it open.

The room was dark and it reeked with the putrid stench of mottled blood and rotting flesh. Tyrone saw a large shape covered with a sheet, lying on a filthy, red-stained army cot. He thought it was a corpse and took a step back. Then the shape turned in his direction and moaned.

"Coach?" whispered Tyrone. He moved forward and saw what was left of Digger Dawkins. One of his hands was gone, its red, raw stub clearly visible. A dirty bandage partially covered the place where his right ear had been; dried blood stuck to the side of his face and matted his gray hair. There was an empty socket where his right eye had been torn out, a piece of filthy cotton crammed into the hole. Tyrone felt a charge of fear and horror as he

stepped closer and saw Dawkins's other eye fill with
tears.

"Oh, Coach. Jesus."

"Touch me," said Dawkins in a faint, pleading voice.
"Please."

Tyrone hesitated before reaching out and placing a
hand on Dawkins's forehead, caressing it gingerly.

Dawkins mumbled something that Tyrone couldn't
catch. He leaned even closer, the odor making his stomach rise. "What?" he whispered.

"He tore my body," Dawkins mumbled. "I'm all
gone."

Suddenly there was a crashing noise. Tyrone jumped
and shouted in fear. It was Walid, returning from the
kitchen. He had dropped the tray on the floor, and he
was yelling at Tyrone. "Get out of there, get out right
now! This is not for you. Get out, get out!"

Tyrone stared at him and said, "Man, what are you
doing?"

"This is not for you," Walid repeated. "Leave the
room at once or I will call the guards."

Tyrone gave Dawkins a last look and did as he was
ordered. Feeling faint, he plopped down in one of the
square easy chairs in the living room. Walid bent over,
collected the fruit from the floor, placed it back on the
tray and brought it to him. "Here," he said, "eat this. It
will make you feel better."

"What have you done?" Tyrone repeated.

"It is the commandment of God," said Walid. "He
guides my father."

"God told him to cut that old man into pieces? What kind of sick God do you pray to?"

"Do not blaspheme," said Walid in a harsh voice. He struck out at Tyrone's face, but Tyrone caught the blow in midair and threw the boy to the floor, jumped on top of him and pressed his forearm against his windpipe.

"You gonna cut me up next?" asked Tyrone.

"I have been protecting you," Walid gasped. "I will not let this happen to you."

"What you gonna do, disappoint God?" Tyrone pressed harder, tempted to break the boy's neck and worry about the guards afterward. Nothing they could do to him would be as bad as what he had just seen.

"Please," Walid said, fighting for breath. "Let me go." There was a pleading sadness in his voice that convinced Tyrone to loosen his grip.

"You think this is right?" Tyrone demanded in a low, insistent voice that sounded familiar to him. Fleetingly he recognized it as the voice of Rasheed, the same tone he had used that day with the Rivers brothers.

"It cannot be wrong," said Walid. "It is my father's will."

"Your daddy's crazy, man," said Tyrone.

"Do not speak that way about my father," hissed Walid, struggling to get free.

Tyrone tightened his grip again. "This ain't you, Walid. You're a good kid. Look me in the eye and tell me you think this shit is right."

Their faces were inches apart now; Tyrone could smell the garlic on Walid's breath and see the big, oily pores of his skin. The boy glared at him with murderous ferocity, his eyes like the eyes of his father that first night. And then, slowly, painfully, the fierce look dissolved into tearful pools of brown. His voice was choked as he said something in Arabic.

"What's that?" asked Tyrone.

Walid swallowed again and again, trying to make the words come out. Finally he said, "No, Tyrone. It is not right. Allah forgive me, but what my father has done is not right."

CHAPTER TWENTY-SEVEN

ON WEEKDAY MORNINGS, BEFORE GOING TO HIS JERUSALEM office, Yoav Kedmi played tennis at the Ramat HaSharon Country Club, not far from his house. He was an excellent player, but he could rarely beat his driver, Gali, who had been a nationally ranked amateur before joining the police force. They were in the second set when Kedmi looked up and saw the thin, unathletic figure of Benny Rosenthal crossing the court toward him.

"Got a few minutes?" he asked.

"Sure," said Kedmi. "Want to go up to the club-house for a coffee?"

"Out here is fine," said Rosenthal. He was wearing street clothes and heavy black shoes.

A smiling Gali approached, holding out his racket. "You wanna play?" he asked Rosenthal.

"Game's over for today," Kedmi said. "I'll meet you at the car."

"You're not bad for an old guy," said Rosenthal as they watched the driver walk away.

"I'm out of shape," said Kedmi, patting his large stomach. "Sure you don't want some coffee?"

"I had coffee at home," said Rosenthal. "We need to talk about your friend."

"Okay. What?"

"I want him out of the country," said Rosenthal. "The best thing for him to do is leave, right now."

"Why's that?"

"The Old Man," said Rosenthal. "I talked to him."

"You're not going to tell me what this is about?"

Rosenthal gave his friend a level look. "I think you already know what it's about, more or less. Later on I'll be able to tell you more. Not now."

"If you cooperate with Rasheed, you'd have some control over him," said Kedmi.

"I can't cooperate with him, and neither can you. And if he goes poking around on his own, it could be dangerous."

"Dangerous," said Kedmi.

"Tell him to leave, Yoav," said Rosenthal.

"I can't," Kedmi said. "He's already gone."

"Where?"

"What do you care?" said Kedmi. "He's not here. That's what you wanted, right?"

"Why'd he leave?"

"I convinced him it would be the best thing," said

Kedmi. "I've been at this game awhile, Benny; I knew something was up."

"And so he left? Just like that?"

"Rasheed's a pro. He knows there's no way he can do anything here without help. I just explained to him he wasn't going to get any. After Friday night, that was pretty clear."

"You gave him good advice," said Rosenthal. "He'll be much better off staying clear of this."

"I hope so," said Kedmi, wiping sweat from his broad forehead. "I really do."

"You're a good friend," said Benny. He didn't say if he meant to him or to Rasheed.

Everything revolves around friendship, Kedmi thought, alone in the backseat of the air-conditioned Volvo as it made the climb to Jerusalem. Everyone was everyone's friend. The country was so damn small, people so interconnected, that it sometimes seemed to him that Israel was one long strand of friendship DNA, linking everyone to everyone. Here political enemies were friends. Cops and robbers were friends. Business competitors were friends. Opposing counsels were friends. The tax crook and the tax commissioners were friends, the corrupt official and the investigative reporter, the cheated husband and the man his wife was cheating with. Friends, or if not friends, cousins, in-laws, army buddies, ex-classmates, neighbors. Nothing could be understood without understanding this national DNA of friendship.

Kedmi was a friend. He liked people, derived pleasure from helping them, making their lives happier. But it was a delicate balancing act. Everyone wanted a senior police officer as a friend, and every friend eventually wanted a favor. If what they asked wasn't illegal, or absurd, Kedmi obliged. A friend needed to impress his bank manager? He and the friend stopped by the bank and invited the manager for coffee. A subordinate's mother-in-law needed a serious operation? He called the head of the hospital, with whom he had gone to grammar school, and asked to bump her to the head of the waiting line. A neighbor wanted to get his son into an elite combat unit? He picked up the phone to the army chief-of-staff. These were the sorts of favors an Israeli like Kedmi, a *bachur tov,* a good guy, did for his friends.

The favors were freely given but nothing was accepted in return. Kedmi knew all too well the traps and temptations confronting a cop. He had Ruthie do all the family shopping, insisting that she pay in full and save her receipts. He accepted no gifts, no gratuities, not even the customary perks deemed natural to a man in his position. He cultivated a reputation for scrupulousness that shielded him from shady propositions—in thirty years on the force, he had seldom been offered a bribe and only rarely pressured by superiors or politicians.

One by one he had watched more brilliant colleagues fall into the friendship trap. Gross, fired when he got caught burying traffic tickets for his uncle, the deputy finance minister. Lev-Amitz, canned when it came out that he had accepted free room and board from his friend, the manager of a resort hotel in Eilat. Stiglitz, demoted because he had recruited a couple of off-duty subordinates to help his brother-in-law collect a debt. They were all gone now, the victims of friendship. And he was here, in the backseat of the big, comfy Volvo, Israel's number one law enforcement official—and, at the age of fifty, finally asking for favors.

His decision to play the friendship game was not based on the fact that he liked Rasheed Holliman. He was doing it because three prominent Americans had been kidnapped on his watch, on his turf, not in Gaza or Nablus or some other shithole, but right off the street in Tel Aviv. And when he realized that Rosenthal and the prime minister didn't intend to do anything about it, that they had a private agenda of their own, he had decided to cash in the chits accumulated over a lifetime of friendship and use them to find the hostages.

First he had contacted Noni, a senior official in the Mossad who had been his friend since they had served together in the same paratroop company. He needed a name in Beirut. Noni gave him that name.

Next he had called Maurice "Momo" Azulai. Momo was a gifted cop, son of immigrant Moroccans, whose promotions had been held up by the Romanian clique that dominated the department in the seventies. Momo owed Kedmi his present rank as chief of the northern district. It was he who had arranged for Rasheed Holliman to cross into Lebanon the night before.

Two members of the Israeli border police had escorted Rasheed through the security zone. They were

Druze, members of a Galilee clan that Kedmi had once helped obtain a business license for a fish restaurant. The Druze delivered Rasheed to a Maronite Christian cabbie who drove him up to Beirut, to the Mossad's man in the eastern part of the city. The only thing Rasheed knew about the man was that his name wasn't Pierre, because that's what he called himself.

There were many observations Rasheed made about Pierre—that he was in his late thirties, dark-skinned and mustachioed like an Arab despite his European name; that his apartment, grungy on the outside, was elegantly decorated with furnishings that looked like they belonged in a French drawing room; that he spoke almost flawless English with a slight lisp; and that he seemed not a bit nervous by Rasheed's visit—but none of these observations interested him much. Rasheed wasn't in Beirut to make new friends or independent assessments. This was foreign terrain and he wouldn't be on it long enough to understand it. Rasheed knew that Kedmi had confidence in Pierre. That was sufficient.

Pierre offered Rasheed a chair, a snifter of Calvados which he accepted gratefully, and a Gauloises, which he declined.

"Will it bother you if I smoke?" Pierre asked.

"Go right ahead."

"Some Americans find it annoying."

"Not me," said Rasheed. He watched the Lebanese light his cigarette with a gold Ronson, inhale deeply and expel the smoke with indolent ease. He didn't seem in a hurry, and Rasheed didn't intend to push him. He had plenty of experience with informers in Detroit, but the world of Middle Eastern espionage was new to him, and so he waited patiently until Pierre said, "I believe I have what you want."

"Here in the apartment?"

"No, but he will be here soon. In no time at all you will be on your way back to Dixie."

"Dixie?"

"That is what the American correspondents here used to call Israel," said Pierre. "They thought it was a code, as if we stupid Lebanese were incapable of understanding their subtleties. Of course that was in the days when there were many foreign correspondents, before the 1982 war. They used to stay at the Commodore Hotel and drink in the bar there. Have you heard of the Commodore?"

Rasheed shook his head.

"It is of no consequence, except that the man you will be meeting was a habitué. He drank himself to death, in a manner of speaking."

"You gonna introduce me to a dead man?"

Pierre blew a cloud of French smoke into the salon and chuckled. "Physically, he is alive. Spiritually?" He waved his hand airily.

"In the islands they call them zombies," said Rasheed. "The living dead."

"Here they are called expatriots," said Pierre. "This one is an Englishman named Edgar Perkins. He was once a very brave man. He won many awards for journalism in Vietnam. And then he came here, in the seventies, to cover the civil war. In those days he was much admired by his colleagues."

"What happened?"

"He developed bad habits," said Pierre. "It is an easy thing to do in Beirut. He drank too much. He smoked too much hashish. He sniffed too many powders. He fucked too many young boys. And then he made the worst mistake one can make in this country—he developed hubris."

"Yeah, that's a bad one," said Rasheed.

"You see, he was a stringer for European newspapers and magazines. One day he came upon an interesting story about Rifat Assad. And he published it."

"Excuse my ignorance, but who's Rifat Assad?"

"The brother of the President of Syria. The Syrians controlled most of Lebanon then, as they do today. They grew poppies in the Bekaa Valley and shipped them to Sicily for processing, and then to America. It was their most lucrative export crop, and Rifat Assad did not like it when Mr. Perkins published his story."

"Drugs and the First Amendment don't mix," said Rasheed.

"No. And unhappily we have no amendments in Lebanon. In any event, one day Edgar was leaving the Commodore Hotel bar when he was picked up by some of Rifat's people. They took him away. He was gone for some weeks. When he returned, he was broken."

"This Rifat sounds like a bad man," said Rasheed. "How come Edgar's still breathing?"

"As an example to the others," said Pierre. "Night

after night he sat at the bar in the Commodore, reminding the reporters of their professional limitations."

"He's British; why didn't he just go home?"

"The West is a place for the strong and healthy. Beirut is better for a broken Englishman. Here he still has some worth."

"He works for y'all?"

"He works for everyone and no one," said Pierre. "He is a freelancer in the most accurate meaning of that phrase. His value, you see, is simply that he is an Englishman. That makes him respectable enough to deal with Westerners who cannot see how ruined he is inside. In short, a perfect go-between."

"Doesn't sound too trustworthy."

"Only a fool would trust Edgar," said Pierre. "But that is not to say that his information is necessarily incorrect."

"And in this case?"

There was a long ring on the intercom. Pierre glanced at the closed-circuit television monitor and pushed a button. "He is here," he said. "You can judge for yourself."

"No, I can't," said Rasheed.

Pierre smiled. "You do not suffer from hubris, I see," he said approvingly.

Edgar Perkins looked, to Rasheed, both better and worse than Pierre's description. Rasheed was an expert at sizing up white lowlifes—not only had he dealt with the white criminals of Detroit but, as a precinct captain, he had been required to evaluate the readiness of his troops, many of whom were alcoholics or dopers. At first glance, Edgar looked more together than many of them. He was tall, thin and surprisingly well groomed, wearing a freshly pressed light blue button-down shirt, chinos and some kind of Weejuns knock-off loafers. His drawn, ruddy face was closely shaved and his brown hair had been recently cut. It wasn't until Rasheed got a close look at his eyes that he understood what Pierre had meant by the word *ruined*.

"Welcome," Pierre said, greeting him as if he were the British ambassador. "Please meet my friend. He is an American."

"God bless America," said Edgar. "Home of the free and all that."

"Right," said Rasheed. He watched Pierre pour Edgar a large glass of cheap whiskey and serve it to him with self-effacing graciousness.

Edgar hoisted the glass, tossed down the three ounces of liquor, handed it to Pierre for a refill and said to Rasheed, "Are you from New York?"

"Detroit."

"Ah, the Motor City. Motown. Murder Capital USA. The Beirut of North America." He paused, having exhausted his stock of information about Detroit.

"My friend is the brother of Tyrone Holliman," said Pierre, handing Edgar a fresh drink.

"Oh?"

"He is looking for him," said Pierre. "I thought you could help."

"I'm a reporter," said Edgar "If I knew where the

Americans were, I'd have a fucking scoop, wouldn't I?"
He was slurring his words and his tight smile was lopsided.

Pierre sighed. "The videocassettes that have been
given to Reuters and the AFP—" There was no need for
him to finish the sentence; Edgar Perkins understood
that Pierre knew that he was the one who had been
hawking the cassettes to the agencies. He didn't bother
asking how Pierre knew this. In Beirut it was rude and
often dangerous to inquire about the source of a man's
information. He gulped down his second drink, held out
his glass for a third, fired up a Gauloises and waited. "Do
you know in advance when they will arrive?" asked
Pierre politely.

"A few hours, usually."

"They are brought to you by one of the kidnappers?"

"No," said Edgar. "A chap from the south. He
doesn't know where the hostages are. He's strictly a
messenger."

"This chap from the south, is he a Shi'ite?"

"Christian," said Edgar. "Good bloke."

"Where do you rendezvous?"

"He comes to my flat."

Pierre gestured to Rasheed. "I would like for my
friend to meet him," he said. "I will gladly pay for the introduction. Ten thousand, American."

"Ten thousand American? For an introduction?"

"In cash," said Pierre. "On one condition. Your

friend from south Lebanon will not know he's being introduced."

"I told you he's a good bloke," said Edgar.

"Nothing's going to happen to him," Rasheed said. "Nobody's going to hurt him."

Edgar stared at Rasheed for a moment with a puzzled look, as if he were trying to decipher some long-forgotten language. "Hurt him? My concern is that no one put him out of business. He and I have a lucrative relationship."

"He'll never know it was you who fingered him," said Rasheed.

"Do I have your promise as an American on that, old boy?" asked Edgar, draining his glass and looking to Pierre for a refill.

"Swear on the flag," said Rasheed.

"Long may she wave," said Edgar. He gave Rasheed another lopsided grin, downed a fourth glass of whiskey, closed his eyes and fell fast asleep on the Louis XIV sofa.

It took two days for the bloke from the south to arrive with the latest videocassette. Like the others, it was homemade and featured the masked man with the scalpel. He ranted about the bombing of Iran, the perfidious Zionists, the Satanic Edward Masterson and the *jihad* against the infidels. "Your tongues will be silenced," he screamed, and with that, he had sliced off Digger Dawkins's tongue with a powerful slash of his knife.

Rasheed was driven, at Pierre's instruction, to a crumbling neighborhood on the western, Muslim side of

Beirut. His driver was the same one who had brought him to the Lebanese capital. They waited until the bloke from the south emerged from Edgar Perkins's dilapidated building and drove off.

Rasheed's cabbie, displaying a professional competence wholly at odds with the garish mirror hangings in his Mercedes and the wailing, Arabic music on the tape deck, trailed the bloke's Citroën past the airport, down the coastal highway to a winding, eastbound side road that circumvented the Israeli roadblock. It was growing dark, but Rasheed's cabbie drove with his lights off, smooth and quiet, keeping just out of sight. When the bloke turned into the town of Marjayoun, the cabbie kept driving south, toward the lights of Israel, and crossed the border without formalities. He stopped at a roadside cafe to make a phone call while Rasheed wolfed down a wilted omelette sandwich. Then they drove to a small, red-roofed cottage in a residential neighborhood of Kiriat Sh'mona. There, in the living room, Rasheed found Yoav Kedmi waiting for him.

"How was the trip?" he asked.

"You got a hell of a driver," said Rasheed. "I've seen some tails, but this guy's a master."

"And your stay in Beirut? Was it worthwhile?"

"You tell me," said Rasheed.

"Very worthwhile," said Kedmi. "We already ran the plate. We know who the delivery boy is."

"You can run Lebanese license plates?"

"Israel controls part of Lebanon," said Kedmi. "It's complicated. Should I explain it?"

"I'll take your word for it."

"Okay. I think we also know who's delivering to the delivery boy. He has a sister who works in a hotel here. Somebody must bring her the tapes, she gives them to her brother, he takes them up to Perkins and Perkins sells them to the wires. Simple."

"Not too simple?"

"What do you mean?" asked Kedmi.

"This backwards strategy of yours worked so easy, it makes me wonder why they needed you to think of it in the first place. How come Pierre or whatever his name is didn't come up with it on his own?"

"When you say 'they,' who do you mean?" asked Kedmi.

"Whoever Pierre works for," said Rasheed.

"He works for the Mossad," said Yoav. "And the Mossad is like the Shin Bet—it reports to the prime minister."

"So Pierre only finds out what he's asked to find out," said Rasheed.

"More or less," said Kedmi.

"Well, if he works for the Mossad, how come he did this for us?" asked Rasheed.

Kedmi smiled. "Friendship," he said. "Welcome to Israel."

CHAPTER TWENTY-EIGHT

THE SEVERED TONGUE OF DIGGER DAWKINS, SHOWN COAST TO coast, galvanized public opinion. The CNN/USA poll showed that more than 90 percent of the American people wanted war, although only 31 percent favored reinstituting a draft. President Masterson wasn't thinking about a draft, though; the American military, even after its post–Cold War downsizing, was more than able to pound Iran and its allies into the sand.

Still, the congressional debate didn't go as easily as Masterson had hoped. The Speaker was right—there were too many members of both houses whose youthful avoidance of Vietnam made it difficult for them to vote for war. As the maneuvering on Capitol Hill continued, the only person more frustrated than Edward Masterson was Dr. Abu Walid.

"These Americans will sell their own mothers before

protecting their honor," he had complained to the Deaf and Blind Sheikh. "How shall we make them fight?"

"The answer is to show the whole world they have no manhood," said the sheikh through the mouth of the boy, now a teenager. "Strip them naked and castrate them in front of all humanity. That will kindle their rage, and their rage will consume them."

"I see," said Abu Walid.

"No," said the sheikh. "But you will. Go home. Allah will give you understanding."

With that assurance Abu Walid had returned home. Within minutes of arriving he sensed an undercurrent of tension. Although he and Walid kissed and hugged in the usual way, the boy seemed cold and remote.

The doctor banished the guards, brewed tea with *nana* mint and served it to Walid, an extraordinary gesture of respect and affection by a father. "You are troubled," he said. "Did something happen while I was gone? Was there a problem?"

"What you are doing to Coach Dawkins is wrong," Walid blurted. In seventeen and a half years he had never once disagreed with his father, but he felt now that he had no choice. "He is an innocent victim. The Koran forbids the torture of the innocent."

"I see," Abu Walid said, "that in my absence you have become a great and wise sheikh."

"Even a simple boy such as I can see it is wrong."

"And your own father cannot? He needs instruction from a simple boy? Is that your meaning?"

"I would never presume to instruct you," said

Walid. The words were polite but there was a note in the boy's voice that sent a chill through his father—the sound of rebellion. It recalled for him the day he had confronted his own father with the news that he was leaving for America to become a modern man of science. His father had reacted with angry words that had caused a schism not healed in the old man's lifetime. Abu Walid couldn't bear the thought of a similar outcome.

"Walid," he said softly, "do you know what is happening in the world? The American Satan is bombing and attacking the false believers of Iran. The great lie of Shi'a is dying. Even as we speak, their Congress is debating a declaration of war. All because of what I have done to this American coach."

"Yes, Father," said Walid. "But—"

"And do you know what will happen when the American Satan strikes Tehran? A billion faithful Muslims will rise as one and liberate us from the influence and power of the infidels. All because of what I have done."

"Yes, Father," Walid said. "But—"

"Do you remember the faith of Ibrahim, willing to sacrifice his own son?" The doctor closed his eyes and began to recite from memory. "*My son, I dreamt that I was sacrificing you. Tell me what you think. And he replied, Father, do as you are bidden. God willing, you shall find me steadfast.*" He opened his eyes and held Walid with his stare. "If Ibrahim was prepared to sacrifice his beloved son, why should I not sacrifice this stranger for God?"

"You intend to kill him, then?"

"If necessary. It is the commandment of the Deaf and Blind Sheikh."

"Must you do this, Father?"

"We must do it together," said Abu Walid. "Are you steadfast, Walid? Like the son of Ibrahim?"

"I—I—Father, what will become of Tyrone?"

"With God's help, his life will be spared. The next video should be the last one required. And then Tyrone can be released. We are not barbarians, after all, that we hold innocent men for no purpose."

"Do you give me your word you will not harm Tyrone?"

It was an insolent question, implying that Abu Walid needed to swear an oath to his own son. But the doctor responded not with anger but by reaching out and gently stroking the boy's cheek. "I give you my word," he said.

It was the first time in his life that he had ever lied to his son.

CHAPTER TWENTY-NINE

CARL BERGER WALKED INTO THE DENNY'S IN BETHESDA, AS INstructed, just after the breakfast rush. As he scanned the room for Ellen Dawkins and Jamil Imami he heard a man's voice, accented and bubbly, calling his name. Berger turned and saw a jowly round-faced guy with a small mustache under his large hooked nose and a broad smile on his thick, red lips, waving to him. Berger walked over and the guy stuck out a short arm, exposing three inches of snowy cuff under his dark blue Armani jacket. "Hi," he said. "I'm Jim. Ellen's friend."

"Jim?"

"My English name. You know how Americans are, they can never remember foreign names, and if they remember them they can't spell them. 'Is that Jameel with two ee's?'—that sort of thing. So I use Jim because it's easier. Well, usually it's easier, except when I meet somebody like you, who knows my Arabic name is Jamil, and I have to explain why I use Jim. Then actually it would be easier to just say Jamil. But I feel we may have occasion to speak on the phone sometime, and if I call up and say Jamil, your secretary will put me through the two ee's rigmarole. This way if she says it's Jim calling you'll know who she means. I've already ordered coffee and pancakes, as you can see. What will you have?"

"Ah, just coffee," said Berger. Jamil, Jim, whatever he called himself, sounded like a Pakistani rug salesman on speed. "Where's Ellen?"

"She sends her regrets. The tape of her father's most recent amputation upset her."

Berger watched Jamil shovel a large forkful of pancakes and syrup into his mouth. "Glad to see it hasn't put you off *your* feed," he said.

"In my part of the world, you can't let atrocities spoil your appetite. You'd die of starvation."

"How did Ellen get in touch with you?"

"In fact, it was I who called her. A friend in need is a friend indeed, as they say. I thought perhaps I could be of help in the present situation. I am uniquely placed, you see. I hope that does not sound immodest; it is simply a fact." He hoisted another forkful of pancakes into his mouth, gave it a perfunctory chew followed by a powerful gulp and daintily patted his lips. The whole process took approximately three seconds.

"What kind of help can you be?"

"Unfortunately, I can no longer free Ellen's father

unharmed," said Jamil, slurping his coffee. "But he is still alive, and that is something. And there are the others—"

"You have a magic wand, Mr. Imami?"

"Irwin, please. Jim Irwin. Imami is even harder for Americans than Jamil. But I have already explained that problem to you. So I am just Jim Irwin here." He took another enormous bite and, mouth still full, said "I-R-W-I-N," spraying the letters in Berger's direction. "No, I have no wand. But I have useful contacts."

"Why don't you use them, then?"

"If I had a clothing store, would I give away my suits? If I owned a cafe, would I hand out free cakes? If I were the head of an airline, would my friends receive tickets? If—"

"Got it," said Berger. "How much?"

"One," said Imami.

"One what?"

"One favor," Imami said, slurping more coffee and wiping his rubbery lips once again. "I want American citizenship."

"I work for the White House, not the INS," said Berger.

"I assume you have looked at my FBI file," said Imami. "You can see that any application of mine for citizenship is not likely to be accepted. Jamil Imami is considered an undesirable alien. Jamil Imami is considered a threat to the national security of your country. Jamil Imami is—"

"I saw the file," said Berger. "It's not so bad." It wasn't, either. Imami had contacts with radical Palestinian

groups in California in the eighties, and he had been
under government surveillance, but he had never been
arrested, much less convicted of any crime. Interpol had
nothing on him, either. Even the Israelis barely remembered him; their records showed he had spent 1976 in
Nablus Prison for membership in an illegal organization,
and nothing since. Still, Imami was right. In the current
anti-Arab atmosphere, he had no chance at all of getting
citizenship. "I'm surprised you'd want to be an American."

"Why? Che is dead. Mao is dead. Arafat might as
well be dead. Even the USSR is dead. The revolution is
over, General Berger."

"Not the Islamic revolution."

"The Islamic revolution is a joke," said Imami.
"Play-acting, pretend, nonsense. The Russians, with all
their nuclear weapons, could not withstand the United
States. What do the Islamic countries have? Nothing. No
science, no technology, no economy. Their rulers are fanatics and criminals and their generals are the loyal, in-
competent cousins of fanatics and criminals. If it weren't
for oil, they wouldn't have money enough to buy even
food. It is all a mirage, General Berger, a desert dream."

"Those videos are real enough," said Berger.

"The man with the knife? Yes, he is real. But the
camera that takes his pictures is made in Japan. The
scalpel he uses comes from Germany. All he can make is
trouble, gory pictures, nightmares. And nightmares are
not real. They amount to nothing. Less than nothing."

"I know some right-wing Israeli generals who sound like you," said Berger.

"So what? Truth is truth, no matter where it comes from. A brilliant student comes to America and studies science. Then he returns to his country. Do you know what happens to him there?"

"What?"

"If he is lucky, he will be given a job counting boxes in a warehouse for a few years, until the authorities are certain that the Western ideas he has acquired are harmless to them. Then he will be given a scientific job. If he is in Saudi Arabia, he may be a physicist but he cannot say openly that the world is round. If he is an Iranian biologist, he must deny that man is evolved from lower orders. If he is anyplace in the Dar al Islam he must not utter a word against the literal truth of the Koran. No, General Berger, the Islamic revolution is doomed. I have already served in one losing cause. I am too old and too tired to serve in another."

"So you want to become an American citizen."

"Yes, Jim Irwin, American citizen. I have a business opportunity in Utah. A friend from Berkeley, a health food store owner, believes that there is a market for hummus and tahini and tabouli among the Mormons. To pursue this opportunity, I need citizenship. And I am prepared to pay for it."

"By doing what?"

"I will find the hostages for you. If I fail, you lose nothing. But if I succeed, and even one of the hostages returns alive, you arrange for me to stay permanently."

Berger stared at Imami for a moment, and then nodded. For all he knew, Imami could go to Cyprus or someplace, sit around hoping the hostages got released and
then come back and take credit for it. But so what? There
were already two hundred and fifty million Americans.
One more retired radical hummus entrepreneur couldn't
do any real harm. He doubted that the tubby ex-terrorist
could find his ass with both hands, but it didn't really
matter. For now, his major service would be to keep
Ellen Dawkins and her sharp tongue off the talk shows.

CHAPTER THIRTY

RASHEED CHECKED INTO THE HOTEL IN KIRIAT SH'MONA AS Reverend Maurice Williams. As far as the apathetic hotel staff knew, he was an American clergyman on a pilgrimage to the Holy Land. The driver who had taken him to Beirut was now his Israeli guide, equipped with an official touring car and a silly cap that looked like an upside down bell.

For two days they drove around the Galilee while one of Kedmi's men watched the hotel. Rasheed swam in the Sea of Galilee, washed his feet in the Jordan River, ate lunch at a dude ranch owned by an American from Chicago and climbed the Mount of Beatitudes. On the second night, while they were visiting in Nazareth, the driver got a call on his cellular phone: Ahmed had arrived.

Ahmed, using his Israeli papers, checked into his usual room, lay undisturbed on the bed and fell asleep thinking about the pleasures of paradise. In the morning, Maryuma arrived with her cleaning cart, right on schedule.

"I have another package for you to deliver," he said.

"I've got to stay over," she said, slipping the bundle into her cart between the sheets and towels. "I won't be going home for two days. Is that soon enough?"

"I guess so," said Ahmed. "Don't open the package or tamper with it in any way. If you do, I'll find out."

"It's men's business," said Maryuma. In the past she had been curious about the packages, but afraid to explore their contents. Now she didn't even allow herself to wonder. The deal she had struck with the police—keeping her job in exchange for alerting them to Ahmed's arrival—was a piece of good luck. If there was one thing her life had taught her, it was that she couldn't count on an overabundance of good luck.

Maryuma carried the package down the hall and gave it to the undercover cop in Room 216. Then she returned to her cleaning duties. She suspected that she'd never see Ahmed again, but she didn't care; he was nothing to her except one more horny man who played with himself in bed and left semen stains on the sheets.

Rasheed and the driver waited for Ahmed to check out and then followed him in the tourist limo. He took a circuitous route, driving west all the way to Acre on the Mediterranean and then down the coastal road. Just before Haifa, he pulled the Subaru over to the side, near a group of hitchhiking soldiers. They crowded around his open window. "Jerusalem, guys," he called in Hebrew.

Two soldiers climbed in the backseat. They were carrying M-16s, but Ahmed could tell from their shiny boots, fresh uniforms and soft bellies that they were not real soldiers, only clerks in uniform. He made a point of picking up soldiers whenever possible. Talking to them helped him keep his Hebrew sharp and his slang up to date. It also gave him a perfect cover. More than once he and his uniformed passengers had been waved past a security roadblock.

When he was a boy, back in the seventies, the Israeli soldiers in Gaza had seemed like fierce, cruel warriors. But during the Intifada, the soldiers he had skirmished with in the streets had been a disappointment. He had expected them to react to the stones and curses with fearsome power, but mostly they had just fired tear gas and rubber bullets and made sure they stayed out of range of Palestinian rocks. The realization that Israeli soldiers weren't so tough was reassuring but, at the same time, vaguely disturbing. It made him wonder how they kept defeating the Arabs in battle.

The hitchhiking soldiers he gave lifts to mostly confirmed his opinion that there was something wrong with the Israeli army. He checked his rearview mirror and saw that the two he had picked up today were already asleep. One had a boy's face, thick glasses and a silly looking crew cut. The other, slack-jawed and tubby, hadn't even bothered taking the magazine out of his rifle before dozing off. Ahmed knew from experience that if he let them, they'd sleep all the way to Jerusalem. He also knew that if he woke them up and got them talking, they'd tell him what unit they were in and where their base was and anything else he might want to know. It would be the easiest thing in the world to kill them if he felt like it. He could imagine plunging his knife into the flabby belly of the fat kid in the back, now snoring lightly; or bashing in the skull of his crew-cut buddy. Of course he would do no such thing. He was on a mission, and such self-indulgence was out of the question. They didn't know it, but they were as safe with him as in an Egged bus—safer, because he was a careful driver. Later he'd wake them up, talk a little Hebrew and see what they thought of his Sanderson tape. For now, though, he was content to simply cruise along, daydreaming about paradise and the seventy-two virgins.

When Ahmed picked up the soldiers, Rasheed's driver snapped open his cellular phone and made a call. He spoke in Hebrew, alerting other units. There were undercover cars along the route and a succession of helicopters floated innocently above the highway. Rasheed, who had done his share of tailing, was impressed by the professionalism of Kedmi's operation.

The white Subaru entered Jerusalem from the west. A police checkpoint stood at the side of the road, but the three uniformed officers ignored the car as it drove past. Ahmed dropped the soldiers off across from the main bus station and drove on into the Jewish downtown section. He parked in a lot a few blocks from the Arab part of town, left his Israeli papers and his yarmulke in the glove compartment, and locked up. Later someone would

come by and get the Subaru; Jerusalem police were suspicious of cars left in parking lots overnight.

Ahmed stopped at a kiosk near the Government
Press building, got a 7-Up and a tuna sandwich to go,
and walked up Jaffa Street toward the walls of the Old
City. His real papers were in order in case he got
stopped, but he didn't want the hassle. No one would
suspect a man walking along eating a tuna sandwich.

It took Ahmed just less than ten minutes to reach
the teeming parking area in front of the Nablus Gate, the
main entrance to the Old City. His Peugeot, with its east
Jerusalem license plate, was waiting. He climbed in and
drove to Abu Walid's place, just east of the ancient walls,
on the road to Jericho. When he reached the compound,
he turned in without bothering to even check his rearview
mirror. It never occurred to him for a moment that he
had been followed all the way.

CHAPTER THIRTY-ONE

KEDMI AND RASHEED WATCHED THE VIDEOTAPED MUTILATION of Digger Dawkins on the VCR in Kedmi's darkened living room. When it ended, they sat in silence. Both men had spent their lives around scenes of grotesque violence, but neither had seen anything quite like this.

"Meet Dr. Abu Walid," said Kedmi. "And son."

"You got them ID'd already?"

"A friend ran a computer check of Palestinians under twenty-five and over two meters tall. We cross-referenced them with fathers who can perform this kind of operation."

"Doctors, you mean."

"Or butchers. And what came up is Abu Walid. Son of a rich family in Gaza. Spent some time in prison here during the Intifada, nothing major. Oh, and he did his medical studies in Detroit, at Wayne State University."

"Damn," said Rasheed. "How do you know the kid in the video is the guy's son?"

"He told us," said Kedmi. "He kept calling the boy *ibni*—my son."

"Stupid," said Rasheed.

Kedmi shrugged. "With religious fanatics there's a thin line. Just because he's crazy doesn't mean he's not stupid. We know one more thing about this doctor that will interest you. A few days ago he was in Dearborn. He met with a deaf and blind sheikh."

"Yeah, I know the one you mean," said Rasheed. "How did you find that out?"

"Our liaison officer with the FBI is a second cousin of Ruthie's," said Kedmi. "This sheikh's been under surveillance for a long time. The FBI got a report on Abu Walid's visit, but they didn't connect it to anything. After all, he's a Palestinian and a Sunni Muslim. He has nothing to do with Hizbollah or Iran, and neither does the sheikh. In fact, he hates them."

Rasheed smiled for the first time. "Damn, Yoav, you're a one-man police force. They could fire all the cops and just have you and your friends and relatives solving crimes over here."

"Unfortunately, the friendship network runs in all directions," said Kedmi. "I have mine, Rosenthal has his. And in this country, some of them are the same people. It's just a matter of time before he finds out what we know. Not to mention that in two days Abu Walid is going to realize his tape wasn't broadcast. And then—"

"Clock's definitely ticking," said Rasheed. "Question is, what do we do now?"

Kedmi gave his friend a sharp look; it was the first time he had ever heard Rasheed Holliman wonder aloud about a course of action. "Let's start with what we can't do," he said. "I can't order a rescue mission without the permission of the prime minister, which he isn't going to give me. I can't ask friends of mine to help, either. It's one thing to request a favor, but that would be way beyond the limits of friendship."

"So it's just the two of us."

"For the time being," Kedmi said. "Once Rosenthal finds out, you'll have to leave. It would be dangerous for you to stay here."

"Shit," snorted Rasheed. "That little guy?"

"You are not afraid of him," said Kedmi, "but you should be."

"What about you?"

"Me? No, Rosenthal would never dare touch me. It doesn't work that way here. He won't have you killed, either, unless you force him. But he can make Israel a very unpleasant place for you. At the very least, you'll wind up spending all your time trying to stay away from him. That's not the way to mount a rescue operation."

"No," Rasheed agreed. "So, back to my question: What now?"

"How about the Americans? Carl Berger? He was here last week. Do you know him?"

Rasheed shook his head. "I don't, but my mother's been talking with him right along. He'd see me."

"Of course he will see you," said Kedmi. "The question is, will he help you?"

Rasheed thought about that awhile, rubbing his large hands together. "I reckon he just might," he said finally. "You know how to use a video camera?"

"I still don't know how to set the timer on the microwave," said Kedmi. "Ruthie does all that. She films all the grandchildren's birthday parties."

"You think she could handle seeing the tape we just saw?"

"Ruthie can handle anything," said Kedmi.

"How many VCRs you got?"

"Just one."

"Need two," said Rasheed.

"There's another one in my office. I can get Gali to bring it over."

"Good. And tell him to bring three blank cassettes and today's newspaper. You got an English paper in this country?"

"The *Jerusalem Post*."

"Fine. Have him bring that. Now, what's the quickest way to get to the States?"

"Airplane," said Kedmi. He was beginning to resent the peremptory way in which Rasheed had taken over.

"Won't Rosenthal's people be looking for me at the airport?"

"Nope," said Kedmi.

"How do you know?"

"Because you flew out of here to New York the other

day. I had a friend in the border police at the airport put your departure in the computer."

"So, I'm not here, huh?"

"You're in Detroit, as far as anybody knows."

"Can you get your friend at the airport to work his show again tonight, let me fly out in secret?"

"Not unless I know what you're planning," said Kedmi.

"Same thing I've been planning since Tyrone got snatched," said Rasheed. "I'm planning to save his skinny black ass."

"That much I know. But since my fat Jewish ass is involved, I want more information."

"Why not just leave it up to me?" said Rasheed.

"The last time I did that, I almost got shot."

"Relax, Yoav," said Rasheed, a slow smile spreading across his face. "This time, the only one gonna get shot is me."

CHAPTER THIRTY-TWO

AFTER THE MUTILATION, DR. ABU WALID SAT DOWN TO HIS evening meal as if nothing extraordinary had happened, but Walid could barely look at the spicy chicken musakan. Visions of Deacon Dawkins's tormented face flashed through his mind, and he couldn't forget the coach's moans of anguish. When Walid had dropped the hemorrhaging organ on the floor, his father had grunted with amusement, picked it up and casually dropped it in a jar of solution. "Keep this as a reminder," he said to his son, "of how shriveled and harmless is the manhood of the Great Satan."

"Yes," Walid had said, unable to form even a simple sentence. It was at that moment that he realized Tyrone was right: His father was truly insane.

"If this is not enough to convince the Americans to

fight, we will skin him alive, like a rabbit," Abu Walid had said. The word *we* had sent a shiver through Walid.

And so Walid sat at the table, watching his father gulp down the tender bits of chicken, holding the meat in the same hand that had, an hour before, performed the ultimate mutilation on Digger Dawkins. Walid moved his food around on the plate, unable to eat. His mind was clouded with terrible thoughts of suicide, escape, betrayal. The one thought he didn't permit himself was of raising a hand to his father; that, he knew, would be impossible.

Abu Walid looked across the table and saw the look on his son's face. He was proud of the boy's sensitivity and, at the same time, of the obedient way he had performed. In a perfect world, the kind of world he was now creating, such awful tests of faith would be unnecessary. At the end of the great war, when the Christian Satan and the False Muslim Believers had destroyed one another, young men like Walid would be free to lead lives of peace. But for that to happen, they must first become warriors, learn to harden their hearts. Today Walid's heart had been hardened, and while it grieved his father to see his pain, he knew that soon a protective layer of tissue would grow in the boy's breast, shielding him from his childish sentimentality.

"Tomorrow you will have the day free," Abu Walid said. "You may play basketball if you like."

"Thank you, Father," said Walid, forcing himself to smile.

"The guards tell me you are becoming a very good player."

"I am improving."

"I am grateful to the American for coaching you. Does he read the Koran I gave him?"

"Yes," said Walid, although he had no idea if it was true.

"Perhaps he will become a believer and remain with us permanently," said the doctor. "You would like that, would you not?"

"Yes, Father," said Walid.

"Does he speak to you of Islam?"

"We speak only of basketball," said Walid. "As you have instructed."

"Well," said Abu Walid, pulling back from the table. "It is a beautiful night. I am going for a walk, to look at the stars. Will you accompany me?"

"No, Father," said Walid. "I am tired. I would like to sleep."

Abu Walid bent over and kissed his son on both cheeks. "I am proud of you, Walid," he said. "You are all I hoped my son would be. When you sleep, dream pleasantly."

"Thank you, Father," said the boy. The one thing he was certain of was that his dreams that night would not be pleasant ones.

CHAPTER THIRTY-THREE

THE SEVEN-HOUR TIME DIFFERENCE BETWEEN TEL AVIV AND Washington enabled Kedmi and Rasheed to fly all night and still reach the American capital before 8:00 A.M. They checked into the Washington Hilton as Reverend Maurice Williams and Mr. P. Almoni, the Hebrew version of John Doe.

By the time Berger arrived at the hotel at nine, Rasheed and Kedmi had already showered, dressed and eaten a room-service breakfast. Both felt fresh; they shared the cops' ability to rest under pressure, and they had both slept soundly on the flight.

Berger, by contrast, seemed haggard. His skin was blotchy, his eyes red and his shave uneven. Ever since the start of the crisis with Iran, he had barely slept. The president was working him hard, pushing him, the other members of his senior staff and the Joint Chiefs. Moving the country to a state of declared war was heavy work, and Berger had done more than his share of the lifting.

"The coffee's still hot if you'd like some," said Kedmi, after introducing Berger to Rasheed.

"Please."

Kedmi took a cup from the room-service tray and poured with a surprisingly dainty touch. He handed the coffee to Berger as Rasheed took a small Sony tape recorder from his jacket and placed it on the table.

"What's that for?" asked Berger.

"I'm sure you've got one too," said Rasheed. "We might as well be open with each other."

Berger reached into his cowhide attaché case, produced his own recorder and set it on the coffee table next to Rasheed's. "Now what?"

"Now I'm going to show you a home video," said Kedmi. "Part of it is a little rough to watch, I'm warning you now." He popped a cassette into the multi-system VCR they had brought from Tel Aviv and pressed the start button. Rasheed's face appeared on the screen. He was holding a copy of the *Jerusalem Post*. Slowly, the camera zoomed in on the headline—MASTERSON TO CONGRESS: DECLARE WAR NOW!—and yesterday's date. Then he began to speak:

"My name is Rasheed Holliman. This tape is being made in Tel Aviv, Israel. As you can see from the newspaper, today is the eleventh. What you are about to see next is a video clip made by the terrorists who kidnapped my brother Tyrone Holliman, Coach Digger Dawkins and Greg Bannion."

There was a brief break in the tape and then a shot of Digger Dawkins lying on a table, flanked by two masked men, one large, the other enormous. The large man faced the camera and intoned, "In the name of Allah the All Merciful, we are sending our answer today to the American Satan. It . . ."

"Where did you get this?" asked Berger.

"Just watch," said Kedmi.

". . . will show them, and the entire world, that they are not men but eunuchs, infidels to be despised, not feared." The camera panned to the devastated face of Digger Dawkins and then slowly down his body, until it stopped at the place between his legs.

"Oh, my God," said Berger. He watched as the masked man took Dawkins's shriveled penis in his hands and, with a quick, expert thrust, severed it. He held it aloft, like a trophy, for what seemed a very long time, then handed it to the enormous man next to him, who promptly dropped it on the floor. The camera veered away for a moment and then returned to the man with the scalpel. "If all American hostilities are not immediately halted, and our holy brothers released from Israeli prisons, and if the arch-criminal Masterson does not beg Allah's forgiveness, we will continue to show the world the vengeance of God. The choice belongs to Satan."

Kedmi hit the pause button, leaving the blurred image of the masked man frozen on the screen.

"That's the worst thing I ever saw," said Berger, instinctively holding his hand on his own crotch.

"Where did you get it? Why hasn't it been shown, like the others?"

"Keep watching," said Kedmi. He hit the pause button and the face of Rasheed Holliman appeared once again on the screen. He was still holding the *Jerusalem Post*.

"This tape was obtained by me, with no government help," Rasheed told the camera. "The terrorists don't know I've got it, but they'll know something's wrong in two days when it is not given to the wire services in Beirut.

"These terrorists are not Hizbollah members and they do not represent Iran. They are not in Lebanon, as they claim. They are a group of Palestinians led by a doctor named Abu Walid. They are holding the hostages just outside the walls of Jerusalem.

"This information has been conveyed, by me, to Brigadier General Carl Berger, the security adviser of the president of the United States. The American government now knows the true identity of the kidnappers and the whereabouts of the hostages. I have reason to believe that the American government has not tried to find them up until now, and has encouraged the Israelis to do likewise."

Rasheed nodded to Kedmi, who once again hit the pause button. There was a long silence as they waited for Berger. Finally he exhaled deeply, making a sound someplace between a sigh and a groan. "You have no proof that President Masterson has any idea these hostages aren't in Lebanon," he said.

"That's true," said Rasheed. "But whatever he knew before, he sure as hell knows now."

"You can't even prove I've seen this tape," said Berger.

"Don't have to," Rasheed said easily. "Not that anybody would doubt it. But unless I get what I want, it's going on the six o'clock news, coast to coast, tonight. I got somebody with a copy waiting on me in New York. They don't hear from me or something happens, you gonna be one famous motherfucker."

"You're talking about blackmailing the president of the United States," said Berger, emphasizing each word carefully.

"Call it any damn thing you want," said Rasheed. "Long as you got the message."

"This is a national security matter," said Berger. "It's much more complicated than you understand—"

"Man, save the bullshit for the trial," said Rasheed, his voice growing hard for the first time.

"It's not bullshit," Berger said, the words sounding hollow to him. "There's a great deal at stake here." He turned to Kedmi. "You, of all people, should understand the importance of fighting Islamic terrorism."

"I'm with him," said Kedmi, pointing to Rasheed.

"Well, your prime minister isn't," Berger snapped.

"That's why we here with America's greatest motherfucking home video," said Rasheed. Kedmi noticed that Rasheed's ghetto accent was growing thicker, his words more profane. He was talking to the adviser of the president of the United States the way he talked to hoodlums in Detroit; street talk. "You want to kick Muslim ass, that's your business. I don't give a shit about Iran, Iraq, Palestine or Pakistan. I do give a shit about getting my brother back in one piece. Once I've got him, and I'm talking about in the next forty-eight hours, you can have the tape and figure out another way to start your war. If not, all y'all's going to jail, 'cause the shit you trying to pull here makes Watergate look like the god-damned Constitutional Convention."

"I see," said Berger. "I'll have to talk to the president."

"Take the tape with you," said Rasheed. "Tell him I ain't playing. I want an answer by five this evening. And that answer better be that the Israelis are going to cooperate. Oh, and get us a plane for going back, a military jet. We lose time heading east and those commercial planes fly too slow, trying to save gas."

"I'll be in touch," said Berger stiffly. He picked up the tape and moved toward the door.

"Carl?" said Kedmi.

Berger stopped and turned. "What?"

"I was just remembering what an arrogant schmuck you were in Tel Aviv," he said slowly. "You're much more of a mensch when somebody's got you by the balls. I just wanted you to know that."

CHAPTER THIRTY-FOUR

IT WAS WARMER THAN USUAL, ALMOST HOT, DESPITE THE DRY crisp breeze that blew through the deserted compound. The sky, as always, was pure blue; in all the days they had been coming out to the court, Tyrone couldn't remember seeing a single cloud.

Walid bounced the ball high, around his waist, once, twice, three times, and tossed it toward the basket. It caromed off to the left. He and Tyrone both went for it. They met, almost chest to chest, and Walid whispered, "My father's going to kill you."

Tyrone felt the court tip and he stumbled slightly. He had wanted to believe that Walid could protect him. That illusion was now gone. He regained his balance, put his hand on the boy's shoulder and said, "When?"

"Soon, I think."

"He tell you that?"

"No. But I know. I can tell. We've got to do something."

"We," said Tyrone, which in his language meant, "You and me on different sides of this motherfucker, white boy." He looked over at the guards. Moonpie and Spaceman were on duty again today. At the moment they were squatting on the ground, playing shesh-besh on a beat-up board, Arabic music blaring from the car radio.

"We will escape together," said Walid. He felt a physical wrenching in his stomach as he spoke, aware that his words constituted a betrayal of his father. It was as though he were pronouncing some unforgivable curse against God himself. And yet, he was certain that he could not witness, let alone participate in, the killing of Tyrone Holliman.

Tyrone searched the boy's face. "Where we at?" he asked. In the past, Walid had refused to answer that question. Now he said, "Jerusalem."

"*Jerusalem?* You mean to say Jerusalem is right out there?" said Tyrone, gesturing beyond the compound with his eyes.

"Yes."

"Shit, I thought we were in the desert someplace," Tyrone said. "How far to help?"

Walid shifted the ball from hand to hand, pondering the question. Who would help? The Israelis in west Jerusalem? They would save Tyrone but arrest Walid, maybe kill him. The Arabs? They might return him to his father. The only place he could think of was a Greek Orthodox church up the road toward the city, near the garden of Gethsemane. He had never been inside, but he had often seen black-robed monks in the courtyard. Once, years ago, one had smiled at him. "There is a church, about five kilometers from here," he said.

"How far's five kilometers? How many miles?"

"I don't know," said the boy. "Not so far. We could run there in fifteen or twenty minutes." He glanced nervously in the direction of the guards, who were still busy at their game.

"What's on the other side of these walls?"

"Nothing. A field, some houses. A dirt road that runs past an olive grove. It is about two kilometers to the main road. Then there will be traffic."

"Two kilometers take what, six, seven minutes?"

"About that long. I'm not certain."

"How do we get out, though?" asked Tyrone. "Is there any chance the guards will let you go? Tell them you taking me someplace, want to show me something?"

"They will not let us leave the compound," said Walid. "It is my father's order."

"You know how to use one of those machine guns?" Tyrone asked, nodding in the direction of the AK-47s that were leaning against the car.

"Yes," said Walid.

Tyrone took the ball and began dribbling; he did his best thinking with a basketball in his hands. The courtyard was more or less the length of a regulation basketball court, its entrance maybe twice the width of the Peugeot. He dribbled and tried to picture in his mind

how he could spring loose. He turned to Walid and motioned with his eyes for the boy to guard him.

Walid assumed a defense stance and moved with
the ball as Tyrone bounced it across his body, from side
to side. "If there was gunfire, would someone be likely to
hear it?" Tyrone asked.

"No. This is an isolated spot. But please, Tyrone, I
do not want to shoot."

"Relax, baby. All I need for you to do is aim, make it
look good. Can you do that?"

Walid nodded.

"And then hop in the car and we'll book out of
here."

"They will run after us," said Walid. "Call my father."

"Not if we got the guns," Tyrone said. "Tell them to
come over here."

Walid gave Tyrone a long, cautious look. He was
losing control over his life, putting his confidence in the
American. He hoped what he was doing was right, because he was certain that, if he displeased Allah, he
would be punished with death. He called to the guards
in Arabic. They looked up from their shesh-besh board,
saw him gesturing and ambled over, assault rifles slung
over their shoulders.

"All right, all right," called Tyrone energetically,
bouncing on the balls of his feet in an excellent imitation
of the rah-rah style of his high-school coach, Mr. Van
Ness. "Yo, Walid, I want you to translate for me. Tell
these guys I need them to help us with a drill."

Walid said a few words in Arabic and the two small

guards began to grin. They had been watching the action for days and were clearly delighted to be allowed to join in.

"All right, say yeah, okay, here we go, now we gonna practice a fast break off the backboard," Tyrone said. He took Moonpie by his shoulders and positioned him facing the basket, about twelve feet away. "You stand there, and don't let Walid get past you," he instructed. "If he tries, you jump in front of him and knock the ball away. Understand?"

Walid explained in Arabic. Moonpie nodded vigorously and said, "Okay, Johnny," which was the extent of his English.

"Good, all right, now we movin'!" hollered Tyrone, clapping his hands loudly. "Walid, tell Spaceman here to get in the same position, only on the other side. And if I try to get by him, he knocks the ball away from me."

Once again Walid translated. Spaceman ran to the spot Tyrone pointed to and assumed a defensive position like the one he had seen Walid use.

"Spaceman look like Scottie Pippen on defense," said Tyrone. "You understand what I'm saying, my man?"

The guard gazed at him blankly and smiled. "Basketball," he said. "Yes."

"Got us a couple naturals here," said Tyrone to Walid, talking even faster now, slurring his words. "You sure that's all the English they know?"

"Yes," said Walid.

"All right. Now, I'm gonna try to dribble past Spaceman. Tell him to swipe the ball away." He began bouncing it high, within a foot or so of the guard, teasing him. Spaceman reached out awkwardly as Tyrone bounced the ball through his legs, went around him, picked up the dribble, raced ten or fifteen feet toward the Peugeot, stopped and trotted back.

"Not bad for a first try," he said, tossing the ball to Walid. "Okay, see if you can get past Moonpie. Take it through his legs, same as I did and run almost to the car. Then turn around with a smile on your face."

Walid bounced the ball high, the way Tyrone had, daring Moonpie to take it. When the guard lunged, he smoothly pushed the ball between his legs, cut cleanly around him, picked up the dribble and broke for the car. Tyrone was fixed on the reactions of the guards, but he couldn't help noticing how smoothly Walid had executed the move. Their practice sessions had made a big difference in his game, no doubt about it. If they got out of here, Tyrone could think of half a dozen colleges that might be interested in a kid like him.

Walid dribbled back, smiling as he had been told, and tossed the ball to Tyrone. Moonpie said something to him in Arabic. "He wants to take a shot at the basket," said Walid.

"Sure, why not? Only tell him he's got to take off that rifle. Can't shoot with a thing like that over your shoulder. It might go off and blow him away."

As Walid translated, a look of uncertainty came over Moonpie's round face. He glanced at Spaceman, who shrugged his shoulders. Walid said something more in Arabic and both guards seemed to relax; they unslung the AK-47s and lay them, banana clips up, on the side of the concrete court.

Tyrone tossed the ball to Moonpie, who held it awkwardly in both hands and pushed it up in the direction of the basket. "Airball," called Tyrone, flipping it back to him. "Try again. Shoot harder."

Walid translated and Moonpie nodded. This time he threw so hard the ball hit the top of the backboard, and Spaceman laughed; the sound startled Tyrone, who had never heard him so much as giggle before.

"Okay, your turn," he said, passing to Spaceman, who caught the ball against his chest. He eyed the basket narrowly, took a running start and heaved. The ball flew toward the rim, bounced once and fell through. Spaceman jumped in the air, screamed something in Arabic, and held out his hands to Tyrone for a high-five.

"All right," said Tyrone, slapping his little palm. "We got a new thing now, the chest bump. I'll show you." He took him by both shoulders, bent low so they were the same height and jerked him forward, bumping chests. "Tell him he just got an NBA salute," he instructed Walid.

Moonpie started babbling in Arabic. "He wants another try," Walid said.

"Give the man a try," said Tyrone. After glancing briefly at his weapon, Moonpie took the ball from Walid, bounced it with both hands and approached the basket. He stopped, put his feet together and once more pushed the ball up toward the hoop. Tyrone, seeing it was overshot, leaped easily into the air and rammed it through. "Assist for Moonpie," he called in an announcer's voice.

"All right, baby, give me the chest bump." He grabbed Moonpie, whose face was split by a huge grin, slammed their bodies together and then pivoted, smashing an elbow into his cheek. Tyrone was shocked by the force of the blow; it felt like he had broken his elbow. The little guard crumpled to the concrete, unconscious and bleeding, as Tyrone screamed, "Get the guns!"

For a moment Walid and Spaceman stood in stunned silence. Then both broke for the rifles. Spaceman got there first, grabbed his gun and pointed it wildly in Tyrone's direction. Walid said something sharp to him in Arabic, walked over, picked up the second AK-47 and aimed it at Tyrone. He stood there for a long moment, staring into the face of the American. Then he pivoted and, with a savage blow, smashed the stock of the rifle into the side of Spaceman's head.

Tyrone let out a long breath. "For a minute I thought you were back on the reservation," he said. "Let's get the fuck out of here."

Walid looked at the two unconscious, bleeding guards. "Do you think they are dead?" he asked.

"Naw, man, they'll recover. Come on." Tyrone slung the rifle over his shoulder and sprinted up the court to the Peugeot. "Hop in and let's go," he yelled, pointing to the driver's side.

"I don't know how to drive," said Walid.

"Yeah, well, I do. All you gotta do is navigate the raggedy bitch. Come on."

As they climbed into the car, Tyrone saw a dazed Moonpie trying to get to his feet. "Damn," he said, feeling the throbbing in his elbow. "Go on over there and put him back to sleep."

"I can't," said Walid. There was a boyish, beseeching look on his face that Tyrone didn't want to argue with. He climbed out of the car, ran over to the guard, hit him across the head with the rifle, watched him go out and then sprinted back to the Peugeot.

The keys were in the ignition, and the engine started right up. Tyrone slipped it into reverse, swiveled his head to the right to get a better view and began easing the old car through the narrow exit. Suddenly he felt sharp, cold metal on his neck, turned and saw a knife, attached to Ahmed's hand, sticking through the open car window, right on his throat. For a split second he considered flooring the car, but he wasn't sure he could get it through the exit before Ahmed slashed his head off. He stopped and very carefully slipped the Peugeot into neutral.

Ahmed and Walid were screaming at each other, Arabic words that sounded like throat-clearing, and then Walid said, "You must get out of the car or he will kill you."

"You gonna get me out of this?" said Tyrone, but he already knew the answer—it was in Walid's panic-filled brown eyes. Tyrone climbed out and faced Ahmed, who had a pistol in one hand and the knife in the other. His face was calm, almost friendly; it was the look Tyrone remembered from the night he had carved up Bannion. He saw the hand with the pistol rise. His last thought was that he was going to die in the Holy Land. Somehow, it wasn't much consolation.

Ahmed worked quickly and efficiently. He kicked Tyrone in the groin, doubling him over so he could reach his head, smashed him across the temple with his pistol and dragged his body to the rear of the car. With surprising strength he hoisted the body into the trunk, which he locked. Only then did he come around the side of the car to Walid and say, in a respectful voice, "Thank God you are all right."

"Yes, I am all right," said Walid in a dull tone.

"Fortunately, I was passing by," said Ahmed. They both knew this was a lie; no one merely "passed by" the deserted compound. Ahmed had been assigned to keep an eye on these practice sessions since Dr. Abu Walid had returned from Detroit. He hadn't asked why, because it wasn't his place, although he had his suspicions. As usual, he thought, the doctor, his patron, had acted with wisdom.

"Otherwise, he would have succeeded in abducting you," Ahmed added.

"Abducting me," said Walid. "Yes, I see." He paused and said, "The guards have been injured."

"I will attend to them," said Ahmed. He left Walid and walked over to the guards. The boy was too stunned to go anywhere now, Ahmed was sure of that. Especially with his American friend locked in the trunk.

Moonpie and Spaceman were both unconscious, sprawled on the hard concrete. When they came to they

would be able to tell the story of what actually happened—a story that Dr. Abu Walid would not like to
hear. Ahmed bent down and, with his hunting knife, cut
Moonpie's throat. Then he did the same to Spaceman. He
felt no remorse about killing them. They were dead, anyway; Abu Walid would certainly have executed them for
allowing his boy and the American to escape. Besides,
they were merely guards, foot soldiers, and therefore dispensable. Until today Ahmed, too, had been a guard, but
he was now the man who had saved the life of Dr. Abu
Walid's son. A different man.

Ahmed went down on his haunches and wiped the
blood from his knife with the tail of Spaceman's shirt. A
great reward was in store for him. Dr. Abu Walid would
surely give him the price of a bride. His mind swam with
the joys of daily sex, sex on demand, sex as his right. He
didn't think about the sex producing a son, because he
didn't expect to live that long. But a single virgin on earth
would hold him until he reached the seventy-two virgins
awaiting him in paradise.

While Ahmed took care of the guards, Walid sat in
the Peugeot, trying desperately to sort out his feelings.
He had rebelled against his father, and it was over; the
most momentous act of his life had lasted barely a
minute. It was all so powerful, so vivid and so brief that
Walid wondered if he had imagined it. But then he saw
the sweat stain Tyrone had left on the driver's seat and he
knew it was real. The dream—of freedom, girls, music,
laughter, basketball, a life of his own—that dream was
over. Allah had intervened. Walid knew with absolute

certainty that his fate would be to follow his father, just as he knew that Tyrone was fated to die.

Perhaps, he thought, Tyrone was already dead. He hoped so. Abu Walid would welcome his son with kisses of relief and stage a joyous feast to celebrate his rescue. But he would know the truth, and he would punish Walid in his own way, by demanding an act of absolute contrition. With a deep dread, Walid knew precisely what that act would be: His father would make him kill Tyrone Holliman.

CHAPTER THIRTY-FIVE

WHEN BERGER GOT BACK TO HIS OFFICE IN THE WEST WING of the White House, he found a large stack of messages. Distractedly he glanced through them. Toward the bottom of the pile was one that caught his eye. It read: "9:13 A.M. Jim (Jameel) Irwin. Needs to speak to you urgently." There was a number, with a Maryland area code.

The president was on his way back from Camp David. In a short while Berger would have to tell him about Rasheed's video. He dialed the number, hoping Jamil had news that might soften the blow.

Jamil answered on the first ring. "I see you got my message," he said.

"Got it."

"I told your secretary 'Jim,' but then I began to think that you must know more than one Jim, so I added

Jamil, just to make certain that you would know who it was who was calling. I'll bet he spelled it with two ee's."

Berger glanced at the note, saw he was right, and frowned. "What's urgent?" he asked.

"Not for the telephone," said Jamil. "I must tell you this in person."

"Sorry," said Berger. "I've got a meeting with the president in fifteen minutes. You got something to tell me, tell me."

There was a pause, and Jamil asked, "Is this phone secure?"

"Of course it's secure," said Berger. "I'm the president's security adviser, for Christ's sake."

"All right, I was merely asking. You see, in my world, there can never be too much caution. Sometimes even the slightest slip can—"

"Get to the point," Berger snapped. Seeing the tape—and anticipating Masterson's reaction—had jangled his nerves. "What did you find out about the hostages?"

"About the hostages, regrettably, nothing. Not a word. My sources have no idea where they are, and believe me, my sources are excellent. But I have discovered something else, something of supreme importance."

"I'm listening."

"It concerns a group of men who are planning an act of retaliation for the bombings in Iran."

"What retaliation?"

"They are going to blow up the Washington Monument."

"That's impossible," said Berger. Jesus, he thought to himself, the FBI intelligence was right.

"Yes, you must be right," said Jamil. "Just as it was impossible to blow up the World Trade Center in New York. I am sorry to have troubled you with such a silly story."

"Wait," said Berger. "It was just a figure of speech. Who are these men? Where are they? When's this supposed to happen?"

"Right now they are in the Washington area. When will they attack? This I am not positive about."

"What group are they from?"

"They call themselves the Oppressed Victims of All Humanity."

"The Oppressed Victims?"

"It sounds better in Persian," Jamil assured him.

"Persian? Not Arabic?"

"In Arabic, all pathetic phrases sound appropriate," said Jamil. "We have a long, sad history—"

"I mean, they speak Persian? They're Iranian?"

"Iranian military intelligence," said Jamil.

"You're certain?"

"Positive. They intend to show America that Iran, too, has a long arm."

"How did you find out?"

"Does it matter? As long as the information is correct?"

"I guess not," said Berger. "How do we get to these guys?"

"First, you must get to me. You recall our agreement, U.S. citizenship for information. This is worth as much as the hostages. More, but a deal is a deal. Besides, it will give me pleasure to begin my American life by defending a national monument. And so I ask no more than what we agreed to. And no less."

"Fine. But I have to know now. This morning."

"It is not that urgent," said Jamil. "I believe you have a little more time. A few days at least."

"No, now," Berger insisted.

"All right. Please arrange my naturalization papers and a passport. You can leave the picture blank, I'll fill it in later. Most of my old pictures don't really do me justice. They have a radical tinge that no longer expresses the true me. I'd like a new image for my new citizenship. Also, a letter from you, handwritten, thanking me for my great service to America's national security."

"I can't get all that stuff together in a couple hours," said Berger.

"Whenever you are ready, I'll be here, at this phone," said Jamil. "Except perhaps at mealtimes."

"What if I just get the FBI to pick you up?"

"You mean by tracing the number? Please, General Berger, I am now a health food entrepreneur, but I have not forgotten the skills of my previous profession. If you have me arrested, I will say, through my lawyer, that it was a misunderstanding. You and I are old friends—several people who saw us dining together at Denny's the other day will confirm that. Also, if I am arrested, it is entirely possible that someone will alert the Iranians.

They will abort their attack on the Washington Monument. They will, however, find an alternative target."

"Just a minute," Berger said. He put Jamil on hold and buzzed Andy Stubbins. "I need a U.S. passport for somebody and naturalization papers within one hour," he said. "Find out how it's done. Call Naturalization, State, the CIA, whatever, but find out. And then get whoever can arrange it on the line." He clicked off, and returned to Jamil.

"All right, I'll do my best," he said.

"I am certain that it will be more than good enough," said Jamil. "Please make everything out to James Erwin—that's with an E. It looks more distinguished than with an I, don't you think?"

"E," said Berger, writing it down.

"For place of birth, write Montreal. And for my age, thirty-four. It is a slight exaggeration, but harmless."

"Okay," said Berger. "Got it. Anything else?"

"Yes. You will need my birthday."

"Which is?"

"The fourth of July," said Jamil Imami. "Naturally."

It was almost eleven when President Masterson's helicopter returned him to the White House from Camp David. Berger met him at the landing pad. "Carl, you're a mind-reader," said the president. "I was just going to send for you."

As they walked together toward the Oval Office, Berger said, "There's something you should know. Two things."

"Good news or bad news?" asked Masterson with his quirky smile.

"Both, I think. It's getting hard to tell them apart."

"That's my job," said Masterson.

Berger cleared his throat nervously. He prided himself on his oral briefings, which were terse and well organized. But he had never been called upon to deliver this kind of news to the president of the United States. All he could think to do was to start at the beginning, with that morning's meeting with Holliman and Kedmi. As he talked, he could see Masterson absorbing every word, his face puckered as if he were sucking in the information. There were no jokes now; for once, Berger felt as though Masterson was truly the commander-in-chief of the most powerful nation on earth.

By the time Berger was finished with his briefing, they were seated in the Oval Office. Masterson leaned forward in his chair and said, "Holliman and the Israeli have us over a barrel, is that right?"

"It appears that way, yes sir."

"Okay, Carl, here's what you do when you're over a barrel. You roll with it." He pressed the phone console. "Get me Prime Minister Peled. And I want the head of the FBI here in ten minutes."

"Yes sir," said the secretary. A few moments later, a red button flashed. Masterson pushed it and said, "*Shalom,* Natan, how are you doing?" He pressed the speaker button so that Berger could hear the answer, which was a long, barking cough followed by a weak, "Fine."

"Natan, I've just received some interesting news," he said. "Apparently our hostages are now being held in Jerusalem."

"Our intelligence believes it is Beirut," said Peled, in his slow, thickly accented English. "As you know."

"We're quite positive," said Masterson. "In fact, one of your people, Police Chief, ah, Kedmi, helped put us in the picture." Masterson looked at Berger for confirmation, and he nodded, impressed by the president's memory.

"Kedmi? I don't know about this," said the prime minister.

"I'm certain you don't," said Masterson. The line was secure, but not from each other's recording devices, which is why both men spoke elliptically. "We just found out about it ourselves. It seems that Holliman's brother has intercepted one of the terrorists' tapes, and he has an address to go along with it, a place near Jerusalem on the road to Jericho, if I'm not mistaken." Once again he looked at Berger, who consulted his notes and nodded.

"That is a new story," said Peled.

"Yes, precisely. You see, Natan, what I think happened is that the hostages *were* in Lebanon, as our intelligence thought, but somehow, because of our military actions against Beirut, they managed to slip out of the country and into this Arab neighborhood in Jerusalem. Is that possible?"

"I suppose so," said Peled, although he didn't. Still, Masterson was leading up to something, and as prime minister of Israel he had long ago learned that when the president of the United States led, you followed—at least part of the way.

"I'm sending Carl Berger, my top security aide, to Israel today, along with Kedmi and Holliman," said Masterson. "Of course your people will be in charge of the rescue operation, but he will have my full authority. Especially since I'm apt to have my hands full with other matters. And so may you."

"What other matters?"

"The scenario we discussed is becoming a reality. I believe that by tonight, or tomorrow at the latest, the Congress will declare war on Iran. Which means implementing Operation Lionheart."

There was a spasm of wrenching coughing on the other end of the line. Masterson put his hand over the speaker and mouthed the words *Lung cancer.* Then Natan Peled said, "You're going ahead with it?"

"It seems we've uncovered yet another act of Iranian aggression," said the President. "The Congress will move now, I'm quite sure of that. You'll need to be prepared as well."

"We've been prepared for some time," said Peled.

"Secretary Malthus will be in touch with Defense Minister Bar-Chen within the hour regarding coordination," Masterson said.

"And the hostages?"

"I leave that up to you. Your forces are the best in the world when it comes to that sort of thing."

"We will do our best to bring the hostages out alive," said Peled.

"I'm sure you will," said Masterson. He was pleased to see that the old farmer had gotten the message: The kidnappers he wanted dead.

"Mr. President, it is a great thing that you are doing," said Peled. "Israel is with you, rest assured."

"We'll be in touch," said Masterson. "*Shalom,* Natan."

Masterson clicked off the phone and winked. "Catch that *shalom* at the end? You've got to be a real linguist in this job."

"Yes sir," said Berger. The president once again seemed as lighthearted as a man planning a holiday. "Do you really want me to go with them to Israel tonight?"

"You think I was just getting Peled's hopes up? Of course you go. Arrange the plane, take a good one. Be nice to Holliman and Kedmi. And when you get there, make sure things go smoothly. I don't want any kidnappers left alive. If the hostages come out dead, well, that'll be the Israelis' fault. If not, keep them away from the press until you debrief them. By that time, all hell will have broken out over there and the hostages will be yesterday's news."

"Yes sir," said Berger. "Do you want me to wait while you talk to the FBI?"

"Sure," said Masterson. "You can fill in the chief on this guy Imami."

"Maybe I should be the one to deliver the passport and the papers. In person. After all, I'm the one he knows."

"Do what you have time for," said Masterson. "Just

as long as this thing gets done pronto." He looked out the window at the Washington Monument and sighed. It would almost be worth it, he thought, to let the Iranians blow the damn thing up. That would really piss off Congress. Not to mention clear a nice spot on the mall for the Masterson Monument.

CHAPTER THIRTY-SIX

THEY WERE SOMEPLACE BETWEEN GREECE AND CYPRUS, thirty-five thousand feet in the air, when Berger sat down next to Rasheed and said, "Don't you think we should talk about the rescue operation?"

Rasheed, who had his eyes closed, opened them slowly and stared at Berger. "Hell, no," he said. "Far as I'm concerned you're just along for the ride." Across the aisle Kedmi snored softly.

"I don't think you have the right attitude," said Berger.

"Nigger."

"What?"

"The sentence goes, 'I don't think you have the right attitude, nigger.'"

"That's uncalled for," said Berger. "I won't have you talking to me like that."

"Man, we in international air space," said Rasheed. "Up here I can say any damn thing I want."

"Okay, give me a hard time, but we're on the same side. I can be a lot of help."

"You must think I'm simpleminded," said Rasheed. "You and your boss trying to start a war; all I'm trying to do is save my brother. That don't put us on the same side, no way. So you just keep this in mind: You fuck with this operation, endanger Tyrone in any way, and I'm gonna kick your ass. I don't care if you General Berger or General Washington."

Kedmi opened one eye and added, "Or General Electric."

"And he's the damn chief of police, so you know I'm not playing," said Rasheed.

"I take my orders from the president," said Berger stiffly.

"In Washington. Over here you take 'em from me and Kedmi."

Berger leaned back in his seat and closed his eyes. There was nothing he could say, nothing that he needed to say. He didn't mind letting Rasheed and the Israelis run the show; in fact, it was just what he wanted. For all he knew, Tyrone Holliman and the others were already dead. If so, well, too bad. If they died in the rescue effort, then it would be Rasheed's fault. And if they somehow came out alive, there would be time to see to it that they kept their mouths shut.

The plane landed at Ben-Gurion, taxiing to a stop on a remote corner of the runway reserved for private flights. Rosenthal and Stacy, the CIA chief, were waiting on the tarmac.

"Welcome home," Rosenthal said to Kedmi in Hebrew. The greeting was dry, unemotional.

"I hope I didn't get you in trouble with the Old Man," said Kedmi.

"He wasn't exactly pleased. Anyway, he wants to see you now, at the Kiriah."

"The prime minister wants to talk to us," Kedmi said to Rasheed.

"Not him. Just Berger and us," said Rosenthal in Hebrew. "No civilians."

"Rasheed comes, too," said Kedmi in English. "Otherwise, I'll write out my resignation right here and you can deliver it to the Old Man."

"Let me make a phone call," Rosenthal said. He walked ten yards down the runway, took out his phone and dialed the prime minister's office. As he waited for him to come on the line, he looked over and saw Stacy huddled with Berger.

"The shit's really hitting the fan," Stacy was saying excitedly. "About three hours ago the FBI rounded up a bunch of Iranian terrorists in Kensington. Caught them red-handed with explosives and a plan to blow up the Washington Monument."

"You don't say?"

Stacy looked at his watch. "In a few hours, Masterson's going to address a joint session of Congress. It'll be war now for sure."

"I wouldn't be surprised," said Berger.

"You here to coordinate with the Israelis?"

Berger looked at him cryptically and said nothing. Stacy nodded and said, "Got it. What do you want me to do?"

"Take my bag to the hotel," said Berger. "And stay by the phone. If I need you, I'll call."

"Where are you going?" asked Stacy, clearly disappointed at being consigned to baggage handling.

"Wherever they go," said Berger, nodding toward Rosenthal, who had walked back and rejoined Kedmi and Rasheed.

"The Old Man's steaming, but he says Holliman can come along," Rosenthal told Kedmi. "You got balls, Yoav, I'll say that."

"Say it in English," Kedmi said. "I want my homeboy to hear it from the horse's mouth."

They drove in a convoy to the prime minister's Tel Aviv office, near the Ministry of Defense. Rosenthal led the way in an unmarked white Mitsubishi. Kedmi and Rasheed followed in Kedmi's Volvo, with Gali at the wheel. Berger and Stacy, in a Pontiac, brought up the rear. At the gate, a uniformed soldier peered in, said a few words to Rosenthal, checked his ID against a list on his clipboard and waved them all through.

Natan Peled was waiting for them along with the army chief-of-staff, Danny Bar-el. As they filed into the Old Man's spartan office, he didn't bother to rise, shake hands or even smile in welcome—he merely stared at Yoav Kedmi through bright blue eyes while Rosenthal introduced Rasheed and Berger.

"What did you do?" Peled asked Kedmi in Hebrew.

"What I thought was right," said Kedmi. "You can have my resignation now if you want it."

"First things first," Peled said. Switching into English he said, "We have a problem. We have to get the hostages out."

Rosenthal smiled to himself. This was vintage Peled, blunt and decisive-sounding without revealing anything. All he knew for sure was that the Old Man had done a one-eighty after talking to President Masterson. He surmised that Holliman and Kedmi had something on Peled—otherwise, neither would be sitting here.

"We'll get them out," said Bar-el. "My guys are already on full alert." Bar-el was a cocky little man of fifty with short blond hair, a mischievous smile and a reputation for daring tactical solutions; his "guys" were Sayaret Matkal, an elite antiterrorist unit.

Rosenthal eyed Kedmi expectantly. The police had its own elite unit, Yamam, and it usually fought bitterly for choice assignments. But it was Rasheed Holliman who spoke.

"I got a problem with that," he said.

"*You've* got a problem? Excuse me, but who are you?" demanded Bar-el. Rasheed let the comment pass, gazing steadily at the little general until Bar-el blinked and added, in a more conciliatory tone, "All I said is that we can get them out."

"Yeah, but you didn't say anything about getting them out alive."

"That's obvious," said Bar-el. "Of course alive, if pos-sible."

"Uh-uh," said Rasheed, shaking his head. "With all due respect, you gonna want to protect your troops, not take unnecessary risks. And sometimes that leads to peo-ple getting carried away. I don't want Tyrone getting burned up like those holy rollers down in Waco."

"We're a little better than the Americans at these things," said Bar-el. "We don't get carried away."

"Hey, I'm sure y'all are some serious professionals. But push comes to shove, you're gonna do what's best for your own people. It's just natural."

"You think the police would do a better job?" asked Peled.

"Same problem," said Rasheed easily, as if he dealt with prime ministers every day. "Yoav knows how I feel."

"Then who do you think should handle it?" asked Bar-el. "The Boy Scouts?"

"Me," said Rasheed.

"You? All alone?" Bar-el began to chuckle, inviting the others to join in. Berger smiled. Rosenthal saw Peled shift his gaze to Rasheed Holliman and, for the first time, really look at him.

"We're not talking about the Normandy invasion here," Rasheed said. "This is basically just a barricaded hostage situation, six or seven guys in there with auto-matic rifles. It doesn't require the whole damn army to deal with it."

"How do you know how many of them there are?" asked Rosenthal.

"Before we went to Washington I gave orders to put the place under surveillance," said Kedmi. "I asked for some aerial photos and pictures of the house. It's not that big. And I had somebody check on the electrical and water consumption. Six, seven people, not including the hostages, that's what I'd estimate."

"We don't even know where the house is and you're taking aerial photos?" demanded Bar-el. "Who gave you permission to use the air force?"

"Nobody gave me permission to do anything," Kedmi said. "You don't have to make big noises here, Danny; I'm in trouble even without your help."

Rosenthal stole a look at the prime minister, whose expression remained blank.

"This is crazy," said Bar-el, pointing at Rasheed. "This man is a foreigner. A civilian."

Rasheed turned to Peled. "Let Kedmi round me up half a dozen menfolk and I'll bring the hostages out. Alive. No muss, no fuss." He looked from Peled to Berger and added, "No leaks and no publicity."

The word *publicity* had the desired effect on Berger. It was a threat, no question about it; a copy of the cassette was still someplace in New York. But it was also an opportunity. Rasheed Holliman was hinting he'd let Masterson spin the story his way—that the terrorists had been in Lebanon until recently—if he cooperated.

"It's out of the question," Bar-el said dismissively. "Rambo."

"What do you think?" Peled asked Kedmi.

"I agree with Rasheed," said Kedmi.

"Where would you get the . . . what did you call them?"

"Menfolk," said Rasheed. "It's a Detroit police term, meaning badasses."

"Where would you get these badasses?" Peled asked, enjoying the new word.

"My guys," said Kedmi. "Volunteers."

"Volunteers," Peled repeated. Rosenthal saw that the old farmer was intrigued with the idea. "How soon could you put it together?"

"We don't have much time," said Kedmi. "I'd want to go in tomorrow."

"You can't be serious," Bar-el said.

"I don't see an objection from our point of view," Berger said. "Speaking unofficially."

The prime minister looked at Rosenthal. "*Nu?*"

It was clear to Rosenthal where Peled was heading. "I'd like to go along," he said.

"I'd go along myself, if I was younger," said Peled. "But this is Kedmi's show. Okay, Yoav, go ahead. But tell no one. Choose your own men. Rambo will go along as an observer. Listen to him all you like, but the final responsibility is yours alone. Understood?"

"Yes," said Kedmi.

"Good. I want to see the final plan. Do nothing without my approval. And another thing: absolutely no press of any kind. If word leaks, the operation's off. Questions?"

Kedmi shook his head. The others remained silent.

Only Bar-el spoke. "I want it on the record that I oppose this," he said.

"It's on the record," said Peled, a ghost of a smile on his thin, hard lips. He had been in politics thirty years, and he still didn't know exactly where the hell the record was.

CHAPTER THIRTY-SEVEN

THERE WERE TWO HOOKERS ON THE CORNER, STANDING SIDE by side, Russians from the look of their blond hair and pale skin. It was early morning, drive time, and the whores on Shmuel HaNavi Street were busily checking out the passing cars for horny husbands on their way to work after a frustrating Thursday night. When Ahmed cruised by slowly, in the white Subaru, they smiled, and he smiled back.

"Good morning, girls," he called in Hebrew.

"Good morning, sweetie," they answered in a heavy-voweled Hebrew that told him he was right: Russians. He preferred them to the Moroccan girls who often guessed, despite his accent and his skullcap, that he was an Arab. Not that they wouldn't go with him—Arabs were their best customers, along with Hassidic *yeshiva* boys—but Ahmed resented the fact that they overcharged him.

Russian women worked cheap and didn't make snide re-
marks, at least not in a language he could understand.

"How much?"

"Five hundred shekels," one said.

Ahmed laughed. "I only want to screw, not build a
house."

"Four hundred, then."

"Two hundred," Ahmed said. "For both of you at
once."

The whores talked it over in Russian while Ahmed
waited. He was in a wonderful mood. It was only eight in
the morning, but already he had done a full day's work,
and he had only good things to look forward to. At sun-
rise, he and two of the others had slaughtered Dr. Abu
Walid's fattest lamb, bleeding and skinning it and hang-
ing it in front of the house in preparation for a great
feast. Then he had driven the doctor and his son to the
al-Aqsa mosque in Jerusalem for Friday morning prayers.
And now he was going to fuck two big blondes.

Many Palestinians he knew cursed the new immi-
grants from Russia as Jewish invaders, but Ahmed felt
differently. He thought of them as a preview of paradise,
although the women there would be virgins. The concept
confused him somewhat—he couldn't understand how
the virgins of paradise could sleep with him and still remain pure—but he was content to leave theological spec-
ulations to Dr. Abu Walid.

"Three hundred for the two of us," said one of the
women.

Three hundred shekels was a lot of money, a hundred American dollars. Normally Ahmed would have continued bargaining, but he was in an expansive mood. The previous night Abu Walid had promised him the price of a bride. A bride would save him the cost of whores—in fact, this might be the last time he was forced to pay for sex. "*Yallah*," he said, an Arabic word often used by Israelis. Ahmed enjoyed the irony of sounding like a Jew in Arabic as well as in Hebrew. "Climb in and let's go." But as he leaned over to open the car door, the hookers looked at one another in alarm and started walking quickly down the street. Ahmed turned and saw a policeman in uniform approaching from across the street.

"Good morning, *habibi*," said Ahmed with a smile. His Israeli papers were in order so there was nothing to fear.

"Morning," said the cop. He was older than the policemen Ahmed usually saw, and bigger. "Mind stepping out of the car?"

"What for?"

"I want to see your outfit," the cop said amiably. "I'm into clothes."

Ahmed climbed out of the Subaru, a wide, embarrassed grin on his face.

"You should be ashamed of yourself, soliciting whores with a yarmulke on," said the cop.

"I was going to take it off."

"Do me a favor, lean on your car with your feet spread."

"You must be kidding," said Ahmed in his best out-

raged Israeli tone. Long ago he had noticed that the Jews
talked to people in authority with disrespect.

The cop pushed him against the car and kicked his
feet apart. Quickly he ran his hands up and down
Ahmed's body. The search didn't alarm Ahmed. He was,
as always when he ventured into Jewish Jerusalem, un-
armed.

"Papers," said the cop, and Ahmed produced them;
a full set of Israeli documents. The cop scrutinized them
and said, "Good fakes."

Ahmed looked down the street and saw nothing but
large, concrete apartment blocks and a few women walking with strollers. The cop was twenty years older than
him at least, and probably a hundred pounds heavier. He
figured he could dart past him, race through the alley between the buildings and circle back to Arab Jerusalem,
which was only a few blocks away. There he could blend
into the crowd. He turned, poised to run, and found
himself staring up at a very big, very hard-looking black
man who seized him by his wrists and said something in
English.

"He wants to know where his brother is," the policeman translated.

"I don't know what you're talking about."

"Get in my car," the policeman ordered.

"You can't do this. This is a democracy," said
Ahmed. It was a phrase Israelis used often, a phrase he
himself loved to pronounce, letting the five syllables of
dem-o-crat-i-a rumble around in his mouth.

"He says this is a democracy," Kedmi translated for Rasheed.

"I'll read him his rights in the car," said Rasheed. He smacked Ahmed on the side of his head, making his ears ring as he dragged him to the waiting Volvo.

"You better cooperate with this man, or he'll kill you," said Kedmi. "And I'll let him."

"I am not afraid to die," said Ahmed. Kedmi translated for Rasheed.

"That's 'cause you're one of these fanatical motherfuckers," Rasheed said. "So what I'm gonna do, I'm gonna tell your boss Dr. Abu Walid that the reason his videotape didn't get shown on TV is 'cause you're working for the Israelis. Run you around town in this po-lice vee-hicle, just to make the point, and drop you off at his place. Then he'll kill you in a way you'll be able to relate to."

"That's a lot to translate," said Kedmi.

"Go slow, give him time to digest it," said Rasheed.

"Sure," said Kedmi. He enjoyed working with Rasheed Holliman; it made him feel like a young cop again. Word for word, he repeated the threat.

"What do you want?" Ahmed asked. This time his tone was noticeably less confident.

"Information about the three Americans," said Kedmi.

"I don't know a thing."

Kedmi looked out the window and signaled. Within seconds, two plainclothes cops dressed in T-shirts and jeans ran up to the car. "Take him in and find out what he knows," he ordered. "What, where, how many, you know the drill. And get the layout of the house. As soon as he talks, contact me."

"How hard do you want us to push?" asked the older of the cops, a broad-chested man named Lalo with a single black eyebrow growing across his forehead.

"Whatever it takes."

Lalo nodded. From what Kedmi knew of him, he expected to be hearing soon.

"Dr. Abu gonna wonder why Ahmed's not home," said Rasheed.

"I'll put it out on the Arabic radio that he was injured in a car accident and he's in the hospital," said Kedmi. "They all listen to it; the news is bound to reach him."

"You can do that?"

"Sure," said Kedmi. "In this country, when you've got friends you can do just about anything."

Dr. Abu Walid walked home from al-Aqsa, his son at his side. It was a few miles, but he didn't mind; the day was beautiful, warm and clear, like all the summer days of Jerusalem. Preparations for the feast were under way, in accordance with his instructions. Walid, towering over him, would benefit from the walk. He was fasting today, as his father had commanded. Fresh air, hunger and prayer would put him in the proper mood for what was about to transpire. "How did you like the sermon?" he asked.

"It was fine," said the boy. He hadn't slept all night

and since seeing Ahmed slaughter the lamb early that morning, he had been filled with a nauseous premonition that something dreadful was going to take place.

"Fine?" said Abu Walid. "You have the gift of understatement, like an Englishman." In fact the sermon had been wild, like the mood of the crowd. The High Mufti himself had preached, calling for holy war against America while tens of thousands of worshipers chanted, "In blood and fire, we'll redeem the House of Islam."

"It was very good," said Walid absently. He couldn't forget the night before. After his father had fallen asleep, he had gone down to the cellar. There he had found Tyrone, naked except for a soiled pair of undershorts, his body beaten and crusted with blood, his lips so swollen he could barely talk, his hands and feet bound tightly. Walid shuddered, remembering the look on his face, his hoarse voice saying, "You sold me out."

"No," Walid had whispered. "I was with you. I wanted to escape. It was God's will."

"They gonna do me like they did Dawkins?" Tyrone had asked, making Walid avert his gaze. He knew that what awaited his friend Tyrone was worse than anything that had happened to the old man. . . .

"Tonight we will celebrate," said Abu Walid, reclaiming Walid's attention.

"Father, can't we let Tyrone go?" the boy asked in a voice that skidded into an upper register he hadn't used since entering puberty. "We have won. There is no reason to keep him."

"Those who spread disorder in the land shall be put to death," Abu Walid quoted.

"But God is forgiving and merciful," Walid finished the scriptural injunction they both knew by heart. It was a bold thing to say to his father, but he could not remain silent.

"God grants His mercy to whom He chooses," said Abu Walid curtly.

"Father, please, Tyrone is not to blame—"

"Be silent," Abu Walid commanded. There were things he did not want to hear from his beloved son, confessions that would rend the precious fabric of their relationship. He did not rebuke the boy for being seduced by the American. It was the doctor's own fault for allowing them to associate. Nor did he fault the basketball Negro for attempting to escape; any true man would have done the same. But it was clear to him that Tyrone had been sent by God for Walid's sake. Just as Ibrahim's faith had been tested by God's demand that he sacrifice his own son, Walid would discover the profundity of true belief by taking the life of his friend. That was divine fate; no man could intervene. It was a lesson Walid must learn in order to assume his proper role in the new world they were fashioning.

CHAPTER THIRTY-EIGHT

KEDMI AND RASHEED WERE SITTING IN KEDMI'S OFFICE AT PO-
lice headquarters when Sammy Levy, the head of intelligence, arrived. He was a small, neat, middle-aged man
with keen gray eyes, a salt and pepper mustache and
puffy lips that were set in a satisfied smile. "He talked?"
asked Kedmi.

"He talked," Levy said. "He was a tough one, but he
talked."

Rasheed noted the use of the past tense. "What did
he say?"

"Your brother and the old man are still alive," said
Levy. "They're in the house, Holliman in the basement,
Dawkins on the first floor. Dawkins can't move without
help, but your brother is still in one piece."

Rasheed expelled a long breath; he realized that,

even more than Tyrone's death, he had feared his mutilation.

"What about Bannion?" asked Kedmi.

"They killed him the first night and buried him near
Ashkelon," said Levy. "I've got people looking for the
body right now."

"Make sure there's a total press blackout. How many
kidnappers?"

"The father, the son and five others," said Levy. "All
heavily armed, Kalashnikovs and a lot of ammunition.
Now we've got a sketch of the interior, along with the
photos and the area map."

Levy spread his material out on the long conference
table. Rasheed looked first at the detailed relief map. He
saw that there was one main entrance to the village off
the narrow highway that led down to Jericho; a side road
that ran south, around Jerusalem toward Bethlehem; and,
within the hilly, sparsely populated village, a number of
small streets and scattered houses. Toward the southern
end, on a rise, a limestone house was marked. It was surrounded on all sides by a low stone fence. The closest
building was a small mosque about fifty yards away and
beyond it, clusters of one- and two-story houses.

"Not much of a fortification," said Rasheed, picking
up one of the aerial photos of the building.

"Is it mined?" Kedmi asked.

"No," said the intelligence chief. "Abu Walid sees
patients there. Children play around the house. It's not
mined."

"He's just sitting there, what, two, three miles from

here? Practically out in the open," said Rasheed, shaking his head.

"We have a saying in Hebrew, that it is always darkest under the light," Levy said. "Being in the open is his disguise."

"How about guard posts?"

Levy shook his head. "We haven't spotted any. But in a place like this, they aren't necessary. The whole village is one big guard post. If strangers enter, especially Israeli strangers, word spreads in an instant."

"You think the neighbors know about this?" asked Rasheed.

"They have no idea," replied Levy. "But they will be a problem anyway. If we go in, and they recognize us, they'll come out of their houses and throw rocks, Molotov cocktails, probably shoot as well."

"Sounds like a Saturday night bust at the Brewster Projects," said Rasheed. "How much time we got?"

Levy looked at Kedmi. "Go ahead," Kedmi said.

"Ahmed said they're holding a feast tonight. At the end, they're going to kill your brother and Dawkins. Sometime between nine or ten, I'd guess."

"That doesn't give us much time," said Kedmi. He and Levy bent over the map, studying the terrain, while Rasheed went to the window and gazed out at the brown hills. Big things were happening out there. His country was going to war. Civilizations were about to clash. But it meant nothing whatever to him. All he cared about was saving Tyrone. It was a tiny concern in the grand scheme of things, but Rasheed had long ago decided that he could do nothing to affect the grand scheme. All he could do was protect his brother.

Rasheed remembered the day his mother brought Tyrone home from the hospital. Rasheed was already a young cop, and that week he had scooped up the remains of three teenage boys killed in a drug dispute on Dexter Avenue. He had looked at the baby, young enough to be his son, and vowed that he wouldn't let the streets get him. Over time that vow had become Rasheed's only way of defying the carnage and hopelessness that surrounded him on the streets of Detroit.

After the shootout with the Rivers brothers in the crack house, he had tried to explain this to Kedmi. The Israeli had listened for a while and said, "I understand. You want to save the world."

"Naw, man, you don't get it. All I can do is save my brother."

"It is the same thing. There's a Jewish saying: A man who saves one life, it's like he saved the entire world."

That thought had stayed with Rasheed over the years. And it had made Yoav Kedmi the one man he really trusted to understand what was involved, how impossible it would be for him to allow anyone to hurt Tyrone.

"It's enough time," said Rasheed, turning back from the window.

Levy looked gloomy. "Even for troops trained in this sort of rescue, it takes a long time to plan and coordinate. We've had plenty of experience."

Rasheed glanced at the map of the village. "You guys

know your business, but sometimes too much force in a situation like this is a mistake. What matters is surprise."

Kedmi turned to Levy and said something in Hebrew. The intelligence officer gave the chief an odd look, nodded and left.

"What'd you tell him?"

"That you and I were going to do this alone."

"You sure?" asked Rasheed, the first grin of the day spreading over his face. "Old as you are?"

"I'm younger than you," Kedmi said, returning the smile. "By four months."

"I guess you are at that; I don't think of you that way."

"Thanks. Just for my information, do you have any idea what we're going to do? I don't mean to be pushy, but I am the commander of this operation."

"I don't know yet," said Rasheed. "But I figure we'll come up with something." He reached out and put his hand on his friend's broad shoulder. "Shit, Yoav, between the two of us, we got the motherfuckers surrounded."

Chapter Thirty-nine

WALID HADN'T EATEN IN TWENTY-FOUR HOURS, AND AL-
though it shamed him to think of food at a time like this,
he was unable to ignore the smells of roasted lamb, *zatar*
and thyme, onion and saffron that wafted into his bed-
room from the kitchen where his mother and sisters had
been busy all day. Of course they would not be at the
meal, nor would they serve it—that would be his job.

One of the guards came to his room and said, "Your
father is calling for you."

Walid quickly slipped into his cleanest, whitest *jalabiyya,* a robe so long that his father had joked when it
was made that the tailor had charged twice the usual
price. He fixed his large white knit skullcap on his head
and looked at his bony, boyish face in the mirror. It occurred to him that he would never see this face again;

that the next time he encountered his own image, it would be that of a man who had spilled blood.

Walid went to the kitchen and brought a pitcher of fresh orange juice and a tray of *mezze*—hummus with pine nuts, tahini mixed with parsley, deep-fried *kubeh* stuffed with ground meat and his mother's specialty, artichokes filled with rice. He set them before his father and the three guards who, tonight, were his father's guests. A fourth guard was positioned in the front yard, keeping an eye on the path leading up to the house.

Walid was relieved to see that Tyrone was not present. He had feared that his father would invite him as he had invited Coach Dawkins on the night he had first cut him. But Tyrone remained in the cellar, watched over by another of Abu Walid's men. Later he and the guard in the front yard would be replaced by two of the others, so that they, too, could participate in the feast.

"Sit, Walid, join us," his father instructed. The boy took a chair. His father was speaking in a grand, literary Arabic that the poorly educated guards could barely understand. "Within months, the so-called great powers of the West will lie in ruins," he assured them in a low, hypnotic voice. "That is the will of the All Merciful. The dominions of the false prophets and ayatollahs will crumble into dust. And then the pure shall sweep out of Arabia as in olden days, a conquering army of Allah that will cleanse the earth of nonbelievers and bring a reign of peace."

The guards nodded. The high-flown language was a rare treat, like the crispy *kubeh* and the pungent salads.

They felt honored to serve a man of such erudition and holiness. Walid himself barely heard his father. He was light-headed from his fast, and his mind raced with confusing thoughts. Tyrone in the cellar, naked and bleeding. Hakeem Olajuwon, going up for a Dee-troit slam dunk to the cheers of thousands. Naked, wanton women like the ones on Tyrone's tapes, taunting him with their bodies. The wild sensation of freedom as he ran from the courtyard. He was faint, weak, unable to focus. The room was too hot. He closed his eyes, gripped the arms of his chair tightly and prayed that when the time came, his mind would be clear.

One floor below, in the cellar, Tyrone Holliman took stock of his options. Or, to be more precise, option. At some point they would come for him. He had no illusions now about escape, but he was determined to avoid slow mutilation. He was pretty sure that if he moved quickly enough, he could kill at least one of them with his bare hands—and force them to kill him immediately, with a bullet instead of a knife.

Dr. Abu Walid was his first choice, but he figured the doctor wouldn't come downstairs. Ahmed, who had beaten him bloody after returning him to the cellar, was number two on his list. Tyrone had never killed a man, but he was ready to kill now, to grab one of his tormentors by the throat and splatter his brains on the concrete wall. He hoped he would live long enough to enjoy it.

*   *   *

Rosenthal picked up Berger at the Hilton and drove him to Jerusalem. He didn't like Berger, especially the way he made little demands, like asking Rosenthal to change the Vivaldi tape in the car because he was sick of listening to foreign languages. They were together because of a shared circumstance—Masterson and Prime Minister Peled had ordered them each to monitor Kedmi's operation—but it was a partnership Rosenthal didn't appreciate.

"What did your guy say?" Berger asked as they headed out of Tel Aviv, driving eastward toward the capital.

"That Rasheed left police headquarters a few minutes ago, dressed like an Arab."

"A black Arab?"

"There are black Arabs," said Rosenthal. "Jericho and Tulkarm are full of them. They were brought here as slaves. Just like the black Americans."

"You figure that's how Rasheed's going to try to get into the house?" Berger asked, ignoring the jibe. Rosenthal was the kind of smart-ass Jew he couldn't stand. Three billion dollars a year in foreign aid, and they still pissed all over you.

"It's an old trick," said Rosenthal. "We've got special units that do nothing but go around disguised as Arabs. I'm surprised Kedmi's letting him try something so obvious."

"From what I saw yesterday, it looks like Holliman's in charge, not Kedmi."

"Yoav's easy to underestimate," said Rosenthal.

"Where is he now? Rasheed?"

"Bethlehem," said Rosenthal.

"What the hell's he doing there? I thought the hostages were in Jerusalem."

"Maybe they were moved," Rosenthal said. "Anyway, I've got two men on his tail. They won't lose him. Sooner or later, some troops have to be dispatched. What does he call them?"

"Menfolk," said Berger, imitating Rasheed's Detroit drawl.

"Right. When they are, I'll get a report and we can join the parade. From a discreet distance, of course. That way, if things turn out wrong, we'll be there to sweep up the pieces."

"I should be back in Washington," said Berger, "instead of riding around playing cops and robbers."

"Use the phone," said Rosenthal, gesturing to the cellular in the backseat. "Call Masterson and tell him."

"Should I call collect?" Berger said, but Rosenthal didn't seem to get the point. What he said was, "Better not. He might not accept."

Kedmi's Volvo rolled into Bethlehem, past the tomb of Rachel. Gali checked his rearview mirror and saw that the Shin Bet car, a white Ford Escort, was still on his tail. "Are you comfortable back there?" he said over his shoulder to the large black man in the backseat.

"Man, turn on the air," said the passenger. "I'm burning up inside this nightgown."

Gali switched on the air conditioner. "The bedouins are wearing wool in the desert," he said.

"Do I look like a damn bedouin to you?"

"To tell you the truth, you look like Aretha Franklin in that *shmata*," said Gali.

"Shit, too," said Corry Robinson. He had narrowly missed making the Lakers. If he had he wouldn't have been in Israel, playing for a second-rate team like Hapoel Jerusalem. In the NBA they paid you, on time, in full; here the team was two months behind and not even apologetic. He had been thinking about suing, but this was an easier way to get the money, just getting dressed up like an Arab and being driven around. Levine, the Hapoel general manager—accompanied by a big bald cop with hairy ears—had given him a cashier's check for forty thousand dollars along with the costume. Tomorrow morning he would go down to Bank Leumi and cash it. He had never heard of a cashier's check bouncing, but he figured if there was a way, Levine would find it. "How much longer we gonna be cruising around like this?" he asked.

"Until I am getting a call," said Gali to the decoy. "When it is all over."

"When what is all over?"

"I don't know," said Gali. He looked in the rearview mirror and saw the Shin Bet car, still following. "And neither does anyone else," he added with a satisfied smile.

CHAPTER FORTY

SHORTLY AFTER SEVEN, KEDMI AND RASHEED SLIPPED OUT A side entrance of police headquarters. They wore black suits and white clerical collars supplied by the undercover unit, and were accompanied by a small, swarthy man called Abu Musa. He was a familiar figure in east Jerusalem and the West Bank, an Arab tour guide who specialized in showing Christian pilgrims around. He was also familiar to Kedmi by his Hebrew name, Moshe Sass. It was Kedmi who had recruited him as a police undercover agent twenty years ago, after he had come to Israel from Aleppo, Syria, where his father had been the Jewish community's last kosher butcher.

Abu Musa inspected their clerical costumes with a practiced eye; over the years he had escorted enough Christian clergymen to become an expert. "Very authentic," he said to Kedmi in Arabic. "One hundred percent."

Abu Musa's Hebrew was excellent, but Arabic was his mother tongue.

Rasheed looked at his friend. "You having second thoughts, Yoav? Shit, man, you the national chief of police, not some cowboy. It's not too late to get one of these young studs to take your place."

"No second thoughts," said Kedmi. "Believe me, this is the biggest adventure I have had in years. Also, my last."

"Why last?"

"Peled will fire me tomorrow," he said. "He no longer trusts me."

"Can't really blame him," said Rasheed.

"No. Well, let's get moving," said Kedmi.

They climbed into the rear seat of Abu Musa's green Mercedes limousine, which had east Jerusalem license plates, Islamic prayer beads dangling from the rearview mirror and an inscription on the doors, in Arabic and English: PALESTINE TOURS. Abu Musa doused his lights and slid out of the police compound, heading for a back road that led to Abu Walid's village. Although it was still early evening, it was quiet. "Palestinians go to bed early," Kedmi explained, as Abu Musa parked in front of a stone house near the entrance to the village.

Within seconds, lights came on in the house, and a man appeared in the doorway. "*Ahlan*," he called in Arabic. Welcome.

"*Ahlan*, Abu Zakki," called Abu Musa. He climbed from the car, walked over to the man and kissed him on both cheeks. They were old friends, the tour guide and

Abu Zakki, who, as head of the largest clan in the village, held the office of *mukhtar* or honorary mayor. Over the years Abu Musa had often brought pilgrims to visit, and protocol dictated that they stop first at Abu Zakki's for a cup of coffee and a once-over.

"Excuse the late hour, but I have two crazy men this time," he said. "They believe that the three wise men of the Christians saw the star of Jesus from this village."

"They are welcome," said Abu Zakki. "Please, ask them in."

"Forgive me, but they wish to view the sky from a hill at a certain hour," said Abu Musa. "As I said, they are crazy."

"I see," said Abu Zakki. He had been watching an episode of *Seinfeld*, and he was relieved that he wouldn't have to miss the rest of the show in idle coffee talk with a couple of foreigners.

"But harmless," Abu Musa added. "I will keep an eye on them."

"Shall I send one of my sons to accompany you?"

"Your sons are always most welcome, but there is no need to disturb them at this hour."

"They are sons," said Abu Zakki. "Wait here, I will fetch one." Through the open door he heard the sound of laughter from the television set. "Tell your crazy Christians I hope they see their star."

"Everything cool?" asked Rasheed when Abu Musa returned to the car.

"Yes. He's sending one of his sons with us."

"Why?" Kedmi asked. "Is he suspicious?"

"Why should he be? He knows me," said Abu Musa indignantly. He was such a good actor that sometimes Kedmi wondered who he was actually working for. "The son's job is to tag along and accept a donation at the end of the visit. For the widows and orphans of the village. Don't worry, when the time comes I'll take care of him."

A young man in jeans and a sweatshirt emerged from the house. He was small, like his father, with a black mustache, dark eyes and a diffident manner. If he was annoyed at being sent on an errand, he showed no sign of it. He smiled at the two men in the backseat and said to Abu Musa,"Where do they want to go?"

"Up on the ridge, near the end of the village. That is where they think the wise men saw the star."

The boy shrugged; he was used to foreigners with odd ideas about Jerusalem. "Shall we walk?"

"They're not in very good shape," said Abu Musa. "Let's drive to the mosque and they can walk from there."

"Why not?" said the son. Once more he turned to the men in the back and said, "You are very welcome."

"God bless you, young brother," Rasheed said. "Peace be unto you." He hoped Kedmi's man wouldn't kill the boy, but it was too late to discuss it now. In the moonlight he could see the tower of the small mosque, and beyond it, on a hill, the house where Tyrone was. Somebody else would have to worry about the son of Abu Zakki.

CHAPTER FORTY-ONE

WHEN IT CAME TIME FOR THE MAIN COURSE, WALID WENT TO the kitchen, took the huge silver tray of *mansaf* from his mother, and brought it to the dining-room table. The men gathered around, standing in the traditional way, sniffing the succulent pieces of roasted lamb mixed with saffron rice and garnished with pine nuts.

Abu Walid motioned for his son to take his place next to him. Holding his left hand behind his back, he reached into the stew with his right, plucked out a sheep's eye and popped it into Walid's open mouth. It was an extraordinary gesture of respect, and the others were visibly impressed.

Walid closed his eyes and chewed. It took all his self-control to keep from gagging. He knew, as the guards did not, why his father was honoring him in this way; it was at once sacred and ironic, his way of preparing his son to commit ritual murder.

The men began to eat, holding their left hands behind their backs and using the right hands to roll balls of meat and rice, which they swallowed whole. There was little talking until Dr. Abu Walid turned to his son and said, "Walid, you aren't eating. Are you well?"

"Yes, Father," he said. Suddenly the room began to spin and he fell to the floor. Abu Walid bent over the boy as one of the men rushed to bring his medical bag. By the time he returned, Walid's eyes were open and he was struggling to sit up. "What happened?" Walid asked weakly.

"You went spinning like a dervish," said his father, making the others chuckle. "Perhaps the smell of strong meat has made you giddy."

"I am all right now," said the boy, embarrassed. He rose with his father's help and stood once more at the table.

"Please go and rest," said Abu Walid. "You will need your strength."

"Father—"

"Go, Walid," said the doctor firmly. "Lie in your bed. When the time comes, I will call for you."

Walid did as he was told. The murmured conversation from the next room soothed him and lulled him to sleep. He dreamed that he was in Arabia, at the Kabba in Mecca, surrounded by millions of believers. They jostled one another and somehow he was separated from his father. Then the *muezzin* began to chant the call to prayer.

"*Allah hu akbar! Allah hu akbar!* Abu Walid is the son of a whore. Abu Walid is the son of a pig. Abu Walid is a filthy swine. . . ." The dream seemed so real that Walid opened his eyes and, for a moment, thought he actually heard the grotesque chant coming from the nearby mosque. Then he closed his eyes once more and dozed off, less afraid of his nightmares than of his waking thoughts.

When the *muezzin* began the call to prayer, Abu Walid consulted his watch. It was too early, he thought; too early and too quiet. Normally the call, recorded on cassette and played over tinny loudspeakers, echoed through the village. But this time it was a man's voice, calling softly and, at first, indistinctly. He strained to identify the voice and hear the words. The tune was right, but the words—suddenly he distinctly heard the voice intone, "Abu Walid is the son of a whore. Abu Walid is the son of a pig. . . ." He looked at the guards and saw they were trying to repress laughter.

"Someone is blaspheming from the mosque," he said sternly. "One of the village idiots. Tell Razi to bring him to me."

Razi, the guard outside, was laughing when Abdullah emerged from the house. "Abu Walid says to go to the mosque and bring him the man who blasphemes," he said in a serious voice, but his face betrayed his merriment. Razi returned his grin, picked up his AK-47 and trotted in the direction of the mosque, some fifty meters away. Two meters short of the door, he tripped over a wire and fell flat on his face. Before he could turn over, he was dead, stabbed in the back of the neck by Rasheed. He and Kedmi dragged the body into the mosque, where they stacked it next to the gagged and bound son of the mayor.

"One down," Rasheed said.

"This was the easy one," Kedmi said. He fixed the silencer on his Uzi and said to Abu Musa, "Give us one minute, then start the praying again. Make sure you keep it low and directed toward the house; I don't want the rest of the village to hear."

"What is he saying?" Rasheed asked Kedmi.

"That Abu Walid is the son of a whore," replied Kedmi. "Among the Arabs that's a terrible curse."

"Yeah, I could see how they might not like it," he said, checking the Magnum.

"Race you to the wall," said Kedmi. It had been years since he had actually gone out on an operation like this one. He wished Ruthie could be here to see him; after all this time, he still loved impressing her.

Rasheed and Kedmi sprinted around the mosque and headed for the low stone wall in front of the house. Rasheed got there first, a winded Kedmi sliding in a few seconds later. "You're slow, even for a white man," Rasheed said.

"Damn, it's hot," Kedmi puffed. Both he and Rasheed were wearing bullet-proof vests under their black clerical suits.

"You gonna be all right?" Rasheed asked, looking at

his friend's flushed face in the moonlight. "I don't want you keeling over with a heart attack now."

"Just get over to the side of the house and let me take care of my own business," Kedmi said.

"Whatever you say, Chief," said Rasheed. Nimbly he slid over the low fence and ran in a crouch to the side of the house. When he got there, he signaled with a flashlight, and the wailing from the mosque began again. "*Allah hu akbar! Allah hu akbar!* Abu Walid is a donkey. Abu Walid has sex with monkeys and dogs. Abu Walid is a piece of filth. . . ."

"This is not a prank," said Abu Walid to the guards. Although he didn't know precisely who or what was outside, it was obvious that he was under attack. His first thought was of his son and their sacred mission. Nothing must be allowed to interfere with that.

The guards looked blank, watchful; it was clear to them, too, that something extraordinary was happening.

"Go see who is out there," he ordered two of the guards. "Bring whoever it is to me." He turned to the third guard, a young man with sallow skin and pimples, named Abdullah. "You stay here. I will take Walid to the cellar and send Ali up to be with you."

The two guards picked up their weapons and rushed from the house. Kedmi, kneeling behind the wall, watched them run toward the mosque. They were yelling words of encouragement to one another in Arabic, trying to dispel their fear of the dark and of the unknown infidel in the mosque tower.

Kedmi switched the Uzi to automatic and waited

until the two Arabs were within ten meters of the stone wall before opening fire. They went down under the spray of bullets and he lumbered forward, switching the Uzi back to single shot. He stood over the bleeding bodies and, for safety's sake, put a bullet in each of their heads. Abu Musa was still calling imprecations, but the village was quiet; evidently no one in the houses below could hear the Uzi with the silencer or the soft wailing from the mosque.

One leg at a time, Kedmi threw himself over the low wall and ran to Rasheed, at the side of the house. Once again he arrived red-faced and panting. "Two more down," he whispered breathlessly.

"That means two more guards inside, plus the father and the son," said Rasheed.

Kedmi nodded, signaling with his flashlight for Abu Musa to stop wailing. Nobody else would be coming out now; he and Rasheed would have to go in.

Abu Walid entered his son's darkened room and found him asleep in his oversized bed. He took him by the shoulders, kissed his cheek and shook him gently. "Arise, *ya* Walid," he said. "It is time."

Walid opened his eyes and saw his father standing over him, a wild look on his face. "What is it?" he asked in a thick voice.

"They are coming for us," said Abu Walid.

"Who?"

"The evil ones. Do not worry, my son; God will turn their bullets into water. Come with me now."

Walid climbed from his bed. "Where are we going?"

"Downstairs," said Abu Walid. "To the cellar."

"Father, please—" said Walid in a soft, imploring voice.

"Silence," Abu Walid snapped. "Do as I say." He took his son by the hand and half led, half dragged him down the corridor, past the room with the closed door to the stairs. Then he stepped aside, motioning for Walid to descend first. As he did, he withdrew his gleaming scalpel.

The noises in the house jolted Digger Dawkins out of his stupor. Although he didn't know precisely what he was hearing, he could tell dimly that something was happening. Women screamed in the kitchen. Abu Walid and his son were yelling at one another in Arabic in the hall. He heard the sound of men running up and down the stairs.

For days Dawkins had been lying in his own filth, slipping in and out of consciousness. He had long since taken an inventory of his missing limbs and organs; he knew there was nothing left of him. The only thing that kept him alive was his furious anger.

With agonizing effort he squirmed to the edge of the bed and slid himself onto the floor. His body was so torn and raw that he could not distinguish the particular sources of the terrible pain he felt. For a moment he blacked out, and then came to. Ten feet away, on a low table, was a glass water jug. With tortuous effort he crawled toward it, until he got his remaining hand around it and, using all his strength, smashed it on the tile floor.

Alone upstairs, Abdullah shouldered his AK-47 and looked nervously into the dark yard. The others had been swallowed up by the night, as if by *jinni,* demons. He was not afraid to die a martyr's death at the hands of the infidels; that would ensure paradise. But to be killed by *jinni* could mean being dragged into the pit of hell. He backed away from the window into the corridor, aiming the rifle into space. The demons, he knew, could take any form.

There was noise from below, the sound of footsteps on the stairs—Ali coming up to join him. They could stand together, back to back, so that the *jinni* couldn't sneak up on them. Abdullah began to pray fervently, to keep the demons away; so fervently that he didn't hear the hall door open behind him, or the laborious sound of Digger Dawkins's breathing.

Suddenly he felt a hand around his leg, pulling him to the floor. As he fell, he found himself face-to-face with a monster. It was crusted in blood and it had one horrible blue eye that fixed him with a crazed stare. Abdullah screamed as the monster raised its arm and plunged a jagged hunk of blue glass into his head. As he lost consciousness he heard the monster scream a single, tongueless sound in a language he did not understand. That sound was "Cocksucker."

Ali raced into the room and cut Digger Dawkins down with a single, prolonged burst of gunfire. It was the first time he had actually killed anyone, and he looked at the body with amazement. He was a warrior now. Surely he had guaranteed paradise for himself. It was a warm, proud moment that lasted three seconds, until Kedmi, leaning through the open window, put a .9-millimeter bullet in his chest.

At the sound of gunfire, Rasheed burst through the back door. There were three women huddled in the kitchen. For a moment he considered killing them, but the terrified looks on their faces convinced him they were harmless. "Stay here, don't move," he shouted, and kept running, toward the stairway that Ahmed had sketched for his interrogators. At the cellar door he met Kedmi.

"I'm going down," said Rasheed. "You keep an eye on the door, okay? And call for an ambulance, just in case."

"Abu Musa will do that," said Kedmi. "I'm coming with you."

"No, man, this is my play," said Rasheed. "Besides, I don't want Abu Walid to know that I'm dealing with the Israelis."

Kedmi nodded. "You need me, holler," he said. He went back to the living room and plopped down in a plush chair near the front door, Uzi in hand. Killing terrorists was harder work than he remembered; if any more turned up, he intended to shoot them sitting down.

Rasheed took a deep breath and descended quietly into the dank, dark cellar. He smelled Tyrone before he saw him: a funky, animal smell of urine, blood and fear. Tyrone was trying to cry out, but his voice was muffled by Abu Walid's *kaffiyeh,* which had been stuffed in his mouth.

"*Salaam Aleikum,*" Rasheed called, using the greeting he had heard Muslims in Detroit exchange. "I come in peace."

"Put down your gun," said a voice from the darkness.

"No problem, brother," said Rasheed, laying the Magnum on the floor. "I'm not here to fight. I'm Tyrone's brother from Detroit. I just want to take him home with me if y'all don't mind."

"Impossible," said Abu Walid. Rasheed could see him now, in a far corner of the cellar. He could make out Tyrone, too, on his knees, hands bound behind his back. Next to him stood the giant son, Walid, with a large knife in his hand. The knife was resting on Tyrone's neck.

"Look, man, I respect what you're doing," said Rasheed in a slow, easy voice. "I can get you and your boy out of here alive. I got a car outside, ready to go. Give me Tyrone and you can head for Lebanon right now. The Israelis think that's where you are anyway. They'll never catch on."

"I have no wish to go to Lebanon," said Abu Walid.

"Jordan, then, Syria, wherever."

"My son and I are going to paradise," said Abu Walid. "But first he must prove himself worthy." He turned to the boy and said, "You know what must be done."

"Father, please, let us go to Lebanon," said Walid.

"Silence," boomed Abu Walid, his voice echoing off the walls of the cellar. "Do not challenge God's will. Do not contradict my commandment. Remember Ibrahim. Make the sacrifice."

"Father, please—" begged Walid.

"Kill him," screamed Abu Walid. "Slit the infidel's throat."

"No, Father," Walid screeched hysterically. "Do not ask me—"

"Uh, uh, uh, uh, uh," Tyrone yelled through the *kaffiyeh*. He was fighting to spit it out of his mouth.

"Silence," commanded Abu Walid.

"Father—"

"Silence, both of you," said the doctor. Suddenly the *kaffiyeh* fell from Tyrone's mouth and, through parched lips, he screamed, "Rasheed, get the old man, not the boy."

As Abu Walid and his son turned their heads toward Tyrone in amazement, Rasheed reached into the pocket of his black clerical coat for the snub-nosed .22 he had picked up in Washington. He held it hidden in the palm of his huge hand and said, "Man, nobody has to die. Let my brother go and we'll all get out of this."

"*Allah hu akbar*," chanted the doctor. "God is great. He demands a sacrifice. *Allah hu akbar, Allah hu akbar*—"

Tyrone looked directly into the eyes of Walid. He saw something there he recognized and he began to mumble. "Two potata muhfucker, two-tone bitch, soupy shuffle muhfucker—"

"You ain't shit," Walid finished in a distant voice.

"*Allah hu akbar,*" screamed the doctor. "Kill him, my son, it is God's will."

"Allah don't want no killing," repeated Rasheed, taking a step closer. "Put down the knife, boy."

"Slice his throat," cried Abu Walid. "Do not defy Allah."

"Allah's the one sent me to you," said Tyrone. "He's the one gave you the gift of basketball—"

"Kill him," shrieked Abu Walid. "Do not disobey."

The boy looked wildly from his father to Tyrone. Slowly he lifted the scalpel over Tyrone's exposed neck.

"Two potata muhfucker," whispered Tyrone, his voice an imploring mumble.

"Kill the infidel," Abu Walid yelled again.

"Nobody needs to die," Rasheed repeated evenly, taking another step toward the boy and fixing his finger on the trigger.

"*Allah hu akbar,*" screamed Walid, and he plunged the scalpel deep into his own chest.

"Walid," cried Abu Walid. He fell to his knees and desperately peered at his son. "You have murdered him," he said.

"He's not dead," said Rasheed. "We need to get him help—"

"I am a doctor," Abu Walid said. "He is gone. You have murdered my son." With a powerful wrench he extracted the bloody scalpel from the boy's chest.

"Nobody murdered your son," said Rasheed quietly, inching toward Abu Walid, who was standing over Tyrone with the scalpel in his hand. "He killed himself. There's no need to hurt my brother."

"He polluted Walid's spirit," said the doctor. "He caused him to defy God and his own father. He will never enter paradise." With a sudden movement he raised the scalpel and brought it down toward Tyrone's neck. At the last moment Tyrone slipped to the left, catching the blow on his shoulder. As he did, Rasheed stepped forward, extended his hand until the .22 was almost resting on Abu Walid's temple, and pulled the trigger.

CHAPTER FORTY-TWO

THE AMERICANS ALL FLEW HOME TOGETHER, RASHEED, Berger and Tyrone up top, the remains of Bannion and Digger Dawkins below, in the cargo area. Tyrone, accompanied by an Israeli army doctor in plain clothes, was too heavily sedated to talk much. Berger spent most of the flight in the cockpit, communicating with the White House. Rasheed took advantage of the quiet and slept most of the way.

About an hour out of Washington, Berger came back and sat next to Rasheed. "The president wants me to tell you how much he admires what you did," he said in a grudging tone. "He hopes to see you as soon as we land."

"Tell him to book himself a flight to Detroit then," said Rasheed. "I'm taking Tyrone home."

"This is a direct invitation from the president of the

United States," said Berger. "He intends to give you a medal."

"Man, the United States has done enough for me and my family," said Rasheed. "You take the medal; you're the one who led the daring rescue operation in Lebanon."

"You understand why that story is necessary," Berger said. "The United States is at war. We can't afford any confusion about the events that precipitated it."

"Man, I told you coming out here, y'all want to have a war, leave me out of it."

"I don't understand you," Berger said. "You saw what these people are. They have to be defeated."

"All I saw was a crazy motherfucker and a bunch of armed hoodlums," said Rasheed. "And a big, gawky boy who didn't have to die."

"You think they're any different from the ayatollahs who blew up our planes and plotted to destroy the Washington Monument?"

"About as different as y'all are from your great-granddaddies," said Rasheed.

"What's that supposed to mean?"

"Nigger," said Rasheed.

"Not that again."

"Look, General, you and Masterson can tell any damn story you want. I'm sure as hell not going to say a word."

"Out of patriotism, I suppose," Berger said.

"Capitalism," said Rasheed. "I got a security business I been neglecting ever since this shit came down. Mostly I work for GM, but I plan to expand. Into defense contracts."

"That's not my area," said Berger.

"You make it your area, or some lucky reporter's gonna wind up with the Pulitzer Prize."

"Blackmail," said Berger.

"African-American mail to you," Rasheed said. "And one other thing—Kedmi keeps his job."

"That's up to the Israelis."

"Use your influence, General."

Rasheed felt a tap on his shoulder. It was the doctor. "Your brother's waking up and he wants to talk to you," he said. "Keep it short, though; he's still sedated."

Rasheed walked to the back of the plane, where Tyrone was lying strapped to a stretcher bed, a tube connected to his right arm. He looked up at Rasheed through half-closed eyes and said, "Hey."

"Hey," said Rasheed, taking his brother's hand. "Everything's cool. We'll be home in a little while."

"Walid?" said Tyrone weakly.

"Dead," said Rasheed. "Dawkins and Bannion, all the Arabs, everybody but you. I'll tell you all about it when you get a little stronger."

"Can I still play?" Tyrone asked.

"Yeah, you can still play," Rasheed said. "You just a little shaken up is all."

Tyrone smiled and closed his eyes.

"Let him sleep," said the doctor.

"Right." Suddenly Tyrone tightened his grip on Rasheed's hand and opened his eyes and said, "You one terrible motherfucker, Rasheed." Which, in Tyrone's language, meant: "Thanks."